Lost in Loch Ness . . .

She heard him scream, though it didn't sound like a cry of pain. It reminded her of the shouts she used to hear on the roller coaster when she took her son to the amusement park.

Suddenly, the vessel tilted another ten degrees or so. It was as if a giant pair of hands had pressed against the starboard side and pushed the boat toward the water. Tally had to grab the winch control panel to keep from flipping over the side. Dr. Castle fell from her seat . . .

Then, just as quickly and unexpectedly, the boat rolled back to an upright position. It rocked toward the starboard slightly, then back to port, then back again before settling. Dr. Castle was on her knees . . .

"Harold!" She shouted.

There was no answer.

Dr. Castle looked at Tally, who didn't need the unspoken order she saw in the scientist's eyes. She punched the button to retract the cables. The winch turned without resistance.

"Harold!" Dr. Castle said again into the radio.

There was no sound. Not even static.

Dr. Castle rose. Like Tally, she expected the worst. Only "the worst" they had imagined was not quite sufficient. Tally had expected the cables to come up without Harold Collins on the other end. They did. But she did not expect to find what she did. The cable hooks were still attached to the rings from Collins's diving suit.

Something had literally sheared them from the plate that attached them to the diving suit.

UNIT OMEGA

JIM GRAND

BERKLEY BOOKS, NEW YORK

This is a work of fiction. Names, characters, places, and incidents either are the product of the author's imagination or are used fictitiously, and any resemblance to actual persons, living or dead, business establishments, events, or locales is entirely coincidental.

UNIT OMEGA

A Berkley Book / published by arrangement with
the author

PRINTING HISTORY
Berkley edition / December 2003

For information address: The Berkley Publishing Group,
a division of Penguin Group (USA) Inc.,
375 Hudson Street, New York, New York 10014.

ISBN: 0-425-19321-7

BERKLEY®
Berkley Books are published by The Berkley Publishing Group,
a division of Penguin Group (USA) Inc.,
375 Hudson Street, New York, New York 10014.
BERKLEY and the "B" design
are trademarks belonging to Penguin Group (USA) Inc.

PRINTED IN THE UNITED STATES OF AMERICA

10 9 8 7 6 5 4 3 2 1

PROLOGUE

THERE WAS A powerful flash and it struck the object. The object changed even before the brilliance faded, and the object itself changed the world.

The object was perfectly round, lacking distinguishing marks or features. It was also infinitesimally small, dwarfed by the molecules of air and rock that surrounded it.

The object was not alive, but it was dangerous. It was not evil, because it did not think, but it was pernicious, because it was one of the most powerful objects in our universe; in any universe. When active, as it was now, it was mightier than all the thermonuclear force generated by every star in any given galaxy during their seventy-million-year life spans.

The object had countless vanes. They existed but were insubstantial. They were defined only by the molecules that could come no closer. Yet the vanes existed. They existed in ways and places the molecules could not.

Time had meaning to the object but offered no parameters. A moment and an eon were the same. Space had meaning too, though the dimensions of height, width, and depth were fundamentally irrelevant. When the object was active, it defined its own time and space.

In a way it was like the sea. In repose the ocean is epic, poetic, and content in its bed. When riled, it is terrifying, ruthless, and boundless.

One morning in September the object suddenly winked to life as it had countless times in the past. The vanes spun. The world changed. Only this was different from other times.

This time Dr. Kathryn Castle witnessed the incredible result.

CHAPTER ONE

HER FATHER HAD been wrong.

When marine paleontologist Kathryn Eugenie Castle was fifteen years old and living in the Kensington section of London, her father had asked her a question. It was a short, simple question, which Jonathan Castle had prefaced by saying that his daughter should ask it of herself every now and then. Kathryn had been very interested and very attentive: over Mrs. Letty Castle's delicious shepherd's pie the Scotland Yard inspector had promised his daughter—*assured* her in his quiet but insistent way—that the answer was among the most difficult in the world.

The question was simple:

"Kate," said the broad-shouldered man—he was the only person who called her Kate, and the only one she permitted to call her that—"Kate," he asked, "what do you know absolutely?"

There was a knowing twist at the edge of her father's strong mouth when he asked that. Being a very smart fifteen, and knowing that her father was a skilled interrogator, Kathryn sensed that it was probably a trick question. If she said something like, *I know that the sky is blue,* or *I know that drinking water will quench my thirst,* her father would have answered, "At night?" or "When it is bubbling hot for tea?"

Rather than answering, Kathryn asked her father to tell her what *he* knew absolutely.

He replied without hesitation, "Just one thing. I know that I love my two girls."

That made Kathryn smile, and made her mother and father smile too. She told her father she would like to think about her answer, though she assured him that she was confident of her own love for them as well. The word she used was "reciprocal," which she had just learned in Mrs. Wilmington's English class.

And Kathy did think about the question, for the next thirty-eight years. Through school, through Oxford, through years of working in deserts that were once the bottoms of vast prehistoric seas.

The answer so far, was that Kathryn Castle knew nothing else absolutely. Nothing but love for her parents and, later, for her husband, Del, and their son, Gary. But love was an easy answer because, if it was real, it was given absolutely. There had been times when she had thought she knew things absolutely. For instance, that light always traveled in a straight line. Then she'd learned about the gravitational lens effect, when extremely dense objects in space bend light from more distant objects. So much for one absolute. She had believed, for a while, that bacteria were smaller than people. Then she had had to revise that: bacteria were smaller than people in size, but not in durability. Nor in power. Then she had had to revise even that because there was some indication that certain bacteria acted in unison, as though they were part of a collective. What if the collected collective were larger than a human being? It was improbable, but it was not impossible.

For most of her life Kathryn had been pretty sure that happiness was better than sadness, until four years ago, when her husband and son had been killed in a car crash outside the British Museum. Afterward, she discovered that happiness made her feel guilty. How could she be happy when they were gone? Sadness, on the other hand, kept the loss alive. And the sense of loss was the only part of them she had. So she held on to that. It was strange, it was unexpected, but it was something else. It was one more thing that Kathryn did not know absolutely.

Over the years, though, Kathryn had closed in on one other target. Something she had wondered about since she had taken out a library book about sea serpents when she was five or six years old. Something of which she was ninety-nine-point-nine percent certain.

After a lifetime of study, hundreds of hours of on-site research, analyses of sonar mapping, of underwater photography and videography, of chemical study of the water and endless hours of personal surveillance, Kathryn believed with near-complete certainty that the infamous Loch Ness Monster was a myth. A trick of waves or floating logs or other detritus.

Two things had convinced her otherwise: First, there was the strong memory of her father's wise, wry smile when he had first asked his question. As if he himself suspected there was nothing but love that could be known absolutely.

Second, and more important, something had happened on the surface of Loch Ness on a gloomy morning in September. Something that had happened when she had been out in the boat, just for a row and a think. Something that had caused her to look up from the pages of the *International Science World* magazine she had been reading.

Kathryn Castle had seen the Monster.

CHAPTER TWO

IN THEORY, AT least, it was a dream job.

Twenty-seven-year-old Harold Collins had been hired— "engaged" as the Secretary-General had called it in his letter of employment, which was now professionally framed and displayed on Harold Collins's mother's living room wall— to head a new research department for the United Nations. That in itself was flattering. But what made it special, what had made Collins accept, was that this was not going to be just another government office to promote existing science or study better ways of doing the same old, same-old.

"Oh no," United Nations Assistant Deputy Secretary-General Samuel Bordereau had assured his old friend. Assured him in that silky, seductive French accent that turned even a suggestion into a cause, an idea into a duty. "You will have the opportunity—no, the mandate— to challenge the way we look at our world."

What scientist could resist the dual offers of patronage and freedom? Especially from a man of vision and some power. Unfortunately, what Bordereau had never been was a man of detail.

Harold Collins had finished at the top of his class at MIT. By the end of his last year of graduate study he had already been offered work on a soon-to-be-up-and-running state-of-the-art cyclotron project in Tempe, Arizona, an assistant professorship at the University of Paris, and a project-leader post at the Ben Abah nuclear research facility in Tel Aviv. Those offers had flattered and intrigued him, but they had not inspired him. He yearned for something expansive, revolutionary. Before the surprise call came, inviting him to visit Bordereau in New York, Collins had actually been considering working as a short-order cook and writing science fiction. The young quantum physicist could become the next Isaac Asimov or Arthur C. Clarke, other scientists who had made good. Collins wondered if he even had a choice. His brain didn't merely proceed from thought to thought. It leaped. It surged. It was hungry to *know*. The call from Bordereau was like the burning bush speaking to Moses. It gave Harold Collins his mission. A dream. Rocks he could use to leap and surge across the rivers of knowledge.

At least, in theory.

Collins went to New York, and after a short chat with Bordereau, the deal was done. Actually, it had been done before Collins had boarded the Amtrak train from Boston. Bordereau was a one-time foreign exchange student who had stayed with the Collins family in Stamford during his junior year of high school. Collins had gone to stay with the Bordereaus in Paris the next three summers, driving, diving, climbing, and adventuring throughout France. The men were like brothers.

"Batman et Robin," the Parisians had called them. Together and close, but very different. Tall, elegant Bordereau with his confident manner, bell-clear voice, and mind full of literary scholarship and quotations. And short, wiry Collins with his buzz-cut hair, unquenchable curiosity, alternately glib or serious depending on his comfort level—serious when he was on firm social or intellectual ground, glib when he was not—and rapid speech that struggled to keep pace with that even quicker mind.

Bordereau told him that the new division he was being asked to head was named the United Nations Institute of Technology, Omega. Bordereau had added omega, the last letter of the Greek alphabet, to indicate that the organization would be the "last word" in collecting and studying scientific phenomena from around the world. Bordereau—a Sorbonne graduate who had majored in political science and minored in literature—felt that the United Nations needed a clearing house for what he called "undiscovered realities," the mysteries that constituted civilization's modern folklore.

Collins felt it was an enlightened, almost heroic concept. An effort to collect, compare, and understand the unexplained.

"I want to place them in global context," Bordereau said, "to see why people around the world experience variations of the same modern myths instead of radically different ones. Do UFO sightings in Argentina and West Virginia have something in common that only a good scientist might think about, such as increased sunspot activities or lunar phases? Are leprechauns and space aliens actually the same beings, reinvented by different cultures in different times? Are reports of the Himalayan yeti and America's Sasquatch linked to people whose diets or local air or smoke from a certain kind of wood burned in a campfire cause them to hallucinate? Are poltergeist disruptions in Siberia and Baja, California, and Maine linked to sudden drops in temperature, low-intensity earthquakes, or unannounced weapons tests at nearby Russian or American or Canadian military bases?"

All of that was possible, but Collins had another thought, one that he kept to himself but which intrigued him even more.

Were any or some or maybe *all* of these things real?

That was what had really attracted the quantum physicist to this post. That big leap. Suppose the explanation for these phenomena was that there *was* no "other" explanation. That there really was an Abominable Snowman or mental telepathy or a spatial distortion in the Bermuda Triangle that chewed up planes and ships. The chance to expand the boundaries of known science without being hindered by international boundaries was a gift.

A dream.

In practice, however, UNIT Omega was a dream from which Harold Collins had been quickly and roughly shaken awake.

No, the young man had to admit by the end of just his second day on the job. It was a dream from which he had been dragged, then tossed into a cold shower and forced to look at the ugly realities of bureaucracy, apathy, and geography.

The bureaucracy was the United Nations organization itself. As Collins discovered, "Batman" Bordereau spent most of his time settling arguments between delegations about procedure. The issues themselves were never solved; the issues were rarely even addressed. Departments were supposed to function autonomously, but Collins did not have the money to do so. In fact, his department was so far off the radar that most members had never even heard of it.

The apathy was caused by the fact that UNIT Omega had been founded in a flourish of Bordereau's youthful, forward-looking, somewhat funky enthusiasm—like the man who proposes to a lady when they're both drunk, and she accepts. Which is also a form of being "engaged," albeit another not particularly happy or successful one. As it happened, Bordereau proposed the office to the United Nations Internal Office Panel over a wine-flavored working dinner. Though the UN Office of Scientific Development's rubber-stamp had okayed UNIT Omega, no one had bothered to come up with the money to fund it. This became apparent to Collins on day one, when he tried to order a subscription to *Worlds of Tomorrow* magazine. His twenty-five-dollar request was rejected. At Bordereau's suggestion, Collins went to see Deputy Ambassador David Khama of Nigeria, head of the Internal Budget Committee. The diplomat politely informed Collins—every unpleasant word or deed was done politely at the United Nations, Collins discovered—that his group had elected to limit funding for UNIT Omega to Collins's salary and one thousand dollars in pre-approved travel expenses.

"We have to see if it is a viable concept before we allocate more money," Khama had told him.

"But sir," Collins had said politely—instead of yelling *Hey, moron!*—"How can we determine viability without money?"

"You have money," Khama had smiled back. "A salary plus a per diem. Use them creatively."

So much for traveling to the six symposia he had planned to attend, joining museum expeditions, and contributing money and expertise to privately funded teams that could advance his own research.

Finally, there was the sad geography of the department. The only office space available for what was appropriately called a LAG, a "low action group" like UNIT Omega was in an office in sublevel three. That was the bottom floor of the building, located two stories below the surface of New York's East River. Two elevators serviced this section. One elevator was for the twenty-odd people who worked in the basement. The other, larger lift was for the custodial staff. They stored their mops, cleaning fluid, and rat traps there.

The young man had one immediate neighbor, Patricia Arroyo of Peru, who headed the one-person Domesticated Animal Rescue Office. The young lady was the daughter of the Peruvian Ambassador and the wife of the Spanish head of UNICEF. So at least she had money to help flood-orphaned cats in China or dying horses at drought-choked ranches in Argentina. She also had people who came and visited now and then. Collins didn't even have a secretary to talk to. And he didn't speak Spanish, so he couldn't eavesdrop.

So Harold Collins went from obtaining his PhD to having a dream job for about a day, to sitting in a dreary, windowless office that shook several times an hour. And the shaking was not because of restless ghosts, which he could at least have investigated. Collins had solved that problem within minutes. It was the rumbling of the number seven subway on its way to and from Queens.

Collins did not want to give up. Not yet. If nothing else he would learn how bureaucracies functioned—or didn't. He spent the bulk of his workday creating files and databases, trying to do the job that he had been hired to do. He cruised the internet for stories to bookmark. He read and clipped articles from newspapers and scientific periodicals. And he stayed in regular e-mail contact with people whose enthusiasm fueled his own empty tank. These included the handful of professors from MIT and Columbia—where Collins had done his undergraduate studies—who shared his enthusiasm for the unexplained; the heads of slightly off-center scientific groups from the ESP research center at Duke University in North Carolina to scientists in the SETI network, the globe-girdling Search for Extra-Terrestrial Intelligence; and smaller, fringe organizations that investigated cursed Egyptian tombs, haunted lighthouses, and alien abductions.

For four months the highlight of Collins's every day was when his mother called from Maui. It was good to hear from someone who cared about him, who loved him, who sent her only child chunks of lava because he was a scientist and she thought he might be interested, even though he wasn't a geologist—a distinction she did not make. She always called on Collins's cell phone. For some reason the automated switchboard at the UN had a difficult time distinguishing between Collins's department and the United Arab Emirates.

But it was maddening, and as he neared the half-year point, Collins would have zipped his backpack, turned in his ID badge, and walked away, if not for Bordereau admonishing him to be patient, lecturing him like God from the comfort of his sunlit thirty-second-floor office in the Secretariat building, an office that had a commanding view of the same river Collins spent most of his day beneath.

"Don't forget the dream just because you are awake," Bordereau told him. "Find ways to get back to it."

"Maybe I should try hitting myself on the head with my keyboard," Collins suggested. "That will put me to sleep."

"Don't," Bordereau cautioned. "We can't afford a new keyboard."

He had a point.

Bordereau shook his head and smiled. "It will all change," he assured him. "These things take time."

"So does continental drift," Collins had replied.

"And look what comes of that," Bordereau answered, emphasizing it with fist-rattling passion. The Frenchman opened his fists dramatically, slowly raising his long fingers. "Tectonic crawl creates sky-piercing mountain ranges. It creates mysteries, beauty, majesty. It spawns challenges for men and homes for the gods. Don't look at it as slow, Harold. Look at it as purposeful, deliberate."

Collins should have expected as much from a leader of an organization that responded to international crises with glacial swiftness. But Collins agreed to continue to try it Bordereau's way. If nothing else, he could begin cobbling together ideas for science fiction stories. That was something he couldn't do while bombarding volatile uranium oxide with deuteron.

Then, one morning at eleven o'clock, Collins's world changed, though not as Samuel Bordereau had predicted. By some miracle a caller had gotten through to him. And as Collins listened to the speaker, the small, clean office he was in seemed to become the center of the universe. His tidy desk felt like a command center. His job suddenly had purpose.

A paleontologist was calling from Scotland. She said she had read about his office in a professional magazine. She felt that he was the only one who could help her.

"Why?" he asked.

"Because I have just seen the Loch Ness Monster," the world-renowned scientist told him.

And suddenly the dream was alive and well.

CHAPTER THREE

T ALLY RANDALL LIED.

When she picked up the phone at her office in the American Museum of Natural History on New York's Central Park West, the tall, Vassar-educated twenty-six-year-old said she remembered who Harold Collins was.

She didn't. Not at first. She sat at her desk on the fifth floor of the building, twirling a strand of blond hair that had fallen from her headband, as she tried to place the voice. Actually, the first thing she did was stop thinking about what she was going to do that weekend, which was where her mind had gone as she proofread the photo captions for the November issue. There were not a lot of late-summer weekends left and she wanted to spend them wisely. Which was difficult when you didn't have anyone to spend them with since all your friends were married and off in the Hamptons or the Jersey Shore or wherever else young couples with little kids went, and you didn't want to spend them with your parents who asked why you didn't have one or two offspring of your own.

It was not until Harold Collins asked her how the "old hearth" was that she remembered the intense young physicist from the under-thirty party at the New York Foundation for the Advancement of Science a few weeks before. The man who had looked as profoundly unhappy in a business suit as he said he was working at the United Nations, for something rather ominously called UNIT Omega. The man whose name she hadn't recognized because, now that she thought about it, he had never bothered to give it to her.

The two had found themselves playing wallflowers in the reception hall of the West Fifty-Fifth Street brownstone when he had asked the inches-taller woman what she did. She told him that she was an associate editor at the museum's *Natural History* magazine.

He seemed impressed.

"I like the writing," he said. "Very clean."

"And the subjects?" she asked.

"Well, I have to say I like the pieces on scientists and the scientific process more than the articles about freshwater riches of the Amazon and textiles of the Ryukyu archipelago," he admitted.

She was impressed that he had pronounced "Ryukyu" and "archipelago" correctly. She also noticed, and liked, the brightness of his eyes and the half-smile that never left his mouth, even when she asked what he did and he complained about the endless red tape that lined the corridors of the United Nations as if it were a crime scene.

"Which it would be," he added, "if entropy were a crime."

He had come to the party, he said, to network and possibly get out of the United Nations. But he held back, he said, because his oldest friend had set up the department with him in mind, his mother would be crushed, and he didn't like giving up on anything, especially since, if nothing else, it gave him time to think about starting a science fiction novel. Tally was amazed that the young man had packed most of that into a single sentence. And it was a legitimate sentence, not disconnected babble. She had punctuated it in her head. It worked.

They talked a little about her college years, how she had started out wanting to be a geologist but had switched to journalism because, if she insisted on working instead of marrying the heir-next-door—literally—her parents thought it was a more suitable profession for a smart young lady.

He asked how she liked working for a venerable scientific institution.

"It's very good," she remembered telling him. "Not at all stodgy. It's like a fire in an old, old hearth."

He had liked that description. He had shaken his head enviously. Then, without much more chat, he had left the party in despair, though not before she had given him her business card. Which she had done because there was always a chance he could call her. Cute, smart, available men, even if they were slightly erratic, were still high B-list properties in New York.

Tally was glad to hear from Harold Collins and to learn his name. She told him that the "old hearth" was fine, and she began to think that maybe her weekend would not start out quite so downbeat and aimless. Unfortunately, she was sorry to hear, Collins was calling to ask her a professional question instead of asking her to go to a movie.

"I just got a call from Dr. Kathryn Castle in the Scottish Highlands," he said after the hellos were done and they had each assured the other that they were fine. "Have you heard of her?"

"Absolutely," Tally replied. She covered her disappointment as best she could. Maybe she would ask him out when he hit a period instead of a semicolon. Perhaps his calendar was as empty as hers. "Dr. Castle is one of the world's top paleontologists. Specializes in marine ani-mals."

"Really?" Collins said. "That's interesting."

"Why?"

"Because of the reason she called," Collins said. "I'll tell you more in a second. Do you know anything else about her? Reputation?"

"Impeccable, as far as I know," Tally said. "She became a bit of a recluse three or four years ago after her family was killed in a car crash. But she's still writing provocative papers on the life and times of elasmosaurs and other pre-historic sea creatures."

"So if she called and said that she had seen the Loch Ness Monster, would you be inclined to believe her?" Collins asked.

"She did that?"

"Yes."

"Then I'd make sure it was her," Tally said.

"It was," Collins assured her. "One of the things I did was call her back at the inn where she's staying, just to make sure."

"And she told you she saw the Monster alive, in Loch Ness," Tally repeated with open disbelief.

"Correct."

Tally switched from playing with her hair to twisting the slender strand of pearls she wore. "Dr. Kathryn Castle" and "the Loch Ness Monster" were names that simply did not fit.

"I just want to make sure I've got this right," Tally said. "Dr. Castle wasn't telling you about a giant squid that she or some fisherman reported seeing in the North Sea."

"No," Collins insisted. "She called. Ten minutes ago. To say. She saw. The Loch. Ness. Monster." He added, "With. Her. Own. Eyes."

"Was she there searching for the Monster?" Tally asked.

"That's the funny thing," Collins told her. "Apparently

not. Dr. Castle said she was on the loch relaxing and prov-
ing to herself that there was something she knew absolutely,
whatever that means. Then it turned into a busman's holi-
day, which a paleontologist should have expected taking a
rowboat out onto Loch Ness, I would think."

"Did Dr. Castle say why she called *you*?" Tally asked.

"Why shouldn't she?" he asked indignantly. "That's my
job here."

"I know. What I mean is, had you ever met her?"

"I never even *heard* of her," Collins said.

"Okay. Then I repeat: Why did she call *you*? How did
she know about UNIT Omega?"

"She told me she was catching up on her reading and
had just seen my picture in the 'New Appointments' section of *International Science World* magazine," he said.
"That's why she called. She said she wanted to talk to
someone like me before she went to an established scientific institution that 'lacked curiosity and mobility,' as she
put it. She said she needed sympathetic field help now."

"So she called someone she didn't know to help her
with an impromptu research expedition," Tally said. "Seems
a little strange to me."

"So does the Loch Ness Monster sticking its uncommon
head from the water, looking around, and then resubmerg-
ing with a wake that nearly capsizes Dr. Castle in a rowboat ten meters away," Collins said.

"It would take a big head to do that," Tally said.

"Very," Collins said. "But one of those things happened.
The first one. She called me. What I need to know is
whether the other one did too."

"A minute ago you said one of the things you did was
call Dr. Castle back at the inn to prove it was her. What else
did you do to verify her identity?"

"Well, figuring that this *could* have been a friend of my
sponsor Samuel Bordereau calling from Europe to keep
my spirits up, I asked for the data on her *ISW* mailing

label," Collins said. "She gave it to me. If she had something to hide she wouldn't have."

"Maybe the caller figured you couldn't check it," Tally said. That was the most specious reasoning she had heard in a while.

"Ah, but I could and I did," Collins said. "Before I called you I phoned the person who interviewed me for that news item. They accessed the files and corroborated the information."

Score one for Dr. Collins, she thought. "I don't suppose Dr. Castle took a picture," Tally said.

"No," Collins replied.

"Figures."

"That doesn't bother me," Collins said. "In fact, I'm encouraged by it."

"You are?"

"Yes. Some of the most famous sightings came with photographs that later proved to be hoaxes."

"And you know that how?"

"It's one of the benefits of having a lot of time and nothing to fill it with," he replied. "I've gone all over the internet and built a database of mysteries from around the world and throughout time, including the sightings at Loch Ness. I believe that someone trying to trick me would certainly have spent time putting together photographic 'evidence.' Only someone who had nothing to hide would come to me with just one thing—the truth."

That made sense, as far as it went, Tally admitted. But it wasn't enough to convince her.

"If you've read the reports about Loch Ness, then you also must know that it's a geologically active area," Tally said. "Tremors could have spit up a log or two and caused the wake. Or even a fossilized mammoth skull. Under the right conditions those could have been mistaken for a live sea serpent."

"By an amateur," Collins said. "Not by a paleontologist."

"Harold, I work at a natural history museum," Tally said. "Every paleontologist I ever met would die happy if they could lay eyes on a living dinosaur. That's a strong wish. It could affect the mind. Especially a grieving mind."

"Forgive me, but that's psychobabble," Collins said.

"A disparaging term used to discredit unpleasant psychiatric truths," Tally replied.

"Look, if Dr. Castle's had some hard knocks, maybe her plumb line is a little off," Collins agreed. "Still, I'm willing to risk that."

"Risk what?" Tally asked.

"I'm going over there," he said. "I've got a whopping thousand dollars in my travel fund, and I'm gonna blow it."

"I'm sure Dr. Castle will appreciate that," Tally said, turning some of her attention back to the captions and wondering what else she might do this weekend since Harold Collins was obviously going to be out of town Monster-fishing in the Twilight Zone.

"Well, that brings me to the second reason I'm calling," he said. "No one in the world except Dr. Castle, it seems, has heard of UNIT Omega. Obviously I could use some publicity."

"Obviously."

"But my needs aside, the best part of this is what you stand to gain," Collins said.

"Me?" she asked. "How did I become involved in this?"

"At the party you told me you've written some pieces for the magazine," Collins said.

"Occasional 'Up Front' and 'Endpaper' pieces," she replied.

"No ambition to write more?"

"Of course," she said.

"Fine. If Dr. Castle isn't a loon, you could end up with the scientific story of the millennium," Collins said.

"That 'if' comes with some very long odds," she said.

"But what if it's true?" Collins asked. "What would odds like that pay in career dividends?"

"A lot—" she admitted.

"Exactly."

"—because it *isn't* true."

"Very probably," Collins said. "But you wouldn't bet your life on that, would you?"

"No."

"Then why bet your career?"

She had no answer to that.

"What I'm saying, Tally, is that I would like you to come with me," Collins said. "Cover the inaugural expedition of the first major new international science foundation of the twenty-first century?"

"You mean drop everything and go to Scotland?" Tally asked.

"That's where they keep Loch Ness," he said.

"That's insane," she said.

"Is it?" he asked.

No, she had to admit. *It's just impulsive, which is different. It's also different from what you usually do, and that isn't necessarily a bad thing.*

"Some people would say it's bold and exciting," Collins said.

"Okay. I got to that by myself," Tally admitted.

"So what do you say?" he asked. "I think I've got enough in my budget to cover two coach tickets and ground transportation if you can pick up your hotel room."

The money wasn't an issue. Tally didn't live large and could afford the room. She could also afford the time. Once she finished the captions she was done with this issue. So why was she hesitating?

Because practical people don't circle the globe looking for a mythical monster, she told herself.

At least, that's what her mother would say. That moved Tally a little closer to saying yes.

Tally had never been to Scotland. Even if the quest were a bust, it sure beat the hell out of going back to her apartment in the West Village and amusing herself with a stack of rented movies. And if she couldn't convince her editor that this was a viable story—she wasn't sure of it herself; if the magazine wouldn't give her the hotel money, she'd pay it out of her own pocket. Who knows? She could meet some hot Highlander. Or if they didn't find the monster, an article about the batty, impromptu Nessie hunt with Collins might be saleable to *New York Magazine* or *Time Out*. Something like, "Stalking the Plesiosaurus: A First Date I'll Never Forget," or "The United Nations Goes Mesozoic."

Except for the fact that Harold Collins was desperate, and desperate men were driven by every part of them but the brain, she couldn't think of a single reason not to go.

"Let's do it," she said in a burst of exuberance.

"When can you be ready?"

"In about two hours," she said. "I need to finish up here and pack."

"Great!" he said. "I'll get flight times and weather reports and I'll give you a call."

Tally gave the physicist her cell phone number, and he promised to call back as soon as possible.

"And thank you," Collins said. "Thank you very, very much."

"You're welcome," she said, though Collins probably hadn't heard. He had already hung up.

That was something the young woman disliked about scientists. They were not the world's best listeners. For the most part their theories, their ideas were all that mattered. But she was used to that. Her mother, Laurel, shared the shortcoming, she thought. Tally wondered whether she should bother to call Mrs. Thompson Canyon Randall IV. Phone her directly across the park, in her Fifth Avenue duplex, and tell her what she was doing.

"You know you have to," the young woman muttered to herself. Otherwise, her mother would call her apartment, get no answer, and phone everyone in her Palm Pilot asking if they had seen or heard from her daughter.

So Tally called. She told her mother that the magazine was sending her to Europe to interview a leading scientist. She knew that anything short of an A-list society party would bore her mother, so she made the trip sound as prestigious as possible. Still trying to impress and persuade, even though the cause was DOA. Tally promised to call when she got back.

"One down, one to go," she said as she hung up. At least it was the easy one coming up. Tally rose and walked down the creaky, wood-paneled corridor to see her editor, Dr. Kerwin Armstrong. She decided not to ask for expenses. That would have invited questions she wasn't prepared to answer. *"To find a Monster, sir,"* was not a phrase she wished to utter. Tally told the zoologist that she had been asked to go to Europe for the weekend by a great guy she had met. Could he possibly spare her on Monday so she could make it a three-day weekend? The paternal Dr. Armstrong told her to go and have a great time. She thanked him with a heartfelt smile, then returned to her office to finish her proofreading. Part of the smile had been for Dr. Armstrong, but part of it was also acknowledging the irony of what had just transpired. Tally had given the story a professional angle for her mother and a personal spin for her employer. The norms were inverted.

Yet somehow that seemed right. A fitting way to start a far-from-normal adventure.

CHAPTER FOUR

HAROLD COLLINS ARRIVED in the reception area of Samuel Bordereau's office and told the Israeli-born secretary that he needed to see Bordereau as soon as possible. Almost everyone who worked at the UN was something-born other than American. Galit Lopatin, a beauty with high cheekbones and exotic eyes, told Harold that her boss was on a conference call but that it should not be a long one.

"It is his weekly briefing from the five international regional commissioners of the Economic and Social Council," she told him in a heavy accent. "They rarely have anything new to report. Each representative complains about underfunding, the disinterest of their host governments, and the fact that whatever they do, the economies of Asia, Western Asia, Latin America, Europe, and Africa all depend on one thing: how well the economy of the United States is doing."

"That's globalization for you," Collins said, not really

sure what he was saying or if the term truly applied. "Fortunately, what happens on Wall Street doesn't affect my budget."

She winked. She knew that he had no idea what he was saying.

A moment later Collins saw the phone light go off on Galit's desk. He jumped past her toward Bordereau's office and opened the door. Galit did not protest. She knew Collins would not have waited for her to announce him.

Collins told his friend what had happened since Dr. Castle had called. As he listened, Bordereau sat back and grinned.

"Well," Bordereau said, self-satisfied.

"Well?"

"I knew you would make things happen somehow," Bordereau said.

"Samuel, this fell on me. It was luck."

"No," Bordereau replied. "It was patience. And I like it, very much. The British Ambassador will appreciate being the recipient of a United Nations–funded undertaking."

"He will? But I'll only be spending a grand," Collins said.

"A grand, a million, pennies collected in a milk container—it's all about appearances," Bordereau shrugged. "Trust me, he will like it. And the fact that the natural history museum is involved gives the expedition prestige. He will talk about your group to others. That will help get you more money. Other nations will want to host your operations."

" 'Operations,' " Collins said. "Three people, a rowboat, binoculars, and a couple of cameras. If that's an operation, it's outpatient at best."

"It's all a question of how you spin it," Bordereau said as he made a note to himself. "I'll see that it's entered in the daily minutes as the first UNIT Omega International Study. You'll file a report when you return, build some momentum. More opportunities will present themselves."

"Or they can be made," Collins said.

"They can be made," Bordereau agreed.

"Like I'm doing now," Collins told him.

"I don't follow."

"I need a favor."

"Big or small?" Bordereau asked.

"I need to borrow Galit," Collins told him.

"For what and for how long?" she called from the outer office.

"For downloading data to diskettes," he shouted back. "I don't have time to go online and collect my files about the Monster. I need to make travel arrangements and get some more background on Dr. Castle."

Bordereau glanced at his watch with a dramatic turn of his wrist. "I think I can spare her for an hour or so."

"Terrific," Collins said. "I'll have my laptop. She can e-mail me any articles that look promising. I'll log on at the airport and collect 'em."

"Fine," Bordereau said. He offered his hand across the desk. "Good luck, my friend. It's nice to see you so excited."

"Thank you," Collins replied. "It's nice to *be* excited," he said as he turned to go.

"Harold?" Bordereau said.

Collins turned back.

There was now a different Samuel Bordereau sitting behind the desk. From his expression, Collins could see that the "political" animal was gone. In his place was the scholarly Samuel Bordereau. The one Collins liked better, felt more comfortable talking to, trusted a little bit more to look out for him instead of for the United Nations.

"Do you believe Dr. Castle saw something real out there on the lake?" the Frenchman asked.

"I hope so," Collins told him. "I mean, wouldn't that be something?"

"It would be," Bordereau agreed.

"But . . . ?" Collins pressed.

Bordereau smiled self-consciously. "Harold, do you know what solving a mystery really is?"

"Probably not, if you're asking," Collins said.

"It's not about the puzzle per se but about the restoration of order," Bordereau told him. "That's how P. D. James perceived it. But Jean Cocteau wrote something that is also true. He said, 'Mystery has its own mysteries, and there are gods above gods.' "

"Puzzles leading to more puzzles," Collins said. "The search for order creating its antithesis."

"Chaos," Bordereau said. "Explorations can go either way."

Now it was Collins who smiled. "You know, I wouldn't make too much of this," he said. "I was pretty gung-ho when I was selling this to Tally Randall at *Natural History,* but now I'm not so sure. While I would love to find a monster, a large part of me—a very large part of me—says that what Dr. Castle saw was probably something else. Something not as sexy or newsworthy."

"The Loch Ness Sturgeon?" Bordereau quipped.

"Reason dictates, does it not?" Collins asked.

"It does."

"Though finding out that it was a shadow of a rock or dark methane gas would still satisfy the UNIT Omega mandate to investigate and explain," Collins pointed out.

"It would. As long as Ms. Randall doesn't write something to make you look foolish," Bordereau cautioned.

"I'm invisible now," Collins replied. " 'Foolish' would at least put me on the map."

"True," Bordereau admitted. "If you find a Monster, I can also guarantee we'll have no trouble boosting your budget immediately. In fact, I'll come to Loch Ness and deliver your check personally."

"I'll hold you to that," Collins said.

Bordereau offered his old friend a hand. "Good-bye, Harold."

"Good-bye," Collins said.

As he walked down the bright corridor toward the elevator, his shoes clapping on the off-white tiles, Harold Collins found himself believing more and more what he had just told Bordereau, which was the same thing Tally Randall had told him. That what Dr. Castle had seen break the surface of Loch Ness was something other than a Monster.

Yet there was still the hope, still the sense of wonder that had first drawn him to science. Still the . . . *wouldn't that be something. . . .*

Still the dream.

CHAPTER FIVE

FAMILY.

It had been there for Kathryn Castle when she was a child, guiding and nourishing her, and it had been there for her when she was a young woman. And now, at fifty-three, it was gone.

There's only the love and the pain of it, she thought. The intangibles of parents, husband, and son. They endured, like ice-bound mammoths, frozen in exactly the state they were in when the flesh had died. It seemed strange to Dr. Castle that spirit should effectively die with the body. Wasn't that supposed to endure and flower?

Instead, the only living connection she had was to a place. Kathryn remembered vividly the first time she had come to Loch Ness. She had been five years old. Her father had promised to take her to Hyde Park one blisteringly bright summer Sunday to go birdwatching, which was his passion. But he had had a case to investigate, a double murder—in the park, as it happened—and so their outing had been postponed. Her father promised to take her the following weekend, but it rained. He told her that rain or shine, the next weekend they would do something "very extra special," as he put it, with warmth and conviction that gave real weight to the words. And they did. On Friday evening Inspector Castle packed his wife and daughter into a taxicab, which drove them to Victoria Station, and the hardy little family rode the train to Edinburgh, Scotland. After the nearly five-hour trip, they rented a sporty Healey roadster and drove north to Inverness.

Apart from visiting her grandparents in Ipswich and Coventry, this was the first time Kathryn had been away from London. It was late in the spring, and her father let her roll down the window. The first thing that struck Kathryn was how different the air smelled here. It was like rolling on the ground in the park, only you didn't have to get dirty. And the smells came *at* you. There was the tang of musty dampness, a hint of musky tree bark, and all kinds of flowers contributing whispers of individual scents. There was something clean and refreshing about all of it. The air also seemed "big" to her. That was how her five-year-old mind described it. In London, the wind moved through buildings, down eaves, up from grates. Here, nothing got in its way and nothing was added to it, like burning petrol or baking bread or fresh fruit from a stand.

Her first view of the loch itself was unmemorable. It was night when they arrived at the Loch Ness Hotel and there was a misty drizzle. There was little to see save for a rippling reflection of the lights from the eighteenth-century stone-built inn, its waterside veranda, and small boats that dotted the loch. What she remembered from that night arrival were two things. One was the sound of the loch. It was a delicate, whispered lapping. It was very soothing, like when it rained in London and she was safe in bed. The other thing she remembered was something less tangible. Her father had told her about the legend of the Monster, adding that he didn't have enough information to say whether it existed or not. Jonathan Castle was not a romantic, and his tone suggested he did not believe. But that first night at the loch, Kathryn felt the way she did at home whenever she walked past the hall closet at night. Eyes half-shut as she shuffled back from the loo, she was certain that a bogeyman was hiding among the linens.

She was certain, at five years old, that something mysterious was hiding in the loch.

When Kathryn got into bed that night, in a room that smelled like moss, she asked her mother to pull the covers all the way up to her chin before she left. The young girl tried not to think of bogeymen and monsters. She shut her eyes and tried to imagine what the loch would look like in the morning.

It will look like a big gray sky with ripples, she decided as her mind wandered into sleep. Like the elephant she saw at the circus. The loch would be cool and flat and vast.

The next morning Kathryn was up before her parents. The window was beside the bed, and sharp morning sunlight slashed across the room. She couldn't wait to see if she had pictured the loch correctly. She knee-walked across the squeaky mattress to the window and parted the white curtains.

"Oh."

That was all she could say. Loch Ness was not what she had expected. It was not a gray sky but it was a rich, serene blue. There was the hint of a rainbow in the distance, between two high hills. The grass along the shore was lush green and sparkled in the sunlight. Eagerly, she twisted back the latch on top of the window and raised it. She could still hear the soft sounds of the water. The air was chilly and didn't seem to have a scent. She sniffed deeply several times to make sure. Except for that mossy smell of the room, there was nothing.

Kathryn dressed and went outside, getting a stern warning from the desk clerk not to venture too close to the water and to button the new sweater she was wearing. The young girl promised she wouldn't do one and would do the other. Then she stepped out the back door and stood in the cool morning. She took small, careful steps forward, swinging under the rail of the deck and walking down a damp, grassy incline. As she squinted out at the big, brilliant loch, she felt as she did when she approached the big doghouse in her Ipswich grandmother's backyard. Like Big Ric, the Irish setter, was going to hear her at any moment and come charging out. Kathryn felt even more certain now that there was something in the loch. She could feel it in her tingling toes, in her rapid heartbeat, in the way her long red hair seemed to rise from her neck. She could almost hear it, something keening inaudibly. But she couldn't move. She felt drawn to the loch, to the mystery, to the unseen. She stopped a few paces from the rocky shore and just stood there. Her legs felt weak. She swayed in that wonderful morning air. She felt as though she was in a fairy tale, with evil just a page turn away.

The spell was shattered when Kathryn's father came out to see what she was up to. His big voice stilled the tingling too as he hoisted her on his big shoulder and carried her back to the inn and breakfast.

"The concierge was worried about you," her father said. "He said the grass is slippery in the morning."

"That's because of the dew," Kathryn said.

"Yes it is. And you might have fallen into the water."

It seemed odd now to Kathryn that she wasn't afraid of the real and present threat but was frightened of the one that she couldn't see. It also seemed strange now, to the mature woman, that here she was, on that very same deck, on a morning like that one so long ago, leaning on the same weatherworn rail and looking out at the same view that had both frightened and mesmerized her as a child.

One thing was different, though. After coming here nearly every autumn since she was old enough to travel on her own, Kathryn had finally beheld the Creature of the loch. She had only seen it for five or so seconds as it had pushed snout-first from the water about thirty meters away from her before falling to the left, like a windshield wiper. It exhaled silently, its hot breath reaching her. It *was* real. The animal did not look like a Mesozoic-Era plesiosaur or elasmosaur or any of the other prehistoric creatures she remotely imagined it might be. Then again, she had only studied the fossils and computer recreations of seagoing dinosaurs. She had never seen one with sinew and flesh, eyes and tongue.

The animal had a flat head the size and general shape of a *Crocodylus niloticus,* a Nile Crocodile. As it rolled to the side, the scientist saw a thick, lengthy neck like a seal and oily black and yellow skin like mottled vinyl. As it vanished in a shallow splash, she saw the hint of a slender ivory tongue and mean snake eyes with lids that blinked upward. And teeth. There were fine, straight, ivory teeth, maybe fifty in all. Above and behind the jaw there appeared to be fleshy slits that could have been gills. They could also have been a lizard's fan, possibly ears, possibly a sexual display. It was too much to take in at once. She was further distracted as a faint but distinctive smell washed over her. It was fresh bordering on tart, like the penetrating scent of ozone.

After the animal's initial disappearance, there was no wake, no further ripples, no evidence that an extremely large animal had been there or remained anywhere near the surface.

Kathryn sat for over two hours waiting to see if the beast appeared again. When it did not, she returned to shore. There had been no one else in the area. No one looking out from the inn. No tours this early, not even her old beau Shep Boucher trying to spend time with her. She had already rebuffed him the night before, at the bar, and once was probably enough. Though there were no other witnesses, Kathryn did not doubt what she had seen.

As she watched the water, she thought about what to do. She could not sit out here day and night. She needed help to find the Monster. Kathryn had to examine the water, try to ascertain if there were cellular residue or submarine conditions that may have contributed to the monster's appearance. Cool currents near the bottom that may have driven the animal to surface. She had to check for tectonic activity. A petrol or chemical spill. Something that may have disrupted a potential food supply.

Telling her story to the local newspaper was out of the question. They would play it up to bolster the legitimacy of the legend and encourage tourism. Her report would be perceived as a stunt. Simply by associating her name with something perceived as fanciful or frivolous would hurt her credibility, especially if it did not attract the resources to help her investigate the sighting scientifically. Nor could she contact any of the international news services, scientific journals, or research foundations. Many of them, from the *New York Times* to the Academy of Applied Science, had already spent hundreds of thousands of pounds on expeditions that had turned up very little. Without a legitimate photograph, without proof, powerful publications and institutions would be disinclined to investigate.

Then Kathryn remembered an item she had read in *International Science World* magazine. It was a small one-paragraph notice about the newly created United Nations Institute of Technology. She went to her briefcase and got the magazine. UNIT Omega was a group that had been chartered to investigate natural phenomena around the world. Perfect. They would have the interest, resources, and presumably the obligation to assist her. Quietly, one would hope.

She had called the United Nations from her room at the inn. After first being misdirected to the office of the ambassador of the United Arab Emirates she was connected with Harold Collins. Mr. Collins sounded young, which meant one of two things: that he was absolutely brilliant or that he had gotten the job because he was someone's son or nephew, with all the talent and ambition that implied. She hoped it was the former, because he also sounded extremely enthusiastic. That is, after initially thinking that someone named Samuel Something was trying to put something over on him.

Collins told her he would call back. Kathryn thanked him for listening and, because whoever he was going to consult would probably think she was a crackpot, was afraid she wouldn't hear from him again. But a half-hour later he rang back and said he was flying right over, along with someone from *Natural History* magazine. Kathryn knew the magazine very well, but she didn't recognize the woman's name. Once again she did the "I hope" routine. She hoped it wasn't some angry young cynic—or worse, a bitter old crank who didn't sit on enough boards of trustees to suit her resume—who wrote acerbic opinion pieces or, nearly as dangerous, a freelancer who moonlighted for the sensational *Weekly World News* or London *Splash*. Tabloid newspapers loved to have real scientists swearing to sightings of ghosts, UFOs . . . or lake monsters.

Once everything was in place, Kathryn wished she hadn't called Harold Collins or anyone else. There had been a large insurance settlement when Del and Gary had died, and since then she had mostly kept to herself, working on remote digs, writing, and pondering. Wondering why that one absolute in her life, love, was so painfully empty. She didn't know if she still had the people skills to handle even a small undertaking like this.

It isn't about you, though, is it? she asked herself.

It's about paleontology. It's about expanding human scholarship. And her instincts had told her to do this. And so she had. Besides, Kathryn Castle's situation was not fraught with options. Nor time. This was the best plan she could think of before whatever was down in the loch slipped away.

Something *was* down there. Kathryn had seen it, heard it, smelled it. It had rocked the water of the loch. And as the scientist sat in the rowboat or stood on the deck, she possessed one additional piece of evidence. It was not traditional science, but it was one more reason she personally believed that the creature was still out there. Her toes tingled and her heart beat faster and the reddish-gray hair on her head stood up very slightly.

Kathryn Castle *felt* it.

CHAPTER SIX

THERE SHE IS, familiar but new, Collins thought as the cab pulled up in front of the West Tenth Street brownstone.

Tally Randall was standing at the curb. She looked just as he remembered her, now that he saw her. About five-foot-nine, slender shoulders, straight blond hair, and pretty as starlight. And obviously well-heeled, judging from the brownstone she was standing in front of. It had to be worth about four or five million on the market. He wondered if a girl like her would ever have gone out with a guy like him if he didn't bring her what was potentially the science story of the new century. As he opened the door and waved, he did something he hadn't done last time they were together. He looked for a ring, wedding or engagement. She wasn't wearing one. At least, he didn't think so. She was wearing four rings, including one on a thumb, but none of them looked "official." When Collins took a moment to mentally flip himself and face the same way she was, he realized that none of the rings was on her left hand ring finger. Besides, if she were married, would she have gone running off to Scotland with a guy she didn't know?

Possibly, he thought, *if she were a serious journalist.*

Not that it mattered. Collins was a middle-class kid from Stamford, Connecticut. Girls like her married position. They joined their lives and important body parts with guys who had names with numerals. He had a better chance of getting a million-dollar-a-year budget than he did getting a date with someone like Tally. Or a second date, surely.

Still, that too was a dream.

All of this careened through Harold Collins's mind as he stepped from the cab. Obviously, a few beats too slow. His driver, an Asian gentleman, had already popped the trunk, left the cab, and was on his way to loading Tally's two small Tumi suitcases. Thwarted, Collins stood by the door and motioned grandly toward the interior.

"Your carriage," he said, though he felt totally foolish actually hearing the words. The romantic notion was all in his head. The gesture clunked and clattered and died on the street in the real world.

"You look happier than the last time I saw you," she said as though he hadn't spoken.

"It's being with you," he said. Even as these words too were coming from his mouth, he couldn't believe he had said something so banal.

"You were with me last time," she reminded him.

"Yes, but now we have something to do other than stand around," he pointed out. He wished he could get back in the cab and start again.

"I can't believe I'm doing this," she said, shaking her head.

"Going?" he asked. "Or going with me?"

"Both," she told him. She grinned. "I didn't mean that as a dig. I'm just not usually this impulsive."

"I'm glad you were," Collins told her. He shut the door

and scooted around to the other side. He jumped in, feeling bad about her non-dig but good about the fact that he'd talked Tally into this. The driver returned.

"And we're going in a cab," she said.

"Excuse me?"

"Nothing," she said.

"I don't follow," he said.

"I usually take a car service to go to the airport," Tally said.

"Ah. Well, I'm on a budget, as I said."

"So am I. But they cost about the same and the sedans have shock absorbers that work." She leaned forward. "No offense, Mr. Chan," she added, reading his name from his hack license.

"The butt always speaks true," he said.

Tally and Collins exchanged looks. Then they chuckled and sat back. The driver pulled away from the curb.

So Tally's comment about the car service wasn't a complaint, it was just information. Still, it made Collins feel stupid.

"So, have you lived here long?" Collins asked.

"In New York, or there?" she asked, nodding toward the building.

"Both," he replied. He wondered if she was being thorny or being an editor, paying careful attention to language. Either way, he would also have to ask precise questions.

"I've lived in New York all my life," Tally told him. "I've only lived in that building since I started working at the magazine."

"Oh. The place isn't yours?" Collins asked.

"The building? I wish," she replied. "What made you think that? Do I look like 'money'?"

Collins was perspiring a little under the arms. He had gone from one pitfall to another, walked straight into the stereotype trap. The clothes, the golden hair, the pearls, the car service. He just assumed the woman was loaded.

"I don't know what 'money' looks like," he lied, because he did. It looked like Tally Randall. He said, with sudden inspiration, "You just looked like you belonged there."

"Greenwich Village, young and hip and vital?" she teased.

"Sure. Yeah."

She smiled at that. "Actually, I rent a room from the owner, Mr. Winston Kolb. He's a retired book publisher."

"Kolb Press, popular science books," Collins said.

"Right. He sold to one of the megaconglomerates and became a patron of art and science," she said. "I was lucky to get in. He usually leases to NYU students, but I was recommended by a staff writer he used to publish. Mr. Kolb said he likes to subsidize 'smart young people'—his words, not mine."

Collins didn't ask if Mr. Kolb was a lech. He wasn't going to go step back into the stereotype trap.

"And Mr. Kolb isn't even a lech, in case you were wondering," Tally added.

"I wasn't."

"He's this really benign gentleman who likes to be surrounded by youth and curiosity."

"That's great," Collins said. "You were lucky to get in."

"I know. I like to think I would have roughed it by living in Brooklyn or the Bronx if I didn't."

"Instead of . . . ?"

"Living with my folks," she said with a small shudder.

"So you have family in the city?"

"My mother and father have a place uptown," she said. "We brunch once a week. If we spent more time together, we'd break more than bread."

There was frost in her voice and a strong period at the end of that sentence. Collins's analytical mind was already putting together a story. Upper East Side money. Rebellious daughter. Tension. If Harold Collins was slightly off-center it was because of his Type-A personality, not because of anything his parents did to him. They were always very loving and very supportive. There was no money, no Harold Senior or I, II, or III whose middle name was written out and whose probably marginal ripples a son was obliged to continue. Whenever he visited his parents, it wasn't an obligation. It was a joy.

"What about you?" she asked.

"My folks live in Maui," Collins told her.

"Now *that's* cool!" she said with a trace of envy.

"My dad was a Naval gunnery engineer who fell in love with a Hawaiian girl. They got married and when his hitch was through he went to work for NordElmer munitions in Stamford, Connecticut. A couple of years ago he had a chance to grab early retirement, so he took it and they went back to the islands. They run a small banana plantation slash bed-and-breakfast."

"You're kidding!" she said.

"Nope. It's a little startling to see my father in a muumuu, but they love it," Collins said.

Tally shook her head. Collins wondered what she was thinking. Did she wish her folks lived like that? Or did she want that in her future? Or maybe she thought it was absolutely uncivilized. He decided not to ask. He hadn't found his footing with this woman.

"What's your story, then?" Tally asked as the cab sped up First Avenue. "How did a physicist come to be hired by the United Nations?"

"It's my friend's fault," Collins said. "When I was a kid we had a foreign exchange student staying with us. Samuel Bordereau, son of one of the most successful toy makers in France."

"Toy maker?" she said.

"Yeah. He created *Les Tetes de Petit Pain.*"

"The Muffin Heads?"

Collins nodded.

"My God, I used to *love* those!" Tally said. "I had the Muffin Treehouse, Muffin Mountain, Muffin Cruise Ship, the works!"

"Which is why Charles Bordereau was one of the most successful toy makers in France," Collins said. "Anyway, Samuel was this really literate, Victor Hugo–reading guy, and I was into science fiction. He had read Jules Verne but that was it. He was always amused by my single-mindedness."

"You're saying you were a geek," Tally said.

"I was a humanist," he replied. Now she was the one doing the stereotyping. *Down Eros, up Mars,* he thought: It was time to take her down. "I was not into the hardware and glittery costumes per se. They were fun, but that was not what science fiction meant to me. I believed in the visions of utopia, in the ways that space and ideas from the future and enlightened extraterrestrials could benefit and elevate humankind. I became a scientist to try and reach some of those places and concepts off the printed page. Reality, not fantasy."

"Somebody's got some passion goin'," she said.

"About this, I definitely do," he said. "Samuel graduated from school and decided to go into politics. But he couldn't be bothered winning elections. When he was twenty-three his father used influence to have him appointed as an assistant to the French Ambassador to the United Nations. When the ambassador got caught in an extortion plot involving security council votes, everyone in the office was cleaned out *except* Samuel. He represented French interests so well over the next three months that the Secretary-General asked him to work on his staff. As soon as Samuel got the chance, he created a department just for me."

Tally nodded. "So, Mr. UNIT Omega, do you have any idea how we're going to go about the search?" she asked.

"I haven't really had time to work that out," Collins

said. "Even though it's been," he glanced at his watch, "a whole ninety minutes."

"Right. Of course. Well, I assume Dr. Castle has equipment—sonar, underwater cameras, sounding charts."

"I'm sure she does," Collins said, though he wasn't sure and he didn't want to scare Tally off by saying anything that started with, *I don't know if* . . . "The important thing is what *we're* bringing to the site."

"And that is?"

"These." He pointed to his eyes.

"Are you serious?" she asked.

He nodded.

Tally pointed to her own eyes. "Harold, *these* don't work well under water that's filled with peat, which Loch Ness is. That's why the National Geographic Society, my own museum, virtually every major scientific and journalistic institution in the world that has gone looking for the monster over the years went with more than just 'these.'"

"Which just goes to show that bigger, more expensive equipment isn't necessarily the solution," he said. "They may even be part of the problem. Maybe the electronics tip off the animal that they're coming."

Tally clearly wasn't sold.

"Look," he went on, "whenever you want to test the validity of an experiment you get the pot cooking the same way you did the first time. We can start by doing the same thing Dr. Castle did. If we get any indication that there's some kind of anomaly in the loch, I'm sure we can also get a wet suit somewhere and have a closer look. I did a bunch of wreck diving with Samuel in the south of France. I can handle that."

Tally sighed. "I have to tell you, Harold, the rush of enthusiasm that has carried me to this point has just flown away."

"Why?"

"Why? Because I assumed we were going to Scotland to take this thing to the next level."

"Which would be?"

"Assuming that Dr. Castle's observation was real and accurate, and going from there. Getting into the water with more equipment."

"I'm not saying we can't do that or won't do it," Collins said. "I was just defending Dr. Castle's methodology."

"Oh. It sounded like you were making this up as you went along."

"That wasn't it at all," he lied. "I felt we could be flexible in our approach because we're not spending thousands of dollars a day. You want to know something funny?"

"Sure."

"The most compelling piece of evidence we have right now is Dr. Castle's phone call."

"How do you figure that?"

"I got to hear her voice," Collins said. "I heard excitement, a little fear, confusion. She called a complete stranger and spilled it all. You don't do that unless you're pretty sure of what you saw."

"Unless you're excited, confused, and afraid," Tally said.

"In that case you go to someone you know," Collins replied. "Dr. Castle went to a resource she thought might be able to help her without judging her. I respected that. And I trusted it."

Tally regarded him for a moment, then looked away. "All right," she said. "I buy that."

"Hey, what's the worst that happens from all this?" Collins asked. "You get a weekend in Scotland, some-expenses-paid."

"The worst that happens is how I feel about myself after letting someone talk me into something that common sense told me was not right," she said. "But you know what?

That's my problem, not yours." She looked at him. "And then there's the upside, remote though it is. We really could find this thing."

"There you go."

"And get eaten."

"That's a possibility," Collins agreed. "In which case I'd have to change my name."

"To what?" she asked.

He replied, "Pete."

She stared at him. "Close-captioned for the slow? I don't get it."

"A homonym for 'peat,' the decomposed organic matter in the loch, which you referred to a minute ago," he said. "That's what I would become."

"Oh," she said. "Harold, I hope this won't ruin the trip for you but I have to tell you something. I really, really, really hate puns."

"I see," he said. Too low-brow, he suspected. Or was he doing the stereotype thing again?

"Correction," she said, almost apologetically. "I don't like jokes as a whole. I'm not a really good audience."

"In that case, I won't crack any more," he told her. "You won't be missing anything. They're usually pretty bad."

Tally thanked him then looked out the window as they entered the Queens-Midtown Tunnel. She suddenly seemed very vulnerable.

A moment before, when Collins saw the young woman's pale eyelids flutter and her mouth get a little sad, he knew that low-brow had nothing to do with it. He suspected that Tally Randall didn't like jokes because she was afraid she wouldn't get them. Even if she did, she probably wouldn't want to laugh. She would have thought it to death and drained it of "funny."

He wondered if that had something to do with upbringing. The pressure of expectations, of being insecure about the right thing to do. That was just the opposite of Collins.

Whenever people told jokes, he got ahead of the narrative, took the clues, and ran to the end. Then, of course, blurted the punch line before the teller did. That didn't made him very popular at the parties he seldom went to, but hey, that was his speed-ahead mind. He couldn't control that any more than Tally could help herself.

Collins sank into the lumpy seat. He gazed out the window as the yellow-orange lights of the tunnel flashed by. It felt good to relax, probably for the last time this week.

Car services, he thought. *Fear of jokes. Sea serpents. Mysteries and knowledge everywhere.*

And the trip had only barely just begun.

This was going to be one hell of a busy *and* interesting weekend.

CHAPTER SEVEN

TALLY OFTEN WONDERED if she was as tough as her name.

It didn't bother her so much that her name was a way of honoring the Randall family business, which was shipbuilding. What bothered Tally was that her name wasn't a sexy part of a ship. A tally is a metal plate attached to machinery bearing instructions for its use. She would have preferred something exotic, like "Bermuda" or "Lateen," after sail types. Or even "Bridge" or "Windlass" or "Port." She had always been partial to Port as a name.

Her father once pointed out with characteristic bluntness that she could also have been "Poop."

But her mother insisted that Tally was the only one that sounded like a name, so Tally it was. A hard brass or iron tablet with writing etched in the surface. Maybe that was why she had become a writer/editor. Words seemed permanent to her. Even when ships went down, the tally often survived. There was one in her father's office in Groton,

Connecticut, from a U.S. naval gunboat that was sunk in the Yangtze River in 1926.

Tally had been tough enough to eschew financial aid from the family. She had been tough enough to resist being affianced to this empty scion or that fierce Bohemian who appealed to her defiant side. She had been tough enough to get her job on *Natural History* against strong competition and nepotistic members of the board. But for some reason she still felt that she had to prove herself. She had no idea against whom or what or why. The need was just there. Maybe because, like Collins, people looked at her and presumed things.

Of course, the big question she had never been able to answer—and maybe that was why she kept pushing—was whether toughness meant a willingness to be confrontational or the ability to ride the currents wherever they went. Probably both, she decided. Like now, for instance. She and Harold Collins had rushed to the airport, made it through security with minutes to spare, then, while he downloaded data from the United Nations, she went to the gate to see if they could do anything about their seats. It turned out that they were assigned to opposite ends of the cabin. There were no other seats available. Tally decided not to fight it, even though she and Harold were paying full fare while people who had bought cut-rate tickets months before held adjoining seats. The two would simply have to get up and swap disks with each other after they downloaded the data, then wait until later to discuss any questions or comments they had. Collins asked if he could take the seat in the front because it was a window seat. He explained that he didn't have a window in his office and this was a real treat. That was fine with Tally. Her laptop was the only window she would need. Upon boarding, Tally went to the back and sat on the aisle beside a balding man with a cheerful smile and a Tom Clancy Op-Center novel. The two canceled each other out. To her right was the lavatory. She wasn't a snob like her parents. She didn't have to fly first class, and she didn't mind screaming babies. That's why earplugs were invented. But the bathroom annoyed her. Every time the door opened she got a whiff of whatever had gone on inside. Over the six-hour flight it was cumulative and unappetizing. Not that she needed an appetite. By the time the flight attendants reached row thirty-two, they had run out of everything but some chicken-and-dirty-rice entree, part of the "Southern Cuisine" menu designed to introduce foreign fliers to American dishes. It was microwave-overheated, and the sauce stuck to the plastic tray. She ate the sourdough bread, carrot salad, and peach crumb pie, which was more preserves than peach.

She didn't complain about the quality of the meal. That required strength. A great deal of it.

Most of the time she simply breathed through her mouth and read up on Loch Ness. The reports pretty much confirmed what she had suspected, that most of the sightings in the thousand-foot-deep, twenty-four-mile-long loch were demonstrable hoaxes or explainable phenomena. The famous 1934 photograph showing the head and neck of the "Monster" was revealed by deathbed confession of the last surviving participant of the scam to be a fake. He said the Monster had been a wood-and-plastic head fitted on a toy submarine. The gynecologist who had allegedly seen the Monster was, in fact, the front man for filmmaker Marmaduke Wetherell, who wanted to wring some money from Fleet Street. Other objects that had apparently been mistaken for the Monster since the first recorded sighting in 565 A.D. were logs, overturned boats, oversized river otters, the wake from passing vessels, and waves caused by geologic activity. That last fact intrigued Tally. The vast trench that contains Loch Ness runs in a nearly perfect line for over sixty miles across the Highlands, following the Great Glen fault. The fault has been active since

Mid-Devonian times, roughly four hundred million years ago, before life had ventured from the sea and established itself on the land. Earthquake-related eddies and wave patterns could explain how "sea monsters" identical to the Loch Ness creature were seen in other bodies of water, most notably Lake Champlain, which is nestled across parts of New York, Vermont, and Quebec. It would also explain how observers might have been subtly unsettled and "open" to seeing a monster.

There had been ten major research expeditions in the twentieth century, beginning with the John Murray Expedition in 1901. None of them had uncovered a monster. Just photographs of gargoyle heads that later turned out to be tree stumps, or computer-enhanced photographs of what were described as flippers that turned out to have been computer-generated fakes.

"What the hell *were* you thinking?" she asked herself as the plane began its descent into Gatwick.

The middle-aged man sitting in the window seat put down his novel and glanced over. "I beg pardon?" he said in a delicate British accent.

"Nothing," Tally replied, frowning. "I'm really sorry. I was just muttering to myself."

"I see," he said. "You'll excuse me, but I couldn't help noticing you've been reading up on Nessie. Taking a trip up there, are you?"

"I am," she said glumly.

"You don't seem happy about it."

"I'm not."

"Business or pleasure?" he asked.

"Business," she said. "No, make that 'insanity.'"

"How so? You hardly seem insane."

"In a moment of weakness I agreed to help a friend look for the Monster," Tally replied. "No, he's not even a friend. He's someone I just met."

"That chap you switched disks with?"

"Yes." She felt herself flushing. "Sorry. It's a stupid story and I won't bore you with it."

"There's no need to apologize now any more than there was the first time," the man said pleasantly. "And I don't find any story 'stupid' if it's real." He held up the novel. "That's why I like these. They take real places and things and make you ask 'what if?' It's a good way to keep your mind fresh."

"I take it you've been to Loch Ness," she said.

"Twice, with my sister's family," he replied. "They live in New Jersey. I'm just coming back from visiting them." He offered his hand. "By the way, I'm Carl King."

"I'm Tally Randall," she said, taking his hand. "Are you from London?"

"Now, yes," he said. "I'm originally from Oxford, though." He chuckled. "I love telling people that. They think I'm some kind of scholar."

"What are you?"

"I'm a rubbish collector, London municipal," he replied.

"Really?"

"Really. And you?"

"I'm a New Yorker," she said, "an editor at a natural history magazine."

"Very lovely," he replied. "It must be fascinating."

"Usually," she said. "Mr. King, do you mind if I ask whether you believe in the Loch Ness Monster?"

"I don't mind at all," he replied. "And yes, I believe in it."

"You do," she said.

"Yes."

"Yet all the evidence I've been reading points against it. Just one hoax or mistake after another."

He leaned toward her conspiratorially. "All a Scottish tourism board plot, eh?" he said.

"I don't know," she replied. "Though I suppose if you've got a good thing going, why kill it?"

"You know, Ms. Randall, I once found a diamond ring

in the back of my lorry," he said. "Good thing too, because a young lady was sorely missing it. It wasn't the kind of thing you ever expect to find among fishbones and wrappings and other discards. But there it was, gleaming like hope itself. I feel the same way about the Monster. Just because there have been flimflams, probably a great many of them, I'll bet that somewhere in all of the rubbish there is one carat of truth. And one is all it takes," he said.

She stared at him. "That's the smartest thing I've heard all day."

"Well," King winked, "I *am* from Oxford." He smiled and went back to his book.

Tally stowed her computer and papers as the landing gear was lowered.

Well that *was unexpected,* Tally thought. But the man was right. The laws of science were always fixed until something came along to change them. Copernicus, who suggested that the sun, not the earth was the center of the solar system. Einstein, who described a special theory of relativity that changed our views of time and space.

Harold Collins, who proved that the Loch Ness Monster was neither a hoax nor a publicity stunt?

It was unlikely. But then, this morning she would have said it was unlikely that she would be on a plane to England that same day.

Or that she would get a lesson in the scientific method from a trash man.

It would take strength and energy to keep an open mind, but nothing she had ever done had been easy. Which, she was beginning to realize, was probably why she did it.

CHAPTER EIGHT

T HE SIX-HOUR FLIGHT from New York passed quickly for Harold Collins. He got blissfully lost in his research material on Loch Ness. He took only a brief time-out to select and eat his meal, pulled pork and cole slaw. Then it was back into the geology, history, and previous Loch Ness expeditions. He was not encouraged by the fact that so many well-financed, well-equipped investigations had failed to turn up anything substantial.

Actually, they didn't turn up anything at all, Collins thought.

Never mind hard evidence. There was not even any credible evidence about the existence of the Monster. In fact, there was actually *negative* evidence. In 1999, a psychologist had stuck a painted two-by-four on a log and towed it through the loch. One observer whom he interviewed later described, in detail, the serpentine neck and head of a sea serpent. People saw what they wanted to see. Including, perhaps, a world-renowned paleontologist like

Dr. Castle. According to the bio from the Contemporary Scientists CD-ROM he'd brought along, Dr. Castle had been rather reclusive since the loss of her husband and son four years earlier. As Tally had suggested, a blow like that could do things to an individual's mind and psyche. It could take monsters that were inside and put them on the outside.

Collins was not looking forward to discussing any of this with Tally. The two sat next to one another on the British Regional Airways hop from Gatwick to Inverness. Tally was on the inside, looking out the window. She said absolutely nothing as the plane took off. Saying nothing was worse than telling him again that she thought the undertaking was futile.

After they had been in the air ten minutes, Collins turned to her. He was about to speak but chickened out. He went to the lavatory instead. He had to decide how he wanted to handle this: apologize and beg for compassion and support or simply try to rah-rah her into action. When Collins came back, Tally was still looking out the window. The view was to the east. He stood with a knee on his seat and squinted past her.

"Can you see the North Sea?" he asked.

Tally turned to him. Her expression was relaxed. He felt a moment of relief. But it only lasted for a moment.

"I don't know," she said. "I wasn't looking at anything in particular. I've been thinking."

"Oh. Is that good or bad?" he asked.

"Inevitable," she replied.

"What have you been thinking about?" he asked. He was hoping he'd get lucky and she'd say she was thinking about an upcoming birthday or even a boyfriend she was missing—something other than the Monster.

"The Vikings and St. Columba," she said.

"Why them?" he asked. Her comment came as a complete surprise.

"What do you think of those sightings?" she asked.

"Well, no one's been able to discredit what they claim to have done or observed," Collins pointed out.

"One of the marine biologists suggests that the Vikings may have seen the prows of ships on a misty morning after a night of too much mead," Tally said. "St. Columba went out in a rowboat sixteen hundred years ago and yelled at the monster, told it never to kill anyone again. How credible is that?"

"I don't know," Collins said. "Some animals respond to loud yelling. It's like gorillas pounding their chests to scare off predators."

"Possibly."

"The accounts say there was thunder and lightning. Maybe that was what really scared the monster."

"How reliable are the translations of specific words in the account of his encounter, anyway?" Tally asked.

"I can't answer that. But the Norse accounts were illustrations."

"According to your files the Vikings also carved images of the giant wolf Fenris, the dragon Fafnir, and other figures of Norse mythology," Tally said. "So that's hardly an endorsement."

"Even so, those are just two of thousands of other sightings," Collins said.

"Sightings of 'objects,' yes," Tally agreed. "But nothing that is demonstrably a monster. Nothing that would convince me, anyway. Those early accounts had a sense of mystery, but they also felt honest. Funny, isn't it, that they should seem more real, considering how old they are?"

"They were unadorned," Collins said. "Maybe the people had no reason to lie."

"Men always have a reason to lie," Tally said. "The Vikings to underscore how brave they were. St. Columba to promote the power of faith."

"Having a reason to lie doesn't mean they *did* lie," Collins pointed out.

"No," Tally agreed. She regarded Collins. "Do you know why I didn't turn right around in Gatwick?"

"There were no flights available?" Collins guessed. His mood was souring. He didn't feel like getting beat up.

"No," she replied. "I hesitated because of a diamond in the trash. While it isn't probable we'll find a monster or solve the mystery, it isn't impossible."

"That's the golden rule of any good scientist," Collins said.

"But I'm not a scientist," Tally reminded him. "I'm a journalist. And I decided something else. Even if there isn't a dinosaur in Loch Ness, there is a story. I don't know what it is—whether it's about Dr. Castle or the scam perpetrated by the Invernessians over the centuries or the desperate brass ring–grab that groups like UNIT Omega are forced to make to get some press, some financing. But a story is definitely out there."

"Hey, that wasn't the reason I came here at all," Collins protested. "It wasn't the main reason, anyway. I'm interested in science first and foremost. Yes, I need publicity and more money to do that. But the trappings don't change the heart, and the heart is about discovery and knowledge."

"I want to believe that's true, Harold, and you'll have your say, I promise," Tally replied.

"Right. As in, 'Does the condemned have any last words?'"

"Not at all," Tally assured him. "But an associate, even a friend, who is a journalist must still be objective. And as a journalist I'm going to work hard to make this trip into something significant, even if there isn't a monster. My shrink calls it 'disappointment management.' Taking a downturn and making it a parachute jump. Something challenging, fun, new, bold."

"I see," Collins replied. "And I'm not supposed to act like a specimen on a slide?"

"I honestly don't know how you should act," she admitted. "All I'm saying is from the time we set down I'm going to be participating, hands-on. But I'll also be watching, listening, thinking. But not just about a monster. I'll also be observing the process and politics of exploration."

"That still sounds like a threat," Collins grumbled.

"Well, it isn't," she assured him.

"I see. Under what conditions—under what *conceivable* conditions—would you write a favorable piece about UNIT Omega or some aspect of this expedition?" he asked.

"I don't know that yet," she replied. "Do you know what you're going to find when we reach Loch Ness?"

"No."

"Well, there you go," Tally replied. "You've got your quest and now I've got mine. It's a different one than I started out with, but I've educated myself and now I have to rethink my goals. Maybe this will be right for *Natural History,* maybe it will be better in some other magazine. I don't know. As for me having some kind of vendetta, you're wrong. You didn't force me to come. It was my decision. But that doesn't mean I only have to write sweet things. What I want to do now is just be professional about all this and see where it all leads."

Collins had to admit that Tally's reasoning made sense. But he still felt as though she was going to find a way to pillory him and the expedition. That all the hoaxes and mistakes of the past would be piled on. Sort of like a reverse Oscar, where the Academy is really rewarding someone for a body of work. The UNIT Omega expedition and Harold Collins were going to pay for Marmaduke Wetherell, the Academy of Applied Science, and everyone else who had ever put forth a bogus monster sighting.

The jet banked west, away from the sea. As it did, Collins clung with increasing desperation to one hope: that whatever personal issues she might have, Dr. Castle was still a reliable witness.

CHAPTER NINE

INVERNESS AIRPORT IS a busy, modern facility that serves London, Edinburgh, Glasgow, Zurich, and the Mediterranean, as well as charter flights. Collins signed for a rental car at the Avis desk in the public concourse. He and Tally gathered their luggage, after which they went to the parking lot to collect the car. Collins took a moment to study a map of the region.

The two-story terminal reminded Tally of a severely flattened baseball stadium. But she didn't contemplate it for long. The air was brisk and salty, and it took her out of the funk she'd experienced during the trip. It reminded her of Coney Island beach, but without the smell of hotdogs and roasted peanuts. Under the faint smell of jet fuel it was pure. That made Tally smile. So did the car they rented. It was a cute, red Citroën Saxo. She folded herself into the tiny vehicle. Tally hadn't been to England in five or six years, and it was a kick getting into a car with the steering wheel on the right side. That made her smile too.

"You sure you can handle this?" she asked Collins.

"Sure. It's just a matter of reversing what you do back home," he said as he examined the dashboard.

"Wait a second. You mean you've never done it before?" she asked.

"Nope."

Tally's smile vanished.

"But don't worry," he said. "I'm good with mechanical things."

"Even when you're jet-lagged and obviously a little annoyed?"

"I'm fine," he insisted. "And I'm not annoyed, not the way you mean it."

"How do I mean it?"

"I'm not annoyed with you," Collins said. "I'm just eager to get this operation underway."

"If you say so," she said. "And you know where we're going?"

"You saw me check the map," he said.

"I also saw you read the data on Loch Ness," she replied. "I want to make sure we get to the same place."

"I'll get us there," Collins promised. "I'm good at reading maps. And by the way, that was a nice one."

"What was?"

"Your dig. It's better than a pun."

"Better?"

"With a dig you do two things: crack wise and tweak someone. If we were keeping score, you'd have snagged a 'two' to my 'one.' "

"I see. Is this a game you and Samuel used to play?"

"Yeah. It was his idea. Everything had to be a competition."

"So now I've got something else to shoot for on my

visit to Scotland," Tally said as she opened the window. "Winning a gag competition."

"I don't want this to be a total loss," Collins said as he started the car. Then he added, "for me."

They pulled from the lot and sped southwest on the A82, which cut through the Highlands to Loch Ness. Upon negotiating several miles of snaking mountain turns, they reached the loch and followed the high road along the northwestern shore. Tally gazed down at the sparkling body of water. Despite her resistance to the idea of the Monster, there was something irresistible about the loch. She had read in the British Regional Airways in-flight tourist guide that Loch Ness was deeper than the North Sea and contained more fresh water than all the lakes of England and Wales combined. The writer suggested that, monster legends aside, the loch had other qualities that contributed to its mystique. The high peat content of the water made it quite opaque. That enhanced the mystery of what lay beneath and gave the surface a unique reflective quality, like a liquid mirror. This area was also the home of the historical Macbeth, whose infamous murder of King Duncan could cast a dark spell on the imagination.

Maybe Tally was feeling the subliminal impact of all those factors. Whatever the cause, something definitely changed once the loch came into view on Tally's side of the car.

"I've come up in the world," Collins said with a little smile.

Tally turned to him. "Excuse me?"

"I left my little office under the East River and now I'm on a road high above Loch Ness," he said. "I know it's only a temporary change, but it's nice."

"I guess it would be."

"The air is different too," Collins said.

"Yes, I noticed that."

"Did you?" Collins said. He threw her a short, curious look. "What about the loch?"

"What do you mean?"

"How do you feel about it?"

"It's magnificent," Tally told him.

"Is that all?"

"I'm not going there," she said.

"Why not? You don't feel anything metaphysical?" he pressed.

"I don't know if I'd call it that," she said.

"What would you call it?"

"I don't know," she said.

"But you do feel something," Collins said.

"I feel 'something,'" Tally admitted. "Maybe *I'm* jet-lagged or maybe it has to do with the spiritual quality of any place where there are big things, like mountains or a large body of water. I feel it when I'm at the ocean, too. I felt it in the Santa Ynez Mountains in Santa Barbara, near the Painted Cave of the Chumash Native Americans."

"So there's nothing unique to this place?"

"I don't know," Tally told him. "Every place has its own history, its own character. But whatever is going on here, I still don't believe it 'must' have something to do with a monster."

"Fair enough," he said. "I've been in lots of epic places too, in the south of France, in Italy, on vacation with my folks in the Rockies. I'm telling you, there's something different here."

"And what would *you* say it is?" Tally asked him. She added quickly, "If you didn't think it was a monster, that is."

"Hold on," Collins said. "I never said I 'think' it's a monster. I just haven't closed the door on the idea."

"But you want to believe that," she said.

"You bet."

"Then you're not an objective participant, which is why I said what I said," Tally explained.

"Tough crowd," Collins observed. "And you said you weren't a nuts-and-bolts scientist."

"I'm not. I'm an editor, and I'm pretty careful about the words I use. So what's your answer?"

"If it isn't a monster?" he said. "It could be the spirit of the place, as you said. It could also be high iron content in the mountains causing a magnetic stimulation of the blood which is affecting the hypothalamus and causing subtle physical reactions. Or it could be a combination of the two."

"You know, there could be something in that," Tally said.

"I know."

"No, I mean pertaining to the Monster sightings," Tally went on. "The hypothalamus controls blood pressure and blood-sugar level. It also plays a part in human emotions and various motor responses."

"Run an article on it, did you?" he asked.

"On the evolution of the hypothalamus, yes," she said. "Wouldn't it be something if an aspect of the local geology caused a physiological reaction that caused hallucinations in certain people? Especially if they were already disposed to see some kind of monster."

"That notion's been used to explain ghost sightings," Collins said. "But a ghost is an insubstantial thing, extremely translucent. The monster has always been described as solid. It causes waves."

"Poltergeists throw things around rooms," Tally said. "And some of them are said to be extremely solid."

"Do you believe in ghosts?" Collins asked.

"No," Tally said. "But I believe that electromagnetic forces can impact the brain. And the brain can create some startling images."

"That can be transferred to film?"

"Yes. But don't try to validate the Monster photos by saying that only amorphous blobs can be transferred to film, therefore some of the Monster images must be real," Tally cautioned.

"I'm not," he said.

"I haven't made a study of spirit photographs, so I can't say whether or not any of those are real," Tally said. "But I suppose that a force strong enough to affect the brain could create stains of some kind on film."

"'Stains'?" Collins said. "Jeez, that's about as unromantic a description of the paranormal as I've ever heard. 'The Spilled Coffee That Haunted Briarcliff Manor.'"

"Well, that's my point," Tally said. "Novels and movies want to perpetrate the romantic view of ghosts. I don't."

"Obviously."

"All I'm saying is that blotches or smears or flaws or even cerebral discharges on film could be interpreted as ghosts and, in fact, could influence what an observer saw or thinks he or she saw."

"Okay," Collins said. "Do you believe in God?"

"That's personal and irrelevant," she said.

"No, it's pertinent," he replied. "It speaks to belief in the unseen. I'm Catholic. I believe in an unseen force. So did Einstein."

"Okay, fine. I'm Episcopalian by birth but agnostic by choice," she said.

"Withholding judgment."

"Absolutely. Just as I am about everything preternatural," she said. "And now that I think of it, that's probably the reason I jumped at the hope that Dr. Castle saw a monster."

"I don't follow," Collins told her.

"I guess if one so-called miraculous being is real, the others might be too," Tally said.

"So if there's a Loch Ness Monster there could be a God."

"I wouldn't trivialize God with that kind of causal agency."

"But proof of a monster would help you to accept things outside your experience," Collins said.

"Perhaps," Tally agreed. She had been looking out at the loch as they spoke. There *was* something different down there. Something she couldn't pinpoint. Something that was more than just the unusual physical characteristics of the loch. The place felt a little more unsettling than it had just a few minutes before. It wasn't just the sparseness of traffic or jet lag or the fact that just a few hours before she had been sitting in the heart of the world's greatest city and now she was in the wilderness. It was a feeling.

"You know, Tally, I don't think we're all that far apart," Collins said. "The only difference seems to be that my arms are opened and yours are crossed. I want to believe and you want to be convinced."

"I don't know you well, but I would probably modify that slightly," Tally replied.

"How?"

"I get the feeling that you *need* to believe."

Collins pursed his lips then nodded. "I'll accept that. I want to believe there's a reason to explore, a place to get to, knowledge to obtain and then build upon. Otherwise, what are we all doing here?"

Tally had no answer to that because she did not disagree with what he had said. The folded arms he referred to were about much more than a "show me" attitude. It was about something she didn't really want to share with Collins. It represented the linebacker side of her nature. It was about defending her ground and gaining independence. In a way she envied Collins his ability to think big. He was looking to unlock the secrets of the universe. She was looking to hold her little plot of individuality.

Maybe that's what's special about this place, she thought as she watched the late-afternoon sun go orange across the loch. Maybe she felt a kinship with the place. It was a long lake landlocked by big mountains and immutable terrain. It was impenetrable from the outside. That was her. That was her *life*. A still soul surrounded by big people, big expectations, big tradition, all of it made of different stuff than she was.

That strengthened Tally's resolve to find a story here. After all, metaphors were a writer's meat. And whatever illuminated this oddly lonely place might well tell her something about herself.

CHAPTER TEN

EXCEPT FOR THE satellite dish attached to the chimney with a bright silver band, the Loch Ness Hotel was exactly what Harold Collins had imagined it would be. A lot of stone, ivy, and dark wood. Despite the fact that the sun was a pleasant tangerine shade, the inn seemed drained of vivid colors. Maybe shadows from the surrounding mountains gave them that appearance. Or, more likely, the color was the blue-gray reflection of the sky from the loch. Whatever it was, fact or illusion, the tincture gave the inn a chilly, foreboding look. Collins's impression of the loch itself was less grim. It was like pale blue satin, oddly comforting. "Oddly" because, if Dr. Castle was correct, it was the home of a possibly carnivorous monster.

Collins pulled into the circular drive at the front of the inn. He followed the signs to the paved parking lot on the side. It felt good to park. Contrary to what he had manfully told Tally, he was tired. And driving had been considerably more difficult than Collins had anticipated. It was an interesting study in physical versus mental reflexes. The physical impetus to make a right turn and stay on the near side of the road actually began, he discovered, under the arms. Along the ribs, actually. It poured through the armpit to the elbow and reached the wrists at about the same time his brain said, *Stop!* It was a constant close-call race. Even when he was just driving along the mountain road, checking out the view, his body tended to drift into a passenger's-side relaxation that, more than twice, nearly sent them into a roadcut. Fortunately, Tally did not appear to have noticed. She had been transfixed by whatever it was that transfixed a Tally Randall.

But they made it, a triumph of attention over reflex and exhaustion. That made Collins feel good, despite the depression of lowered expectations for their mission. Lowered bordering on panic. He was hoping—praying—that things would pick up after they sat down with Dr. Castle. The paleontologist was staying at the Loch Ness Hotel and told Collins to ring her room when they arrived.

He didn't have to. Dr. Castle had been standing on the wooden deck in back of the inn, just a few hundred yards from the loch. She heard the car pull in and walked over to introduce herself.

"If you're not Dr. Collins, welcome to Loch Ness just the same," she said with a half-smile as she approached the car.

"I am Dr. Collins, and please—call me Harold."

The paleontologist smiled. "Very appropriate."

"I'm sorry?"

" 'Call me Ishmael,' " she said. "That's a very appropriate start for leviathan hunting."

"Ah," Collins replied. He hoped that was an indication of scholarship and not utter detachment from reality.

"I'm Kathryn Castle," the woman said, allowing the smile to blossom. "And you can call me Kathryn."

"I'm happy to know you," Collins said. "This is Ms. Tally Randall."

"Just Tally," the young woman said.

The paleontologist exchanged greetings with the young woman. Collins took that moment to study the older woman's face. It was weather-beaten but not unattractive. It reminded Collins, strangely, of the inn. It lacked a certain color, a sparkle. He prayed that her mind and senses were not also nuance-challenged, that she could tell the difference between a monster and a horse or dog out for a swim.

Tally was extremely pleasant as she shook Dr. Castle's hand. The young woman's manner surprised Collins. He had expected her to be guarded at best or patronizing at worst.

Unless it's just me who brings that out in her, he thought.

Dr. Castle helped Collins and Tally take their bags from the car's small trunk. The paleontologist walked between them as they made their way toward the front of the inn.

"Tell me, then. What's your first impression of our fabled Loch Ness?" Dr. Castle asked.

"Imposing but very personal," Tally said.

"Oh," Dr. Castle replied. "I like that."

"I'm not a wordsmith," Collins said, "so I'll just say what I imagine most people say. It's awe-inspiring."

"I haven't done a scientific analysis of what I'm about to say; it's just a gut response," Dr. Castle said. "Most people who come here are impressed by the beauty. But what they talk about more, on the veranda, in the dining hall, along the shore, is the great mystery of the loch."

"You mean the Monster?" Collins asked.

"No. It's more than that," Dr. Castle said. "There's

something here that seems to give even jaded visitors a mystical eye. Their vision starts to go beyond what they can see."

"Let me return the compliment," Tally said. "That's very poetic."

"It struck me that way when I was a child, with a child's innocence," Dr. Castle said. "I've been lucky, or cursed, to hang onto that sense of wonder. That's what has kept bringing me back to this place."

"Is it always the same?" Collins asked.

"The loch? No," Dr. Castle said. "Emphatically no. I've seen the loch in its many different moods. Calm and demure, like today. Brilliant and alive. Bleak and unsettled. Stormy and dark and throwing up driftwood and scree."

"Scree?" Collins asked.

"Loose stones," Dr. Castle told him. "The water can peel them from a slope in such a way that they look like a writhing titan submerging. Believe me, I've seen all the visions and mirages. I've seen the decayed carcasses of fish, dogs, horses, and even cattle that, from a distance, floating on the loch, looked like the bobbing head of a sea beast. As a scientist, I never trust first impressions. I've spent a great deal of time traveling around the world in search of fossils. And one of the things I've learned is that prodigious bodies of water are just like the desert and sky. They are great deceivers."

"Tally said they have a spiritual quality," Collins told her.

"It's a matter of interpretation, isn't it?" Dr. Castle asked. "One man's mirage is another man's hope. It spurs you on regardless."

"I don't follow," Collins admitted. Now he was really worried. If Dr. Castle was getting spiritual on them, they might as well go home now. Collins had no intention of sticking around to hunt for the living embodiment of the ancient elements of fire, water, earth, and air, or anything druidic like that.

"What I mean is, vastness of any kind is a canvas for illusion," Dr. Castle explained. "Human beings have tremendous difficulty absorbing the scope of some things, so the mind looks to create structure and the familiar in anything big and terrifying. For example, that's why we created constellations. To carve the night sky into brain-size pieces."

"Iconography as a yardstick," Tally said. "A connect-the-dots that takes us from one end to the other."

"That's right," Dr. Castle replied.

"Hold on," Collins said. "What you just said would argue *against* the existence of a monster in Loch Ness. If people wanted to populate the loch with something more comprehensible than blackness and mystery, why would they imagine a monster?"

"My point exactly," Dr. Castle said.

"Excuse me?" Collins replied.

"It makes no sense whatsoever to define the mysterious with something equally unknown and terrifying," Dr. Castle pointed out. "Ipso facto, the monster must not be fiction."

Collins did not know what to say. For one thing, the argument made complete sense. For another, perhaps unintentionally, the paleontologist had warned him against prejudging her. She had moved from the supernatural to the rational in one sure, swift step. Collins was surprised, but Tally looked absolutely awestruck. He wondered how many story ideas the young woman had just gleaned from Dr. Castle's observations.

"I've thoroughly and very critically investigated everything this place has ever shown me," the paleontologist went on. "There has always been an alternate explanation to whatever people have seen or heard or even smelled. So much so that just before my sighting—my first, I should tell you—I was on the verge of putting to bed a mental file I've kept open for most of my life. That the *one thing* I knew absolutely in life is that the Loch Ness Monster does not exist. Had I done so, I would have been wrong."

"You're *that* sure you saw the Monster," Tally said.

"Tally, I didn't merely see the animal," the scientist replied. "I heard it sucking air through what sounded like gills but could have been a nasal passage—I did not see it long enough to be sure. I also smelled the Monster. It was a clean, sharp smell almost like ammonia. And I *felt* it. The rowboat rocked in the wake caused by the creature rising and submerging. I don't use narcotics. I rarely even take aspirin, and I never have more than a glass of wine or beer at dinner. This sighting was early in the morning. The creature was as near to me as you are." Dr. Castle began walking forward again. "Unfortunately, I didn't have a camera because, as I said, I went out there to bury a concept, not to prove it. Without that evidence, only you were interested in following up my sighting."

"You're a paleontologist," Tally said. "What about this idea that the Loch Ness Monster is some kind of dinosaur that has managed to survive through the ages, like the coelacanth?"

"First, I have to correct that misconception," Dr. Castle told her. "The coelacanth is not a dinosaur. It is a fish that was thought to be extinct and known only through the fossil record. Most of the members of the order Coelacanthiformes *are* extinct. Only the one species, *Latimeria chalumnae,* was discovered. That happened in 1938 off the coast of Africa. What was special about that fish was that it had come down through the ages relatively unchanged. But so has the cockroach and the gecko. The coelacanth find was interesting, but it was not unprecedented nor was it a dinosaur."

"Well, you know what they say," Tally replied. "As a paleontologist I'm a great reporter."

"Please, no—don't misunderstand," Dr. Castle said. "That wasn't meant to dismiss what you said. But we need to put that find in perspective before we leap to the idea that a dinosaur might be living in Loch Ness."

"Tell me," Collins asked. "Did the thing you saw in the loch look like anything you've ever seen in the fossil record?"

"Possibly," Dr. Castle replied.

" 'Possibly?' So what was all that about the coelacanth?" he asked. "Isn't it the same thing? A life form, presumably lost, may still be alive."

"It's a large leap from a fish in oceans where the temperature is largely unchanged since prehistoric times to a possibly amphibious dinosaur that thrived in a very warm climate with a significantly different atmospheric composition. I don't want to encourage such a leap without more than a single sighting on a foggy morning."

"But it's conceivable," Tally pressed.

"Most things are," Dr. Castle replied. "Unfortunately, just saying that makes the undertaking seem like something from a science fiction novel. I don't want to taint it that way."

"You haven't," Tally assured her.

Now there was a little role-reversal, Collins thought. He was questioning, Tally was defending. Unless she was not sticking up for the idea, just defending another woman against a man. Or anyone against him.

"Again, the idea that this is some kind of lurking dinosaur is not something I want to consider at this point," Dr. Castle went on. "I am very excited inside, more than I can say. But I have to stay grounded. I need proof. Especially if we end up requiring the assistance of other institutions."

"Which brings up something I never really got clear," Collins said. "What is it that you need from us specifically, from UNIT Omega?"

"The reason I called," Dr. Castle said, "what I *hoped* for, was that someone with a scientific background would be willing to help me do something."

"And that is?" Collins asked. "Monitor the site? Run computer projections and do photographic reconnaissance?"

"All of the above," Dr. Castle said. She stopped as they reached the front door of the hotel. "But not from the surface."

"From where?" Collins asked, even though he already knew the answer.

Someone with scientific credentials was going to go for a deep, dark swim.

CHAPTER ELEVEN

TALLY HAD NO idea at first what went through Harold Collins's mind when Dr. Castle told him about her plans for the "expedition," that he was going on a submarine monster hunt. She didn't know whether he was disappointed, excited, or terrified. His expression did not change. But Tally thought she felt a frisson of fear in his voice when he asked how the scientist knew he had the necessary skills. She told him that his résumé was posted on the United Nations website and she had taken a look at it. He listed diving as one of his skills. That's what she was planning: a straight down and up dive.

"A simple one," she said.

Perhaps he is an accomplished diver, Tally thought as they went inside. After all, his father was Navy and his mother was from Maui.

As they registered, Dr. Castle stepped aside to use her cell phone. Tally took the opportunity to ask Harold what his qualifications were. He said that he had done some scuba-diving with Samuel. That was it. Tally didn't know if that qualified him for what Dr. Castle had in mind. And he cautioned her not to say anything to the paleontologist because he wanted to do this.

Fine, Tally thought. So much for the idea that exaggerating on a résumé is a good thing.

After registering, Dr. Castle said that everything was set.

"For—?" Collins asked.

"Collecting the gear," she said. "I thought we had best do that now so there's no delay in the morning."

Tally and Collins put their bags in their rooms, then climbed into Dr. Castle's van and headed back into the hills. This time they traveled south along the eastern side of the loch. They were going to the marine supply store where the paleontologist got her fishing gear. Dr. Castle had not been specific about how Collins was supposed to cause the creature to surface. All she said was that Shep Boucher would have the answers.

Collins sat in the passenger's seat telling Dr. Castle a little about his background and about UNIT Omega. There was more ambition than accomplishment in his recitation, but Dr. Castle didn't seem to mind. To the contrary. She seemed genuinely interested in her passenger and his vision. Tally spoke a little about her own work when asked but was content to sit in the backseat and look out the window. Behind her, Dr. Castle's gear rattled restlessly. Shovels, duffelbags, buckets. There were even harpoons and an airgun.

Despite the racket, Tally was more relaxed than she had been with Collins behind the wheel. She was able to appreciate more of the ancient countryside, the dwarf birch and the delicate white bulbs of creeping lady's tresses, the red deer and European beaver, the glacier-scarred rocks of the ancient hills. Yet Tally was also strangely conflicted. She had arrived at the inn convinced that Dr. Castle was either crazy or hoping to generate a hoax for some unknown reason. Tally no longer believed that. Dr. Castle had been as earnest and probably as articulate as anyone Tally had ever met. Hell, Tally couldn't even think of the woman as a "Kathryn." She commanded respect, was still a "Dr. Castle."

There were other things about Dr. Castle that spoke to Tally. The loneliness in the older woman's eyes? The burdens on her sloped shoulders? Her earth-mother appearance, which was the opposite of her own Fifth Avenue mother? Her cultured British accent? Or maybe they were just feeling and sharing that same strange "something" coming off the loch. Whatever it was, in whatever proportions, Tally wanted to believe the paleontologist and help her if possible. She also wanted to find the story that was definitely here, perhaps in Dr. Castle's life or ideas.

Given the rustic, undeveloped surroundings, Shep's Sea Shoppe was a bit of a surprise. It was a large, modern, one-story showroom with boats, water-skiing equipment, and diving gear visible through the big windows. There was also a giant fiberglass Loch Ness Monster held on the roof by wire. The green sea serpent was smiling. The store was not directly on the loch but was situated on a sharp slope about a quarter of a mile away. A paved path led to a pier in the water which, Tally presumed, belonged to Shep.

"Maybe we ought to just float that in the loch as bait," Tally joked as they climbed from the van.

"It wouldn't have the right scent," Dr. Castle replied. "But it does ululate every hour."

"It does what?" Collins asked.

"It wails," Tally informed him. "I thought you graduated at the top of your class."

"I did," Collins replied. "I must've missed the field trip to the zoo."

"People ululate too," Tally said.

"I wonder if that comes from the same root word as 'uvula,' " Collins remarked.

"No, but that's a good guess," Tally said. "Uvula comes from 'uva,' the Latin word for 'grape.' "

"Is that so?" Dr. Castle asked.

"Yes, which the fleshy extension of the soft palate resembles. 'Ululate' derives from the imitation of the sound itself."

"I'm impressed," Dr. Castle told her. "Very few contemporary magazine editors can pull something like that from the air."

"Etymology has always been one of my favorite topics, even when I was a kid," Tally explained.

"The study of bugs?" Collins asked.

"That's entomology," Tally told him. "Etymology is the study of word origins."

"Obviously, English is an area I need to bone up on," Collins said. "My French is very impressive, though. So is my Hawaiian."

"Latin, French, Hawaiian," Dr. Castle said. "I only speak English. You're making me feel inadequate."

"Dr. Castle, I read your résumé too," Collins said. "That's like a tyrannosaurus saying he's inadequate because he doesn't have a long neck or spiked tail."

"Maybe that's why they were so hostile," Tally suggested. "Neck envy."

Dr. Castle chuckled as they reached the shop. Before they went in, Dr. Castle turned and said there were several things her guests should know about Shep Boucher.

"First, he's missing the last two fingers on his right hand. That's the result of a youthful mishap, trying to unjam an outboard motor that was still in the water. I mention that only because he usually tells tourists the Monster bit them off."

"He isn't serious," Collins said.

"No, but he'll try to make you think he is. Shep Boucher enjoys drama. That's the second thing," Dr. Castle said. "He likes to talk about his experiences at sea. It's easier just to listen and say nothing. If there are no follow-up questions the spotlight dims and he leaves the stage. Finally, and most importantly, please say nothing about the reason we're here. Shep will make sure to tell every tourist who comes by. Monster sightings are always good for business, especially in the off-season, but they're very bad for further Monster sightings."

"Unless the creature's carnivorous," Collins said.

"Even if it is, most sea carnivores are cowards," Dr. Castle said. "They run from flailing limbs or turning boat screws. The only thing that overrides the flight instinct is blood."

Collins's mouth twisted unhappily. "So I should probably not shave tomorrow."

"I wouldn't worry about that," Dr. Castle said. "You'll have a helmet."

A bell jingled as they entered the showroom. The smell immediately reminded Tally of a plastic kiddie pool she had at their old summer estate in Great Neck. That was probably because of all the rubber rafts, flippers, and diving masks Shep stocked. She loved it.

Shep Boucher was the only clerk in the store. After finishing up with a young couple who were renting a motorboat, he came over. Shep was an oak of a man in his late fifties or early sixties. His skin was the color of dark wood and the texture of canvas. His lips were permanently pursed and he had the smallest, squintiest eyes Tally had ever seen. If she had to guess, Tally would have said it was from years of facing a very stiff, salty sea wind. Her dad's face had a little of that from sailing on the Long Island Sound.

"Afternoon, Doctor," Boucher said with a slight nod to Dr. Castle.

"Good afternoon, Shep," Dr. Castle replied. "These are my friends from America, Ms. Tally Randall and Dr. Harold Collins."

"Welcome," he said, looking first at Tally, then at Collins, then back at Dr. Castle. "Is there something wrong with the rower?"

"Nothing at all, though I *will* be bringing it back in the morning," Dr. Castle informed him. "Dr. Collins has to do a little diving in the loch. What can you set us up with?"

"What's he going down for?" Shep asked suspiciously.

"Geological research," Dr. Castle replied.

"I see. How deep you planning on going?" Shep asked Collins.

"To the bottom of Lauderdale Rise," Dr. Castle replied.

Shep snapped her a look. So did Collins.

"That's fifty very murky meters," Shep said. He looked back at Collins. "What kind of diving experience do you have, boy?"

"Enough," he insisted.

" 'Enough,' " Shep sneered. "I don't mean groping for your ducky in the bathtub."

"Neither do I," Collins snapped back. "My ducky floats."

Tally snickered. Two points for Harold.

"I've been wreck diving in the Gulf of Lions," Collins continued. "I'll be fine."

"The Mediterranean?" Shep said. "I sailed there on a tanker. That *is* bath water, boy. Warm and flat-bottomed. You can see for a quarter kilometer in any direction. I dove there twice. Once when a man fell overboard and again when a bastard of a first mate was pushed overboard. I had to jump in and pull 'em out. And I didn't have a fancy wetsuit, just my trousers. You'll need experience and thews to dive the loch. It's got visibility the length of your arm on a good day, when the water's still. And good day or bad, there are rocks and slopes that'll rake your flesh like sharkskin."

"We'll be fine," Dr. Castle assured Shep.

Shep shrugged. "You know best, or so you've always said. So, rock research. I've done a little spelunking and rock climbing—"

"Shep, Dr. Collins came from MIT to check specific areas of strontian granite to study sinistral movement over the millennia," Dr. Castle said impatiently.

"I could do that for you," Shep said.

"It's a little complicated," Dr. Castle assured him. "It has to do with locating specific kinds of rocks."

"You could tell me what to look for."

"You'd have to see if they match at different locations in order to chart the southwesterly motion of the earth's crust," Dr. Castle went on. "I do appreciate your offer, Shep, but it really does require a degree in geology."

"Mr. Boucher, *I* need to do this," Collins insisted.

To Tally, that sounded as if Collins were trying to convince himself, not Shep Boucher.

"Fine," the older man shrugged. "Just trying to save you from failing, drowning, or being eaten by the Monster." He turned to Collins. "It's down there, you know."

"Is it?" Collins replied.

Tally groaned inside. That was a question. Fuel.

"It is," Shep said and held up his right hand. "Lost these trying to swat it away in the peat darkness."

"We'll be more careful," Dr. Castle said. "Let's talk about gear. I'd like to get it together, then get some rest."

"Sure," Shep said. He was still looking at Collins.

"What would you suggest?" Dr. Castle pressed.

"A non-pressurized suit with a wet suit to keep warm. You won't be needing more than that, as deep as you're going."

"Sounds good," Dr. Castle said.

"Up top," Shep said, rapping his own head, "I can give you a nice hard-hat set. An Mk-twelve helmet with a built-in com system."

"Is the air piped from above-water?" Collins asked.

"No," Shep replied. "It's pumped from tanks to a hose in the back of the helmet. A unit on the side of the helmet vents the air to a second hose and out into the water."

"I see," Collins said.

"You've swum with tanks?"

"I've swam with them, yes," Collins said.

"But you probably had a mouthpiece because that's what most amateur divers have," Shep said. "This is different. It's tough to go hyper with a pacifier."

"Come again?" Collins said.

"A mouthpiece regulates your breathing because you can only pull so much air," Shep told him. "Free breathing through a helmet, you can hyperventilate if you panic."

"What are the other features?" Dr. Castle said, refocusing the discussion.

"There's a keypad built into the left forearm, right behind the O-ring connector for the glove. It uses wireless technology to talk to a computer on the surface or receive messages on the display. Just in case you need graphics displays such as maps or blueprints of sunken ships, that sort of thing." He paused dramatically. "It will give you depth in meters or feet and it even has a special key for SOS."

"I'll be sure to bring along pots and pans," Collins said.

Shep and Dr. Castle seemed puzzled. Tally just shook her head. That was no points.

"What else?" Dr. Castle asked.

"The helmet's got a top-mounted halogen torch and a neoprene suit with a nylon shell. It's warm and very flexible. Since it's off-season, I can give you a nice touring boat. It has an automatic cable dispenser for the dive. You sure you can handle that much boat, Doctor? If not, I can get someone—"

"I took a lateen-rigger up and down the Nile," she said.

"Sissy river," he said. "Not like the Amazon."

"No, it isn't," she agreed. "I had to use a canoe there."

Shep frowned. Tally grinned.

"You mentioned the boat has a cable dispenser," Collins said. "What's that for?"

"There are two lines that clip to the side of the suit," Shep told him. "They're made of steel covered in galvanized rubber. Very tough. They keep you stable as you descend. And if something goes wrong—say you black out or are attacked by something down there—they can pull you back up."

"Piece of cake," Tally assured Collins. "I played Peter Pan in college, had that same kind of side rigging, only with piano wire. It's very stable."

"Glad something is," Collins murmured.

Tally winked at him.

"I'll also need the videocamera with a remote feed to the surface," Dr. Castle said.

"Fine. I'll want a deposit for the full replacement price in case rock man loses it. Unless you want me to go with as camera operator—"

"I'll leave the deposit," Dr. Castle said.

"Whatever you want," Shep said. "Follow me and I'll get you everything you need. Except—" he glanced back at Collins and Tally. "Are you two married?"

"No," she said.

"I thought not. Didn't see a wedding band. So don't worry about it," Shep said.

"Don't worry about what?" Collins asked.

"Casualty insurance," Shep said. "You'd have to go up to Inverness if you wanted that. But since this fine lady's not your next-of-kin, it probably doesn't matter."

Dr. Castle shook her head and looked up. Tally shot Collins a little smile. He did not return it. He looked pale, tired, and more than a little anxious. Tally didn't blame him for any of that. Dr. Castle and Shep had just dropped a lot on him, probably a lot more than he had anticipated.

But Tally did not feel bad for Harold Collins. She had once written a series for her college newspaper about the history of astronomy. She had quoted Bertolt Brecht for the piece, something the German playwright had written in *The Life of Galileo*. It was a quote that applied to more than just the study of the stars: "Science knows only one commandment—contribute to science."

Whatever Harold Collins had thought before today, his job was not about extensive training or intelligence or lab skills or coordinating expeditions from behind a desk.

His job—his *life*—was about science.

CHAPTER TWELVE

STANDING IN THE diving supplies corner of the store, on the loch-side of the showroom, Kathryn Castle was surprised by what she suddenly thought, by the unexpected emotions she felt.

She was watching Shep fit Harold Collins with diving equipment when she was surprised to feel tears press against the back of her eyes. For some reason, Dr. Castle could see in the faces and words of these kids the first four figures in Shakespeare's Seven Ages of Man. In Collins's fear and Tally's confidence she saw the infant mewling and puking in his nurse's arms. As Collins tried on his bright yellow gear she saw the schoolboy with his satchel and shining morning face. In the way Tally and Collins smiled and sparred with each other she saw potential lovers. And as the diving outfit came together, Dr. Castle saw in Collins the building of a soldier, a warrior of exploration.

And in all of that Kathryn Castle saw something else. She saw the things she would never experience with her own son.

She continued to watch, relishing Harold Collins's boyish ungainliness as he tried on the weighted boots, the gloves, the helmet. She remembered her own Gary when he was six, trying to put on his football sweatbands and his team jersey. He was all noodle-like arms and clumsy fingers as he attempted to lace his shoes at the end of his long, skinny legs. But when he got on the playing field and began kicking the ball around, Dr. Castle's son became that same little soldier she had just seen in Dr. Collins. Gary had become determined, coordinated, part of a team, a wonderful shadow of the man to come, she thought. Within too short a time he was the man who would never be.

Tears crawled from the sides of each eye. Dr. Castle brushed them away with a finger. She shouldn't be thinking these things, but she couldn't help herself. Memories were all she had left. If she suppressed those because it also reminded her of her loss, she would have nothing.

"Kathryn, may I say something?" Shep asked. He had taken a step back after assembling a suit that fit.

"Is that a question or a preface?" Dr. Castle asked.

"It's a warning," Shep said. "He looks as natural as a trout on a leash."

"He'll do fine," Dr. Castle said confidently.

"I hear what you're saying, but I know what I'm seeing," Shep replied. "Hell, the boy isn't even defending himself!"

"You've got the helmet on him," Tally said.

Shep stepped over and threw the locks to remove the headpiece. He handed the helmet to Tally.

"Tell me, boy," Shep said. "Do you think you can do this?"

"You mean submerge?"

"Yes," Shep said. "Blazes, I *hope* you can take the bloody helmet off!"

"If not, I can," Tally assured him. "It's not like he'll be taking it off when he's alone."

"You never know," Shep said. "The line could snag or

break and he may have to climb ashore somewhere. Do you think you can do that? Can you make your way in an environment that isn't your own?"

Collins looked at Dr. Castle. There was uncertainty in the tightness of his mouth, in the heavy crease of his brow. Perspiration had formed along his upper lip and on his cheeks. It could have been caused by the warmth of the diving suit. Or it could be fear. Or both. Dr. Castle looked back at him the same way she looked at Gary the first time she sent her little striker off to the field. With pride and encouragement.

"I work for the United Nations," Collins replied with a brave grin. "I go where I'm needed."

"This isn't a summit conference on world hunger," Shep said. "We're talking about you, who have dived in sunny blue seawater, going deep into muddy mountain loch terrain."

"The world is my playground," Collins replied.

Dr. Castle was beginning to get a bead on the young man. He was afraid. That seemed to be when he started joking.

Shep regarded the scientist suspiciously. "What the hell is that? Are you being impudent?"

"A little," Collins said.

"Suit yourself," Shep said. "It's your bum. Kathryn, I'll be wanting a deposit for the full amount of the gear."

"I thought you would," the paleontologist replied.

"Well, do you blame me?" he asked.

"Never," she replied.

"I'll write it up and you help him out of the suit. If you have any trouble I want to know it now."

Shep ambled off while Tally and Dr. Castle went over to help Harold Collins from the one-piece diving suit. Tally unbuckled the boots from the rubber cuffs, Dr. Castle worked on the zipper.

"I feel like a banana," Collins said.

"You look damned impressive," Dr. Castle assured him.

"So does a Thanksgiving turkey," Collins replied.

"Stop mixing your food metaphors."

"Stop being an editor," Collins shot back.

"Yikes. Someone's a little sensitive," Tally observed.

"No, scared. Do I take Shep's warnings seriously? About the dive itself, I mean."

"Of course," Dr. Castle said. "One should never be lackadaisical about underwater activities."

"Even if the world *is* his playground," Tally added.

"I was being facetious," Collins said.

"So was I," Tally replied. "Also, I'd think about longjohns. That thing may chafe."

"Believe me, there's nothing to worry about," Dr. Castle went on. "You'll be carrying your own air supply and we'll have two lines attached to you from the boat." She picked up one of the boots as Collins stepped out of it. "Even if something goes wrong—and it won't—you can always just pop the weights. You'll float to the surface in a matter of seconds."

"Aren't you forgetting something?" Collins asked.

Dr. Castle and Tally waited.

"The Monster," Collins said.

"It didn't attack me and, as I said, I don't believe it will attack you," Dr. Castle said. "I'm not even sure the animal *is* carnivorous. I didn't smell fish on its very windy exhalation and, in any case, there aren't enough sea animals in the loch to sustain a creature that size."

"Great," Collins said. "I'm betting my life on a sea creature's halitosis."

"Don't worry," Dr. Castle said. "If I didn't think this was safe, I wouldn't ask you to do it."

Shep returned with the contract. As Dr. Castle reviewed it with him, Collins and Tally finished removing the suit.

"Are you really nervous?" Tally asked.

"Quantify 'really'," he said.

"You are, aren't you?"

"A little," he said.

"Just remember what we were talking about before," Tally said, "how fear might produce false images, projections. You don't want to screw up the experiment."

"That shouldn't matter to you," he said. "You'll still get a story."

"True," she said. "And that would be fine. But there's a difference between a story and what every reporter wants."

"Which is?"

"*The* story," she said as she helped him step from the bottom of the diving suit.

"I take it, then, that something has opened your mind to the possibility of Nessie?" Collins asked.

"Let's just say that I don't necessarily believe in monsters any more than before, but I do believe in something."

"What's that?" Collins asked.

She replied, "Dr. Castle."

CHAPTER THIRTEEN

THE LAST THING Harold Collins recalled from the previous night was opening the door of his dark room and shambling in. Which would explain, he thought, why he was still dressed when the phone rang.

"This is your wake-up call, Mr. Collins," said the cheerful male voice on the other end.

"Thanks," he muttered. Collins did not remember having left instructions to be awakened either.

After three blind tries, he managed to drop the phone back in its cradle, then dropped his face back on the too-hard pillow. It didn't seem very bright out, and he wondered what time it was. He forced himself to turn back to the nightstand. The non-digital clock said six-thirty. Now that he thought about it, Collins could not even remember having discussed with Dr. Castle what time anything was going to happen today. Maybe he just forgot the conversation or maybe she hadn't wanted to bother him with details. Or perhaps she wanted him to think he'd be able to sleep in, wake refreshed and alert, and have time to think about the somewhat insane commitment he'd made.

Obviously, that was not the case.

The smell of his clothes was the next thing Collins thought about. They were ripe. Except for taking off his shirt and pants to try on the diving suit, he had been in these clothes since waking up in his apartment the previous day. His mouth was no cherry Starburst either. And now that he was becoming aware of the rest of his anatomy, he realized it was probably a good idea to skip to the loo.

"One point," he thought.

He pushed himself from the twin bed. His body felt like a wet sponge. Had he *really* agreed to play Ned Land to Dr. Castle's Captain Nemo and go however many leagues under the loch?

Yes.

As Collins shuffled toward the water closet, he felt his forehead and temples throbbing in synch. It was a jetlag headache. He needed coffee, food, something to help rally his scattered resolve. Shep may have been a bit of a loon, but he was right about Loch Ness. It could be out of his class. The Mediterranean had been easy and, in any case, Collins had never gone down alone. He had been with Samuel, who was an experienced diver. Sunshine had been ever-present, like rippling fluorescent ribbon, and there were fish and plants to keep him company. To make it all bite-size, as they had discussed the night before. And he could always see the surface. From everything he had read, Shep was right about Loch Ness. Swimming there was like submerging in black bean soup.

And then there were the vagaries of what exactly Dr. Castle wanted him to do down there. She hadn't said anything more about her plan. Either she was afraid the details would unnerve him further or she really did just want videotape. She could study it, look for traces of a monster, then send a more experienced diver into the drink.

The small lavatory was literally the size of a four-by-four closet with a tiny tub and shower. His underwater United Nations office no longer seemed so small. There was a sign on the bathroom door that warned the occupant to watch out for the hot-water pipe that ran up the wall beside the tub. He burned his thigh anyway. The good news was that it woke him right up.

Collins made his sluggish way into the shower. The water pressure was surprisingly strong for an old inn, and Collins stood with his head inches from the low nozzle. He let the droplets sting his scalp, then his face, then the inside of his mouth. It helped chase away the fog. All he needed now was something to wash away his doubts.

The details of Dr. Castle's plan weren't the only things that concerned Collins. He was worried about failure and also about success. What if they got lucky? What if they found the Monster and it decided that Collins represented a threat to its lair or its offspring or its food supply? What if Collins and dopes like him *were* the food supply? These were questions they had to resolve before Collins snuggled back into the diving suit.

Collins finished up in the bathroom and went to the lobby. It was a small area with exposed stone and a large area rug. There was a big fireplace with a fire and a cart with coffee, tea, toast, and an assortment of scones. Dr. Castle was already there, sitting on an armchair near the hearth. She was drinking tea and writing on a legal pad. She acknowledged Collins with a nod and a smile, then went back to work. She seemed kind of blasé, or maybe she was just preoccupied. Collins walked to the cart and made himself instant coffee. He had never understood why brewed coffee had never made a real foothold in the United Kingdom. Not enough overactive people who needed gassing-up, he suspected. He made the black coffee strong, took a crumbly blueberry scone, then went over to the sitting area. He lowered himself onto an armchair across from Dr. Castle. The paleontologist looked up again. She smiled again, this time bigger and warmer. Or perhaps it just seemed that way because Collins was close enough to see her eyes.

"Good morning," she said. "Sleep well?"

"Oh yeah."

"Sorry I had to leave a wake-up call, but we need to get started early," Dr. Castle said.

"Why?"

"Monster biorhythms," she said. "Most sightings—most of the valid sightings—have taken place early in the morning."

"Interesting. Are we just waiting for Tally?"

"Tally's already here," Dr. Castle informed him. "She went to take a little stroll along the loch. No, I'm just finishing up marking some map coordinates on Lauderdale Rise while you have your breakfast."

"We don't have to wait on my account," Collins said. He started to rise. "I can bring it with me."

"Sit, sit," Dr. Castle insisted. "I wanted to talk with you anyway before we set out."

The scientist capped her pen and pulled the chair closer. Collins washed down the last of his scone with coffee. They didn't make very big scones here, either. He hoped Dr. Castle had packed them lunch.

The paleontologist leaned close. She seemed to be considering her words more carefully than usual. "Harold, Tally and I spoke a little before she retired last night. She obviously has profound doubts about what we're doing, though she was very complimentary about my reputation in the paleontological arena. Working where she does I'm not surprised she knew about some of my work. But I suspect neither of you knows much about me personally."

"Only what we gathered from the online Who's Who references," Collins told her.

"Do you know about the car accident that took the life of my husband and son?"

"Yes," he replied quietly.

"For a woman who deals with extinct life forms, you'd think I would have been somewhat prepared to put death in perspective," she said. "I wasn't. In fact, just the opposite. Years before, I had encountered a fascinating Chinese anthropologist, Dr. Lao Chan during one of my digs in the Gobi Desert. He gave up a professorship in Beijing to live a nomadic existence, spending his life doing field work in the northern provinces. After the accident, I went to visit him and explored various modern and ancient concepts of reincarnation and the afterlife. I had some interesting experiences with him, including one in which he placed me in a trance and helped me to receive visions of a time when dinosaurs lived in the Gobi."

"With or without drugs?"

"Without," she said. "I told you, I don't do that."

"Sorry," Collins said. That sounded a little like a scolding. Collins probably deserved it, though; he was being flip.

"Dr. Chan did it with the power of his voice and his will," she said. "Somehow he connected me to that past time. It was like a dream, only I was completely awake. He says it was a past-life regression, only he skipped the intermediary forms of my spirit and went back to prehistoric earth."

"I see," he said.

In a short while this woman would be lowering the young man into Loch Ness. She would be responsible for bringing him up again. Collins wasn't sure he wanted to know that she engaged in mental time travel.

"I went so far as to submit a paper on the experience to the *European Journal of Paleontological Studies*," she went on. "It was turned down. Word of what I had written made its way through academia and funding for many of my expeditions began to resemble the Gobi, arid and infertile. I can't say I blame the grant writers. To them I was a disturbed woman unbalanced by her loss, a bad risk. Even worse I now had what they regarded as an 'agenda.' I would select research locales and perhaps even skew research to prove some of the visions I had."

"Didn't scientists face that kind of bias when—I forget who it was—they first suggested that a comet or asteroid was responsible for the extinction of the Cretaceous dinosaurs?"

"Luis Alvarez and his son Walter," Dr. Castle said. "In 1980 they hypothesized that about sixty-five million years ago, a four-to-nine-mile-in-diameter asteroid smacked the earth to cause the Createous-Tertiary catastrophe. They were widely denounced."

"But it turned out they were right."

"Yes," Dr. Castle replied. "Years later, scientists even located the 'smoking gun,' the Chicxulub impact crater at the tip of the Yucatan Peninsula in the Gulf of Mexico."

"Out of curiosity, where did you stand on their theory when it was new?" Collins asked.

"Fair question," she replied. "I published a paper arguing that I believed extensive volcanism was what killed the bulk of the dinosaurs, but that an asteroid collision would be a perfect trigger as well as a secondary cause, due to the amount of sunlight-blocking dust it would kick into the atmosphere. It would be especially damaging if it struck near a ring of volcanoes, a geological superstructure that was more common then than now."

"Do you still believe that?"

"I do," she said. "My point is, like them, I was branded."

Collins drained his coffee mug. He turned it around in his hands several times. "I assume you're telling me all this as a sort of 'fair warning.' You're afraid that I may end up carrying some of your professional baggage."

"Actually, that's not quite it," she said.

"Oh?" Collins was totally confused.

"Because of the work I did prior to the Gobi experience, I still have many supporters in the field," she said. "And there are a few scientists who believe that my visions have validity. Or at least, that lucid regressions have a place in scientific research." She put a hand on his. It was warm and soft and motherly. "I'm telling you this as a means of explaining why I didn't simply hire a boat and go down into the loch myself," Dr. Castle said. "I already told you that if we're lucky enough to find the creature, and can't get it to emerge, someone other than me has to see it. I wanted you to know why. Even if I were to take a picture, there have been so many falsified images that mine would be suspect for that reason alone—not to mention getting added scrutiny because of who I am. Critics would say I was channeling a picture from dinosaur-Valhalla, or some such nonsense."

"That sounds like a phrase some smartass might actually have used," Collins observed.

"They did," Dr. Castle grinned. "Professor Archie Ferdinand of the University of New Mexico said it in the keynote speech before the annual meeting of the International Society of Marine Paleontologists. He didn't mention me by name, but everyone knew what he was referring to."

"I hate condescending bastards like that," Collins said. "You hear them in the United Nations commissary all the damn time. 'My distinguished colleague from Peru' this, or 'The esteemed spokesman for the dissidents' that. They make me wish that English weren't the lingua franca over there."

"Wait until it's directed at you," she said. "That said, I care about my reputation, but I'm more concerned with the truth. Otherwise I never would have written about my lucid experience with Dr. Chan. I wanted to assure you of that, but also to explain why I organized our expedition the way I did, with you descending into the loch while I remain on the surface."

Our expedition, Collins thought. The young man liked the sound of that. It cut through everything and reminded Collins why he was there.

"I understand," Collins said. "And look, since we're fessing up, I have to tell you, your pal Shep made me nervous."

"You were anxious anyway," Dr. Castle replied. "I saw it in your face. This is a new experience, very disorienting. Anxiety is natural."

"Sure, but he cranked it up," Collins said.

"Are you still as nervous as you were last night?"

Collins shrugged. "I'm still shaking, but I can't tell if it's nerves or excitement."

"Some of both, and that's good," Dr. Castle assured him. "It keeps the epinephrine flowing, and that will keep you alert. But don't worry. The excitement will take over as we get underway. I don't know why that happens, but it does." The woman leaned close. "And trust me, Harold. I have learned how precious life is. I would not let you do this if I didn't think it were safe." She smiled and rose. "Now let's drive over to Shep's and see if we can't find our dinosaur-killing asteroid."

Collins placed his coffee cup on the cart. He followed Dr. Castle out the back door toward the loch. It was a brilliant morning, and the water looked like liquid mercury, iridescent and rolling lightly.

Loch Ness looked more secretive than it had the day before. That appealed to Collins. He was going to probe the loch's secrets, make it talk. More than that: He was going to investigate one of the greatest secrets of the ages. It was even possible that Tally Randall would think he was hotter than she had at the party where they first met.

Tally was sitting on the waveless shore, typing on her laptop. She gave Collins a big grin as they approached, a we're-off-to-see-the-Wizard look of wonder and disbelief.

"What are you writing?" Collins asked as he walked sideways down the dewy slope.

"Just keeping track of the temperature of the water, the weather, the exact location, that sort of thing."

"Your Dell come bundled with all those tools?"

"No," she said. "I logged on to the NessWatch website before I left my room."

"I guess you're more of a scientist than you thought," Collins observed.

"Or scientists are just closet writers, Mr. Asimov," she said.

That was another good one, he thought. Two more points for Tally Randall.

A small trailer had been attached to Dr. Castle's van. Collins helped her remove it. Then they climbed into the vehicle and headed over to Shep's.

As they did, Dr. Castle was proved right about one thing at least. The balance had shifted. Collins's fear lessened and his excitement grew as "our expedition" officially got underway.

CHAPTER FOURTEEN

THE BOAT WAS a forty-two-meter express cruiser, which, according to Shep, was the best vessel to use on the loch. He climbed on board first and helped the others onto the low-lying, off-white boat.

"You can make your tight turns at eighty-percent full throttle," he informed Dr. Castle.

"Why does that matter?" Collins asked as he followed the women in.

"Well, if you lose something, you can get back to it as quickly as possible," Shep said. He nodded toward the heavy black hoses coiled in the aft section of the boat. "Another motorboat comes along and somehow slices those, or more likely gets tangled in them, you'll want your crew to be able to turn on a spot and try to grab the other end."

"That isn't going to happen," Dr. Castle assured Collins.

"Nothing in life is guaranteed," Shep pointed out.

"Nothing is," Dr. Castle agreed. "But I'll tell you what.

Let's wager on it. If those lines are cut, I'll pay treble the rental fee for today. If they aren't, we get the boat for free."

"Let's not get carried away, Kathy. I didn't say it *will* happen," Shep insisted. "I merely said it *could*. It's just another reason to have an experienced man down there, someone who knows the loch and its moods."

"For the last time, Shep, we only need a scientist down there," Dr. Castle replied. "But thank you again for your concern."

Shep shook his head as he stepped back onto the dock and began handing them their gear. "Are you going to stay on the loch overnight?"

"Probably," Dr. Castle said. "I'll phone you when I decide."

"I'll give you a special rate if you want to commit now," he said as he handed her the key.

"Fine," Dr. Castle said. "We'll take the rate and see you tomorrow, Shep." The scientist asked Collins and Tally to stow the five duffelbags and the diving suit in the athwartship berth. Then she settled in at the helm.

Shep untied the boat from the mooring. "Have a safe journey," he said. "If you need anything, call me."

"I will," she promised.

"I can take one of the other boats and be out in a lightning flash."

"Thank you again," Dr. Castle said. She put the key in the ignition and fired up the engine. She throttled up slowly and moved out onto the lake.

While Collins finished up stowing the gear, Tally came forward and sat in the seat to the left of the helm.

"Is Shep so persistent with everyone?" Tally asked. "Or is it just women?"

"Actually, it's just me."

"How'd you get lucky?"

"He still has a crush on me," Dr. Castle said.

"Wow," Tally said. She had to speak up to be heard over

the wind and the drone of the engine. "How far does that
go back? If you don't mind my asking."

"I don't," Dr. Castle said. "To tell you the truth, I feel
a little guilty about Shep. We had a summer romance
many years ago, before I met my husband." She smiled.
"Shep was a beautiful creature, just like you'd imagine
the sea-god Triton to be. Bare-chested with a curly red
beard and brilliant eyes. He moved with poise and
strength, and it was craving at first sight, lust at second.
His arms made you feel safe and his eyes made you feel
attractive. But what makes a girl happy doesn't always
satisfy a woman. After I met Del, the bar was raised."
The smile broadened. "Delbert Timothy Castle. He was a
shoe salesman at Willbern's, working his way through
school. I was buying a pair of hiking shoes and the way
he handled my foot sent electricity up my leg. He was
very shy and I had to ask him to tea. He accepted, and
that was when I learned that he was working his way
through Oxford, studying geology. That was how I was
able to put together that explanation for Shep last night,
about strontian granite and sinistral movement." The
smiled soured slightly. "I suppose it was rather cruel of
me to use Del's tools against Shep. And I think Shep
knew it. But frankly, a large part of me is still angry that
a man like Del is gone and—well, I was just being a little bitter, I suppose."

"Only in response to his pushing," Tally said. "Not your
fault."

"Thanks. Nice of you to say. But I have to tell you, Shep
has been very nice to me since I lost Del and our son,"
Dr. Castle went on. "But I'm not twenty-two, and my view
of life has changed. Arms don't make me feel safe anymore."

"You guys talking about me?" Collins yelled from
below.

"Not even warm!" Tally shouted back.

"'Cause it's okay if you are!" he said.

"We aren't!" Tally replied. She shook her head. "So—back to Shep. I don't think he's handling rejection very well."

"I agree, but I can't be dishonest. I can't make things better for him. Not without making them bad for me."

Collins climbed back up the stairs. He was pulling on the blue windbreaker he had brought along. "Hey Tally—I thought you were going to help me load all this stuff."

"You were wrong," she replied.

"Obviously," he said.

Collins waited for Tally to continue. She didn't. Dr. Castle continued looking straight ahead, steering through the fine morning mist. Collins made a face and walked to the portside rail, near the ladder. Tally left him alone with his thoughts, though she did wonder what they were. Who was in charge right now, the scientist with a mind of steel or the boy with thews of sponge cake? Or possibly neither. If Tally were in Harold's place, she'd be more afraid of coming up empty than of anything else.

Tally turned her attention back to the loch. Loch Ness was not only different in appearance, it felt different than any body of water Tally had ever been on. The spray had a gritty quality, probably the result of the peat in the water. It had a slick, clingy quality like rainwater that ran from your hair. The air was cool bordering on cold, though the water was surprisingly warm. The ride was also unusually smooth, that could be a virtue of the boat rather than the water itself. And the terrain around the loch was even more magnificent than it had been the day before. The fog gave the mountains a mythic stature. Seeing them made it easy for Tally to understand how the Vikings saw dragons here.

Tally had brought along her digital camera and took a few pictures. They were not for publication but for her own reference. She had learned in college that the mind often remembered events the way it wanted them to be. Tally did not want that to happen here.

"Tell me something, Kathryn," Collins said, turning toward the women. "You talked about the most reliable sightings having come in the morning. Has anyone ever done a detailed chart covering all the appearances of the monster? See if there was anything seasonal or climatic about them? Something pertaining to food supply or spawning, that sort of thing?"

"Yes," Dr. Castle replied. "Dr. Layne Maly, a math professor at the University of Edinburgh, once deconstructed every known sighting of the Monster. He made one chart for the reliable accounts and another that included the questionable sightings. He was convinced that there should be some kind of pattern, as you've said. Unfortunately there was none. If there is a phenomenon in this loch, biological or geological, it is apparently random."

"I don't believe that," Collins said. "Nature is not random. It is predictable, from weather patterns to gestation periods."

"What about extinctions?" Tally asked.

"If there's an asteroid strike, it's governed by celestial mechanics. Again, not random."

"That's true," Tally said. "So wouldn't all that argue against the existence of a creature?"

"Not at all," Dr. Castle said. "I said 'apparently' random. I agree with Harold. Nature is predictable. What Dr. Maly's work did was point out the holes in our Nessie scholarship. Obviously we've missed key components that would help us solve the puzzle."

"Fractal logic," Tally said. "Irregular patterns that are unique to specific situations."

"That's right," Dr. Castle said.

"Of course, the flip side of that is making patterns where none exist," Tally said.

"Example?" Collins asked.

"The unicorn," Tally said.

"Ah, but that was human error," Dr. Castle said. "Those

tales were probably generated by the misassembled bones of prehistoric animals. Eventually they were connected in the proper fashion and a pattern emerged. The evolution of life on earth. Time, patience, and a curious mind will never let you down."

"Speaking of time and patience, how long will it take us to get where we're going?" Collins asked, ambling over. He glanced at the helm gauges.

"Are we there yet?" Tally teased him.

"That was a nag, not a dig. You lose points for that," Collins said.

"Worth it," she replied.

"It will take fifteen minutes," Dr. Castle said.

"And what direction are we headed?"

"Northeast," Dr. Castle said.

"You're sure?" he asked.

"Of course I am. Why?"

"Because your compass is pointing northwest," Collins said, pointing to the gauge.

Dr. Castle looked down. So did Tally. The small, black dial was mounted on the control panel above the wheel. Collins was right. Dr. Castle rapped it with a knuckle. The needle jiggled but remained constant.

"That's very strange," the paleontologist said.

"It's not stuck," Collins observed.

"I take it that hasn't happened before?" Tally asked.

"Frankly, I've never been out on the loch with a compass," Dr. Castle admitted.

"But others have," Collins said. "If this happened with any regularity, someone would have mentioned it."

"That stands to reason," Dr. Castle agreed.

"Does everyone feel okay?" Collins asked.

"How do you mean?" Dr. Castle asked.

"I'm not sure. Anyone feel uneasy or antsy—I can't really explain it."

"I take it you do," Dr. Castle said.

"A little. I first felt it downstairs. 'Below,' I mean."

"It could be excitement or the vibrations of the boat," Tally said.

"I know what those feel like, and this was more," Collins said. He looked toward the shore. "Tally and I were discussing something earlier. Do you know if these mountains have unusually high iron content?"

"Not that I'm aware of," Dr. Castle said. "Why?"

"Sometimes charged ions from solar wind can cause a temporary, localized electromagnetic shift," Collins said.

"You mean they magnetize the mountain?" Dr. Castle asked.

"In essence," Collins told her. "The ionosphere usually keeps that stuff from reaching us."

"Hence, the name," Tally said.

"Right. Sometimes, though, waves of particles do make it through." Collins said. "Maybe that's causing some of what we're feeling. There's iron in our blood cells too."

"You know, now that you mention it, my legs feel a little lively under the skin," Tally said.

"This is interesting," Dr. Castle said. "I wonder if your hypothetical ions could have some affect on the creature. Some animals, especially sea creatures and migratory birds, even dogs and cats, are thought to have a very finely crafted sense of the earth's magnetic poles. It helps them to navigate."

"It's conceivable, I guess," Collins said.

"It's more than that," Dr. Castle said with rising excitement. "It fits rather nicely with something I've been thinking. That out-of-environment forces are the pattern we are looking for. In the past the creature seemed to respond to light—or rather, its absence. The torches carried by St. Columba were extinguished in the water before the monster rose. Cameras using strobes always seem to catch an animal moving away from the light. I went out on an extremely overcast morning. If the creature inhabits an underwater cave, or a series of caverns, then it is accustomed to and most comfortable in darkness."

"I'm confused," Tally said. "How is that going to help us draw the creature out?"

"Also, none of the research says anything about hidden subterranean regions in the hard clay here," Collins said.

"That's true, but we know there are several ancient rifts filled with sediment, and we *don't* know how deep those may go or where they lead," Dr. Castle said. "We're going to place high-intensity halogen light outside those openings. If the creature is down there, it will want to get away from them."

"Possibly, but that won't necessarily bring it from hiding," Collins pointed out.

"I agree," Dr. Castle said. "Fortunately, you'll be down there watching for any movement, any clouds of silt, any sounds, a sudden scattering of local biota. If you catch any of that on the videocamera, it will be raw data that we can use to try and find the pattern."

"Or it could just jump right out and eat me, like it tried to do that friend of St. Columba's," Collins said.

"The annals don't say the creature devoured a man," Dr. Castle said. "They say 'killed.' He could have been crushed or drowned when his boat was overturned. He may have died of fright."

Tally had been watching Collins while Dr. Castle spoke. He seemed to become even more alert as the conversation progressed. Tally was glad to see that, even if the cause was terror. It was a bad idea to send an agitated man into a dark, claustrophobic, unfamiliar environment. He was probably familiar with the old joke about today's careless herpetologist becoming tomorrow's crocodile shit. Having a problem in his own field to ponder, whether it was the contents or the rift or the mystery of the compass, would help him to stay focused.

Tally had another look at the compass. Judging from the

direction of the sun, the needle was still some thirty degrees off. More than that, the feeling Collins had pointed out a few minutes before was growing stronger. The sense of exactly *what* she was feeling also became clearer. It was a kind of soft, electric "fuzz" running through her arms and legs. The feeling was inside her bones—that deep. Logic told her it was probably anxiety, though she usually felt that in the back of her neck. Her natural unorthodoxy and a hint of superstition—which, yes, seemed to come alive here—insisted it could also be some kind of weird reaction to whatever electromagnetism might be out there. Maybe the locals were accustomed to it and tourists ignored it. But Tally was a journalist. A rested one now, who took an objective intellectual stroll around everything she was seeing, thinking, and feeling. And this was definitely new and disconcerting. Something was up.

Or down.

CHAPTER FIFTEEN

I T WAS NOT yet eight o'clock when they passed their inn
and rounded the sharp, jutting edge of a cliff. Dr. Castle
dialed down the throttle as they came to a wider section of
the loch. The paleontologist told her passengers they were
almost at the site of the charted fissures, about one hundred
meters from where she had seen the creature.

Collins did not feel anything more or less unusual here.
He went below to put on his diving suit. He was amazed
that as a pretty consistent "show me" scientist, he had gone
from being deeply discouraged with the evidence to being
wildly intrigued by the place itself. All in the span of less
than a day.

At this rate, who knows where I could be tomorrow? the
young man thought as he sat on the bunk and slipped into
his diving suit. He might be back in the doubter's box or he
could be holding historic photographs of the Monster of
Loch Ness. It was starting to get very exciting. He felt like
he had when he was a kid putting on his snow suit, getting

ready to go out in a yard or two of fresh Connecticut snow. There was a world of magic out there. To discover it, to find that snowman or ice fort, all Harold Collins had to use was imagination and a little shoulder power. He hoped that was the case in Loch Ness as well.

With his boots in one hand and his helmet under his arm, and his oxygen tanks slung over a shoulder, Collins trudged up the stairs. Anticipating this moment, he had thought he might feel like an astronaut marching toward the space shuttle and destiny. He did not. He felt like a seal. One who had trouble keeping his balance on the surging, rocking boat. One who squeaked with each movement because of the tight wet suit. He hadn't even gone in the water, and he knew that Shep was right. This was not like scuba-diving in the Mediterranean. He had to stop and put the oxygen down beside him before it could pull him backward.

"Just as I feared," Tally said as she saw him. She jumped from the chair.

"What?" Collins asked.

"A man who doesn't like asking for help."

"I asked before and you didn't come," he reminded her.

"That was because you didn't need it. Now you do."

Logic only a woman could conceive, he thought. Tally reached out and took the helmet and boots from him.

"To tell you the truth, I didn't think I'd *need* help climbing five damn steps," Collins said as he reached the deck. "Believe me, I'm not a macho man. If I'm in trouble, you'll hear about it."

"Are you sure?" she asked.

"Oh yeah," he said.

Tally put the gear on her chair. The boat slowed to just a few knots and was relatively steady now. The spray had stopped, leaving only the cool air. Despite that, Collins immediately began to perspire. He rattled the rubber collar to get some air into the suit. It didn't help.

"You'll be cool enough once you get below," Dr. Castle assured him when she saw what he was doing. "The temperature drops very rapidly as you move away from the sunlight."

"Maybe that's one way we can track the creature," Collins suggested. "Get a thermalscope down there. Watch for cold spots."

"I thought about that," Dr. Castle said. "Shunning light and preferring cold water do not necessarily follow. I would suspect our creature prefers a moderate environment."

"Why?" Collins asked.

"Prehistoric seas were relatively warm," Dr. Castle said.

"But don't some species of whale dwell in extremely cold climates?" Tally asked.

"They do, but they have a great deal of blubber to protect them. From the brief glimpse I had, this creature did not seem to have a great deal of body fat. Which didn't surprise me, I might add. Most sea giants today are muscular and relatively lithe."

"Isn't that a rather large leap of faith?" Tally asked. "I mean, what held true then might not hold true now and vice versa."

"Streamlining works in the sea just as it does in the air," Dr. Castle said. "Fat leviathans would not survive. And there are indications that sea life in particular has a consistent quality through the millennia. In 1970, we unearthed the partial remains of an adult plesiosaur off the coast of England. The fossils were about two hundred million years old, yet the vertebrae showed a spinal ailment known as Schmorl's nodes. That's a condition common among modern vertebrates."

"So we are probably facing an in-shape monster," Collins said.

"My trainer has always said that swimming is the best exercise," Tally said.

"And veggies are the healthiest food," Collins added. "That's good news for me."

"People, now that all this has been said, we mustn't assume the animal swims a lot," Dr. Castle pointed out. "It could be more like an alligator or a hippopotamus than a plesiosaurus, or possibly an undiscovered cross between two known forms. If there are caverns below, and the creature dwells in them, it could conceivably spend a great deal of time on land, like a frog or salamander. We have to remember to think outside the box."

"Outside the lunch box," Collins quipped.

"Pun," Tally complained.

Dr. Castle ignored them. "There has to be a reason that most of the sightings have been unheralded while methodical, traditional searches rarely turned up any hint of the creature," she said.

"I'll try not to let you down," Collins said.

When they reached the spot where Dr. Castle had seen the animal, she shut the engine and went into the cabin. She opened one of the duffel bags she had brought and took out a laminated map about the size of a place mat. She returned to the deck. Tally and Collins stood on either side of the paleontologist. A narrow, winding fissure had been marked in grease pencil. The middle of the crevasse was marked a dark blue with lighter blue sides.

"This rill was first picked up by sonar in 1987," Dr. Castle said. "It's ten meters deep and one hundred and ten meters long. At its widest point it's seven meters across, about twenty-two feet. That's here, on the northwest side," she said, pointing. "However, you can also see it doesn't change to light blue as it does on all the other sides. That's because the sonar reading did not register rock. The signal was swallowed by what is certainly a massive deposit of silt or clay."

"Wouldn't the sonar signal penetrate that?" Tally asked. "It penetrates the peat in the water."

"Sediment tends to be much denser," Dr. Castle told her. "Depending on the composition it would come back as rock."

"Then how do you know it isn't rock at the edge of the fissure?" Collins asked.

"Because rock would slope up," she said. "It would give us a reading of some kind. Sediment would give us a blank reaction because there's nothing for the signal to bounce off."

"So it's like a sonar black hole," Tally said.

"In a manner of speaking," Dr. Castle agreed.

"Why didn't anyone ever have a look down there before?" Tally asked.

"There was no reason until now," Dr. Castle said. She turned to Collins. "Which brings me to what I would like you to do. I need you to go down to that spot. It's straight down. When you reach bottom, I would like you to shine your light horizontally across the fissure, then angle it down slowly. Watch for any changes as the region gets brighter. It could be that the creature pushes its way through the muck now and then. In that case you may see some indication of a passageway. If you do, mark the spot and we'll explore it in another descent."

"How much air do I have?" Collins asked.

"There's an hour in each tank, plus two minutes reserve," Dr. Castle told him. "It should take us about fifteen minutes to get you down to the site and a few minutes less to bring you back."

"What about the cables?" Collins asked.

"What about them?" Dr. Castle asked.

"Shep was talking about the possibility that the lines could get snarled in something—"

"In the unlikely event that happens," Dr. Castle said, "you pop the cables with the unhook buttons on the side." She pointed to the orange tabs. "Then you drop the boot weights and float to the surface. 'Up' is the only way you can go." The scientist turned to Tally. "Would you mind getting my laptop? It's in the olive green case below."

"Sure thing," Tally said.

The young woman smiled knowingly. Dr. Castle obviously wanted a moment alone with Collins.

The young man watched her go. He had started to breathe more rapidly as the moment of descent arrived. He knew he had to get that under control before he went under. Otherwise he would burn through the oxygen supply much too quickly. Dr. Castle knew that too. She rested her hands on his shoulders.

"You'll be all right," she said.

"I know."

"Have I told you how much I appreciate everything you're doing?"

"Not in so many words, but it isn't necessary," Collins told her. "We're helping each other. Hopefully, we're also doing something for science."

Dr. Castle's expression seemed somewhat melancholy. "I've never relied on someone else to do my research or digging. I've always gone into the desert or up the mountainside or out on the plateau. This is a new experience for me."

"And are you enjoying it?" Collins asked.

"Let's say I'm comfortable with it," she replied. "I haven't known you very long, but I have faith in you. I have faith in *us*."

Collins smiled as Tally came back. She handed the computer to Dr. Castle. She had also brought Collins's gloves.

"I figured you'd need them," she said to him.

"I don't know," he replied. "With all this cross-millennia hybrid species stuff, I was starting to think I might have merman genes. Maybe I'm related to the Man from Atlantis."

"Ooooo," Tally said as she set the gloves on the vinyl cushion of one of the built-in seats.

"What?" Collins asked.

"I used to have a major crush on Patrick Duffy."

"Is that good news or bad news for me?" Collins asked.

"I don't know," Tally said. There was the hint of a tease in her voice, in her expression.

"Come on," Collins pressed. "Give a guy some hope here. I'm about to go into battle with a sea serpent."

"It's really tough to say," Tally replied. "Patrick didn't have all this 'stuff' on. He swam around in his Speedos."

"Jeez. That's setting the bar a little high."

"Sorry," the young woman said. "You asked, I told."

"Yeah, yeah." Collins pretended to speak into a cassette recorder. "Note to self. Go to gym for a year and then purchase Speedos."

"But he also had gills," Tally went on. "That may have had something to do with his sex appeal." She glanced at the hose outlets on Collins's helmet and winked. "There's something seductive about a man who breathes through the side of his head."

Tally helped Collins on with the oxygen tanks while he fixed the hoses to the helmet. Shep had showed them how to make the connections the night before. Collins also checked to find the releases for the cables. The large orange buttons were located below the hooks. They were sealed in clear plastic coverings to keep the water from corrupting the mechanisms. Collins pressed each one once, just to make certain they were working.

The young physicist felt a little better now. There was an escape route. He also felt good about the exchange with Tally. Collins couldn't believe that she might actually have been sort-of, maybe-just-a-little, coming on to him. What she had said about him was probably charity, like a kiss from a USO dancer the night before a big bat-

tle. But even if it was, it was still thoughtful. And very,
very effective. If he were sufficiently brave and charming,
who knows? It might prove to have been a test-drive for
the future.

Once the hoses were attached, Tally fixed the cables
to the side of the diving suit. Collins waited before putting
on the helmet. As soon as they did that, he would have
to go on tank oxygen. Instead, he checked to make sure
the weights on the boots were secure. Then he put on his
gloves.

When Dr. Castle was finished, they ran a check of the
computer system and the communications link. The latter
was run through the ship's radio, which was set to the suit's
frequency. Both were working perfectly. Then Tally went
below to get the videocamera. They made sure the picture
was transmitting to Dr. Castle's laptop, and that the software was saving the images, before powering down to conserve the battery. Collins hooked the camera to his
equipment belt.

The boat was moving to and fro on the gently swelling
surface of the loch. The weighted boots, five pounds each,
helped Collins keep his balance as he walked to the port-
side. With Tally's assistance, he put the helmet on. Dr. Castle turned the air valve on the tank. The oxygen flowed
freely. The young man nodded and Tally helped him lock
the helmet in place. He reached around to just above his
right ear and switched on the top light. Then he turned his
back to the loch and climbed down the aluminum ladder.
Collins had expected to feel claustrophobic when the helmet went on. He did not. It was just the opposite. As he
lowered himself rung by rung into the loch, the world
seemed to open up to him. He was no longer a mere creature of the land but a denizen of the sea.

The Man from Atlantis, he thought happily as he
reached the last rung.

"Good luck!" he heard Tally shout into the radio as he opened his fingers, gave a little jump back, and began his descent.

Whatever trepidation Collins had experienced before left him as he dropped through the murky water.

CHAPTER SIXTEEN

D R. CASTLE WAS settled into her seat at the helm. She was turned to the port side and had the laptop on her knees. The deck radio was set to receive. She had eschewed the headset in favor of the condenser microphone so Tally could hear. To keep from distracting him with surface noise, the RESPOND button was muted. So far, except for a few exclamations of how awesome it was to be down there, how slowly he was sinking due to the peat, and how impenetrable the water was, Collins had nothing of substance to report.

Be patient, the scientist told herself.

The chill wind stirred her hair and windbreaker as she looked over the top of the computer at Tally. The young woman was standing beside the cable drum. A small digital readout on the side monitoring the length of cable that had been played out.

"He's going to be all right," Dr. Castle said.

"Pardon me?" Tally said.

"Harold," Dr. Castle said.

"Oh," she said. "You know it's strange. I'm not worried about him. Not seriously, anyway."

"And you shouldn't be," Dr. Castle said. "Shep may be a little wonky, but his diving equipment is sound."

"I know," Tally said. "And I can't imagine that much is going to happen. Not really."

"You still doubt me?" Dr. Castle asked.

"Not really," Tally said. "But I've had to put what we're doing into perspective."

"How do you mean?"

"I've had to remind myself that what we're looking for is an animal, not a monster," Tally said. "I can't be distracted by what tourist brochures and popular culture have made of this creature."

"Nor should you be," Dr. Castle said. "A lot of that ranges from inadvertent distortion to pure fancy."

"Exactly," Tally said. "Until responsible scientists went to Indonesia for a firsthand look, the Komodo dragon was thought to be an unspeakable monster. At three meters long it's just a very large monitor lizard. The same is true of the giant squid. We have yet to see one alive, but carcasses up to sixty feet long have been hauled from the ocean. If I were a sailor on an old caravel, I certainly would have described that as a monster, the 'kraken' of ancient lore. The mystique about all of these creatures has been the result of their elusiveness."

"True," Dr. Castle said. "But I should point out that the Komodo dragon lives in what was always a comparatively remote section of the world. The giant squid inhabits the depths of the sea. Loch Ness is finite. People have always lived here. There is no access to the North Sea. While I agree that we're operating within the laws of biology, the animal itself may be more like the platypus, the only egg-laying mammal. Unique in every way."

"But still not a sea serpent," Tally said. "Not in the classic sense."

"Not if you mean a supernatural creature, no," Dr. Castle agreed.

"For all we know, someone using sonar in another section of the loch may detect Harold and think that he's the monster."

"What we call 'friendly fire' in the field," Dr. Castle said. "The observer accidentally becoming the observed. Speaking of Harold, how deep is he?"

"Twenty-five feet," Tally reported. "How much are the cables slowing him down?"

"Very little," the paleontologist replied. "Dropping through the first twenty to thirty meters or so is like descending in quicksand. Rising heat carries the peat with it and makes the water extremely buoyant. The final ten meters will go much more quickly."

Dr. Castle made a note of the time and depth in her computer log. "You know, Tally, non-visibility generates myth. Look at cinema stars and reclusive billionaires. The press makes up scenarios to explain them. But supposition doesn't change the truth. It only colors it, often inaccurately."

"I understand that," Tally said. "When I was a little girl I used to devour books about UFOs and extraterrestrials. *The Interrupted Journey*, *Chariots of the Gods*, *Worlds in Collision*."

"How old were you?"

"Ten, eleven years old," Tally said.

"Quite a brainful for a young lady."

"I was fascinated by it all because I wanted to believe in other worlds, better worlds, smarter and more benevolent beings."

"Unorthodox beings?"

"Absolutely," Tally admitted. "Is it that obvious?"

"That you were rebelling against a traditional upbringing?"

"Yes," Tally said.

"Not exactly," Dr. Castle said. "I took one of those

intellectual leaps that make you uncomfortable. You have exceptional sea legs and seem very much at home on a boat. I have traveled on ships manufactured by the Randall Corporation. And your first name is a part of a boat. Am I wrong in assuming that you are part of the New England shipbuilding family?"

"Guilty," Tally said.

"Orderly factories, orderly home—"

"Orderly life," Tally said. "You have the family pegged. And I was the oddball. I was willing to open my mind to new ideas but not to suspend disbelief. But as I read those books, I would try to think of alternate explanations. I would go to our study, to the Encyclopaedia Britannica, and look up how the pyramids were built. Built very obviously by men, not aliens. Or I'd read how marsh gas or weather balloons could be mistaken for flying saucers. I became very disillusioned."

"Yet you still came here," Dr. Castle said. "You still want to believe."

"Yes, I do. Very much."

"So did I," Dr. Castle told her. "But I take a different approach. You went to the outer extreme. You captured wild theories then brought them back to study. I always went the other way. I've used science as a stepping stone in my lifelong search for Nessie."

"Is that what got you interested in dinosaurs?"

"Yes," Dr. Castle said. "And there was always something that kept me going. For example, five years ago Danish scientists discovered a previously unknown life form down a cold well in Greenland. *Limnognathia maerski.* It was only the fourth new creature to be discovered in the twentieth century. They were tiny freshwater organisms that did not fit into any known animal family."

"The operative word is 'tiny,'" Tally pointed out. "It's probably very easy to overlook small creatures inhabiting a remote well. People live on the loch year-round."

"And there are sightings year-round," Dr. Castle replied. "But they're like the Boy Who Cried Wolf. No one comes to investigate anymore."

"Well—not exactly 'no one,'" Tally smiled as she turned to check the depth gauge.

That was true, Dr. Castle admitted. They were here. A shipbuilding scion, an existential paleontologist, and a quantum physicist who worked for the United Nations. She couldn't have put together a less likely team if she tried. Yet it was a team she felt confident about. A team she was proud of, just like the ragtag football team her son had played on, the one that had seized the local title because they were so unorthodox no one knew how to play against them.

The kind of team that won games . . . and made history.

CHAPTER SEVENTEEN

LOCH NESS WAS exactly what Harold Collins had been expecting: dark, particulate swill with heavily filtered light, slightly redshifted by the prismatic effect of the silicate content of the water.

The physicist descended slowly. There was a definite sense of downward motion; it was like riding an elevator on the outside of a building, smooth and frictionless, if not as swift. He was no longer breathing fast, but the sound of it filled his helmet. The light on top of his helmet sent a cylinder of light down and ahead at a forty-five-degree angle. It illuminated matter that looked like algae and minute clumps of fertilizer. The latter was obviously the peat. He also saw the occasional brown trout, as well as thin, eel-like creatures that might have been water snakes, and small fish that looked like large guppies. He had a surprising flash to being in kindergarten for the first time and looking out at the grownup-looking alphabet tacked above the blackboard. It was a tantalizing mystery that he looked forward to having revealed. Yet it seemed *so* foreign.

"Lord god, the things I don't know," he said.

"What's that?" Dr. Castle asked.

"I was just commenting on how little I know about marine biology," Collins replied.

"We're specialists," Dr. Castle pointed out. "We're supposed to know everything about a little, not the other way around."

"Yeah, but this is seriously far from my neighborhood," Collins said. "I move in circles where I know the streets, the houses, the occupants, and what they look like naked."

"Colorful," Dr. Castle said.

"This is exciting, though."

Collins went back to looking. He glanced down at the back of his right forearm. He hit the illuminated button marked with a figure of a diver. His depth and the remaining oxygen supply appeared in the rectangular green window. He pushed the button that translated the meters to feet. He was nearly thirty-five feet down. Ninety-seven point seven percent of his oxygen remained. He felt like a kid with a new toy on his birthday.

That's the second time in the last minute you've feel like a kid, he realized. That was a good thing, he assumed. It meant he was excited and awed. A scientist should be both.

The deeper he got, the thinner the floating material became. He also noticed that the area outside the glow of his headlight had gone from brownish to near black. Obviously, the higher layers of peat prevented sunlight from penetrating here. He wondered what the first people who dove down here had felt, probably in the eighteen hundreds, just holding their breath and swimming down, maybe using nets to scoop up samples for study.

They probably felt scared, he guessed.

Especially if they believed in the Monster. Oddly enough, that was the first time he had thought of the creature since beginning his descent. Visually, the world down here and the physical descent itself were different enough to distract him. Now that the monster was back, it dominated his mind. In that instant, the darkness beyond the cylinder of light became transformed. It went from being impenetrable to being ominous. *Does that mean there is something out there?* he wondered. Or was it something else? The notion that nightmares come at night? Or racial memory, the idea that the fears of prehistoric humans who hid from nocturnal carnivores is imprinted on the genetic code of modern individuals? Or all of the above?

Collins glanced at his gauge. He was forty feet below the surface. How far would that be on land? Less than a quarter of a city block in New York. That didn't seem deep at all. Not to the logical side of his brain. Collins tried to think horizontal, to keep that part of him in the fore.

As he crossed the fifty-feet mark, his feet began to tingle. The sensation quickly spread to his fingertips and forehead. Maybe it was just the result of breathing canned-air. Still, it began to concern him a little.

"Kathryn," he said, "my extremities are feeling a little electrified. Should they be?"

"It could be the increased pressure," Dr. Castle replied. "Or the cold. Your organs start to conserve blood when it gets cooler. That keeps it from circulating to your fingers and toes."

"The feeling is getting stronger," he said. "It's spreading up my legs."

"Do you want us to bring you up?"

"No," he said. "Is Shep a practical joker?"

"Why do you ask?"

"Maybe the wet suit is too tight," Collins said.

"No, he wouldn't do that," Dr. Castle assured him. "He wouldn't play games when it comes to diving. Let me know if you start to feel faint."

"I'm okay. It's just like one of those muscle massagers," Collins said. "I'll let you know if there's a change."

There was. The sensation crept up his thighs, and then along his arms and up to his neck and cheeks. It wasn't painful, but it was slightly distracting, and it was getting stronger.

What if the Monster is a giant electric eel? he thought suddenly.

The darkness suddenly became a whole lot scarier.

But then reason forced itself on him. If the water were electrified, Collins wouldn't necessarily feel it. He was stuffed inside a rubber wet suit and *that* was inside a diving suit. An electric shock would not be able to reach him. He had to stop dwelling on it. He turned outward.

He was sixty feet down. There were fewer large particles in the loch, and very few sea creatures. The water looked more like broth now than like soup. It was filled with a powdery substance, perhaps silt stirred from the floor by currents—or something moving down there. He turned his head to the left and right, then down to shine the light around. He could not yet see the bottom.

Dr. Castle had offered to bring the speargun from her van, but Collins had declined to carry it. He still did not regret that decision. If he saw the animal, he would not shoot at it. Not for any scientific reason, like preserving the last of a dying species. He had never used a speargun and would probably only wound and enrage whatever he was pointing at. That is, if he didn't shoot himself in the leg. And how would he know if an animal were attacking him or simply coming toward him because it lacked stereoscopic forward vision? No, this was one of those risks a scientist simply had to take.

Collins looked at the gauge on his arm. He had nearly reached the seventy-feet mark. It was comforting to know that he was more than halfway to the ridge. He knew what lay above. The second half was probably more of the same. The sense of being in limbo began to pass. As it did, it hit Collins that the Man from Atlantis had nothing on him. At least, not in the courage department. Or for that matter in the being-unique department. The quiet kid from Connecticut, the egghead who liked animated cartoons and comic books way past puberty, who knew more about the space program than his science teacher; that guy was diving deep into Loch Ness to look for the legendary Monster. How many of the tough-guy jocks in school would have the guts to do that? And with a little luck—*okay,* he thought, *a lot of it*—this day could go down in scientific history. As long as he didn't forget to record it—

"Shit!"

He unhooked the videocamera from his equipment belt.

That would have been just great, he told himself. *The monster scoots by while you're thinking about videotaping it.*

The palm-size unit was easy to operate underwater. It had big, luminous buttons and a large viewfinder with a rubber eyepiece that could be pressed against the visor of his helmet. Collins did so, just to make sure that he could, in fact, see. He could. Perfect. He switched the camera to STANDBY to conserve power, but it was there if he needed it in a hurry.

Collins's breathing was so calm now that he barely noticed the sound. The tingling in his extremities had spread to his whole body now, but it remained very low-intensity. It was like white noise, barely noticeable after a few minutes. His body was also fully accustomed to the slow, steady rate of descent. He no longer felt as if he was dropping. He experienced a sensation akin to what he imagined weightlessness to be.

And then, in less than the time it took to think, to try to process what was happening, everything changed.

CHAPTER EIGHTEEN

TALLY WAS STILL standing beside the large winch that was deploying the cables. It was a thick green drum anchored to the deck by a pair of white, hourglass-shaped pylons. It was well-oiled and perfectly balanced; except for the two-hundred-horsepower engine, it barely made a sound. Tally had been watching as the numbers changed, enjoying the clear air and the gentle movement of the boat, when she felt a violent tug. She knew there was a problem even before she heard Collins's message over the radio.

"There's something wrong down here!" Collins shouted.

"Stop the deployment!" Dr. Castle yelled to Tally.

"Done!" Tally had moved to shut the engine even before Dr. Castle instructed her to.

There was a small, gunmetal control panel on the left pylon. The young woman had lifted a clear plastic cover and jammed her palm on the fat green button inside. The cables froze instantly as clamp-locks closed around the drum lips on the bottom of both sides.

"Harold, what's happening?" Dr. Castle asked.

"I'm not sure."

"Is there anything above you? Can you see?" Dr. Castle asked. "Can we bring you up?"

Before he could answer, there was a different kind of pull on the winch, slower and more sustained. The vessel began to list slowly but certainly to the port side. Tally braced herself on the rail. Suddenly, the boat stopped tilting. It remained at a slight angle.

"Harold, talk to us!" Dr. Castle said.

Silence.

"At least let me know you're receiving the transmission!" the paleontologist urged.

"It's incredible," he said softly.

Dr. Castle looked at Tally. "What is?"

"I see stars down there."

"Where?"

"Under me."

"It must be phosphorous," Dr. Castle said.

"I didn't see any record of that in the geologic charts," Tally said. "Maybe something's picking up light from his helmet. Oil or mica."

Dr. Castle held up a hand to silence Tally. The paleontologist was correct. Identifying the substance was not the highest priority right now. There was another tug and the boat listed further. It was now about ten degrees off plumb.

"Harold, you said something was wrong," Dr. Castle went on. "We felt a pull against the drum. What happened?"

"I don't know."

"Did you snag on something?"

"Not that I can see."

"Well, there must be something. We're definitely being pulled up here," Dr. Castle informed him.

"I'm looking up," Collins said. "I don't see anything."

"Something must be tangled in the lines between Harold and the surface," Tally said. "Should I reel him in?"

Dr. Castle hit the mute button. "No! If the lines snap the whiplash could tear his suit."

"Then we should tell him to unhook—"

"Not until we make sure there's nothing above him," Dr. Castle said. "He has air. There's time. We don't want him ascending into an uprooted tree with roots and branches grabbing his suit. If we can't free him I'll call Shep, ask him to go down there—"

Suddenly, the boat listed a few degrees more. The cables were growing extremely taut. Tally could see them tightening around the drum, the rubber grunting and the reel complaining.

Dr. Castle turned the speaker back on. "Harold, can you reach up for me, see if there is any play in the cables?"

"Hold," he said.

The groaning of the cables permeated the entire area. It was like a creaking door opening slowly.

"They're very tight," he said. "I thought you said you locked them down."

"We did."

"I'm still descending," he told her.

"Harold, are you *certain* there's nothing pulling on you?"

"Positive," he replied. "There's nothing but water around me. Here, I'll show you. I'm turning on the camera."

Dr. Castle looked at the computer monitor. She saw the light, the water, the contents of the loch, and the cables leading into the darkness.

"Are you getting it?"

"We are," Dr. Castle said. "Whatever it is must be higher."

"It can't be that much higher. I'm only about seventy feet—wait a second," he said.

"What is it?"

"Get out of here!" Collins murmured. It wasn't a command but a statement of disbelief.

"What?" Dr. Castle pressed.

"This is very bizarre. I'll turn the camera around. The stars are getting brighter and clearer, yet I don't feel like I'm moving any more."

"You must be," Dr. Castle said. "Something's pulling on the cables. It's causing us to tip toward your side."

"I don't understand what it could be," Collins told her. "Hold on. I'm angling the camera down."

"Dr. Castle—please. Call Shep," Tally said.

The paleontologist nodded. Her eyes were on the monitor as she felt her belt for her cell phone.

"Kathryn, are you looking at your computer?" Collins asked.

"Yes," she said.

"Are you seeing the lights?" he asked.

The hazy daylight was making it difficult to read the screen. Dr. Castle used her left hand to shield the monitor. "There's a faint pattern of lights, yes," she told him. "But they can't be stars."

Collins was silent.

"Harold, we'd better get you out of there," Dr. Castle said. "Either you can disengage or I'll call Shep—"

"Hold on. Something's happening!" he interrupted. Then he went silent.

"Harold, keep talking," Dr. Castle urged, exchanging glances with Tally.

"All right. Do you see anything on the monitor?" he asked.

"Just your light and the water," Dr. Castle said, looking down.

"Well, it's incredible down here. Things are turning," he told her. "It's like being on a potter's wheel."

"Harold, I need you to do something for me! I need you

to drop your boot weights and release the cables," Dr. Castle said. "Do you hear me?"

"Yeah. I'm getting nauseous—"

"Harold, *disengage and surface!*" Dr. Castle shouted.

"I *am* surfacing," he said.

"What?"

"I'm coming up."

Dr. Castle was still looking at the computer monitor. She squinted and was able to make out the lights. They did appear to be swirling. "Harold, which way is the video-camera pointing?"

"Down," he said.

"Where are the lights?"

"Up," he told her.

"Harold, you've become inverted somehow."

"I'm what?"

"You're upside-down. You probably became twisted in the cables!" Dr. Castle told him. "That has to be why you're nauseous and spinning. You have to try and right yourself. Can you get your hands on the cables?"

"I don't know—something very weird is happening down here," Collins told her.

"Harold, I need you to pay attention to my voice!" Dr. Castle yelled.

"The stars are turning—"

"Listen to me! Close your eyes. Do you understand? The lights are probably just plankton or phosphorous. They're confusing you."

"Do you still see them on the monitor?" he asked.

She looked. "Yes, I see them," she said. There were streaks of light here and there like yellow streamers. "Harold, are you trying to turn around?"

"I'm telling you, I'm not upside-down. It's like a galaxy now, just whirling—uh-oh."

"What's wrong?"

"I'm being pulled—can't hold the camera."

Dr. Castle was no longer looking at the computer. She was punching in Shep's number. "Harold, focus on my voice."

"Strange . . . head . . . light . . ."

"My voice, Harold!"

She heard him scream, though it didn't sound like a cry of pain. It reminded her of the shouts she used to hear on the roller coaster when she took her son to the amusement park.

Suddenly, the vessel tilted another ten degrees or so. It was as if a giant pair of hands had pressed against the starboard side and pushed the boat toward the water. Tally had to grab the winch control panel to keep from flipping over the side. Dr. Castle fell from her seat, though she managed to grab the computer, protecting it. She lost her cell phone, however, which slid across the deck and off the side of the boat. Then, just as quickly and unexpectedly, the boat rolled back to an upright position. It rocked toward the starboard slightly, then back to port, then back again before settling in.

Dr. Castle was on her knees, holding the computer to her chest with her left arm. She put her free hand on the seat and got back up. She scrambled over to the radio and leaned over the microphone.

"Harold!" she shouted.

There was no answer.

Dr. Castle looked at Tally, who didn't need the unspoken order she saw in the scientist's eyes. She punched the button to retract the cables. The winch turned without resistance.

"Harold!" Dr. Castle said again into the radio.

There was no sound. Not even static.

Dr. Castle rose. She set the computer on the seat and walked slowly toward the winch. Like Tally, she expected the worst. Only "the worst" they had imagined was not quite sufficient. Tally had expected the cables to come up without Harold Collins on the other end. They did. But she had not expected to find what she did. The cable hooks were still attached to the rings from Collins's diving suit.

Something had literally sheared them from the plate that had attached them to the diving suit.

CHAPTER NINETEEN

U PSET BUT REMARKABLY focused, Dr. Castle hurried back to her seat. She leaned over the radio again. "Harold!"

Nothing.

"Harold, are you *there*? Can you *signal* me? A tap, a grunt, anything?"

"What could have caused him to shout like that?" Tally asked. "It didn't sound like he was afraid."

"No, it didn't," Dr. Castle agreed. She waited a moment and then repeated the call. Tally was standing at the port side. She was leaning on the railing, looking for air bubbles, trying to peer through the murk for any sign that Harold Collins might be surfacing. Or some sign of whatever might have torn the lines. There was nothing but the drip of water from the severed cables.

"Harold, if you can hear me—I'm going to have to break contact and call for help," Dr. Castle said. "If you're receiving, don't worry. We'll get you back." She switched off the suit radio and radioed Shep. That was the only frequency she knew by heart. And he was the only man she knew would be at his post. She also knew that he was a professional. He would hustle, even if it weren't Kathryn making the call. And an expert diver who knew these waters was what they needed now, desperately. Assuming that Collins's air tanks and helmet were intact—which was hardly a certainty—they had only about ninety-five minutes to bring him up.

"Kathryn, do you feel strange?" Tally asked.

"What do you think?"

"I'm not talking about Harold. Physically, I mean," Tally said.

"There's Dramamine in the first-aid kit," Dr. Castle said impatiently as she finished adjusting the radio frequency.

"I don't *mean* that!" Tally said. "I'm talking about a kind of pressure, like when you're going up in an elevator."

"No," Dr. Castle said.

The radio beeped once. Shep answered immediately.

"Kathryn, is that you?"

"Yes, Shep. We—"

"Need my help," Shep chuckled. "I figured you'd have trouble with something."

"Shep, Collins is lost."

"Say again?" The seaman's voice was grave now.

"He was down about ten minutes when the cables tore away. His radio is also down."

"I'll be there in ten," Shep said was all business now. "Keep the radio on his setting and watch the water on the side he went down in case there are air bubbles or he tries signaling with his light."

"We are."

"If you see anything, mark the water with dye in the hold. I'll call the local rescue unit while I get underway. Out."

"Thank you and out," Dr. Castle said. She quickly punched in the frequency for the helmet radio. "Harold, are you there? Can you hear me? If you can, try to cast the weights off your boots. You will float to the surface. If not, remain very still with the helmet light on. Shep is on his way. It will be easier for him to find you without clouds of silt."

If Harold was hearing, he wasn't responding. Dr. Castle stared at the radio. Upset as she was, she could not afford to lose control. She had to think, to try and figure out what had caused this. She didn't want to believe that the creature had attacked him. The water would have been disturbed by an encounter like that. The camera would have shown something.

"The camera!" she exclaimed. Dr. Castle picked up the computer and opened the top. She set it on her lap.

"Is the computer still working?" Tally asked.

"I'm checking," Dr. Castle said.

It had gotten knocked around and had shut itself off. She pressed the ON button. The monitor blinked to life.

"Still operational," Dr. Castle said as she rebooted.

"What about the camera?"

"I'll know in a minute," she said. "Though without the light, there probably wouldn't be much to see."

What she really wanted to do was have a look at the "stars" he'd reported seeing, as well as any final images that may have come in after the boat shifted. She would run the pictures through the image enhancers. Perhaps the lights were radioactive or electrically charged in some way and were interfering with his communications. Whatever they were, she didn't imagine they were responsible for cutting the cable, unless they were glittering metal shards of some kind. A mine, perhaps. A torpedo. But from where? Loch Ness was not a terrorist target. Besides, there had not been an explosion.

"There's nothing going on here," Tally said. "Maybe Harold is making his way to the surface at some other location but couldn't tell us."

"Possibly," Dr. Castle agreed. "I'll check starboard."
She rose and set the computer on the seat.

"Kathryn?"

"Yes?"

"There's definitely something in the air," she said. "I felt it from the time Harold and I arrived yesterday."

"What is it?" the paleontologist asked distractedly. She wasn't interested in talking.

"Unease," Tally said. "It's a very physical thing, like the feeling you get before giving a speech."

"I feel sick too," Dr. Castle said.

"But it isn't like that," Tally protested. "It's a tension in my belly, in my shoulders, my legs. I wonder if it's the same thing Harold was describing."

"I don't know. I think we're both just scared."

Or remembering, Dr. Castle thought. The feeling was extremely reminiscent of how she had felt when the call had come from the London police that her husband and son had been killed.

The scientist continued to look across the smooth water. The eastern shore was about two hundred meters distant. The port-side shore was closer, a rock wall only thirty meters away. The surface was disturbingly unrippled. There was no activity on or below it. She was no swimmer, but if there were any kind of visibility she would jump over and try to find Harold herself.

"I wonder if the feeling is stronger on this side of the boat," Tally said.

"I can't imagine what kind of causation could do that," Dr. Castle replied.

"Radiation?" Tally asked. "That could confuse someone, affect the body, induce nausea."

"True, but caused by what?" Dr. Castle asked. She turned and walked toward her.

"Hazardous waste, unknown deposits. I don't know,"

Tally said. "We were ready to believe in an unknown sea creature, weren't we?"

"You have a point," Dr. Castle said. She reached the drum and looked down at the water. "There has been construction at Urquhart Castle. The developers may have inadvertently put something in the loch. Chemicals, possibly, not radioactive material."

"Do you think there could have been bad air in the tank? Harold sounded almost as if he were on nitrous oxide."

"Shep would never have done that," Dr. Castle said.

"Then maybe the air was compromised in some other way," Tally suggested. "He might have been breathing CO_2. Or perhaps he wasn't breathing at all. The air line may have gotten knotted in the cables."

"You know, now that you mention it, I do feel something," Dr. Castle said suddenly. "A sense of being pulled down. I feel it in my feet and my hips, as though my muscles are working against it."

"Exactly," Tally said. "So it *is* this side of the boat. We were being pulled this way too, and Harold said he was being drawn down."

"But he also said he didn't feel anything pulling at him," Dr. Castle reminded her.

"Possibly because he wasn't standing on anything solid," Tally suggested.

"Good point."

"We are," Tally said. "He would have been dragged through the water. I take it that you've never felt anything like this before?"

"Not that I'm aware of," Dr. Castle replied. "But then I'm not usually standing when I'm out here. I'm always sitting in a rowboat."

"I wonder. Are there any power plants nearby?" Tally thought aloud. "There could be some kind of discharge from a generator that caused Harold's suit to short, made him panic."

"There's nothing like that anywhere nearby on the loch."

"No hydroelectric dams?"

"No. The loch would not be a suitable place for anything like that. There's no running water."

"Right," Tally said.

"And the force required to slice this metal," Dr. Castle said, gesturing toward the hook, "this is something else. Even bolt cutters wouldn't have been able to cut them so cleanly." The paleontologist realized that she had sounded like her father just then. She used to listen as he discussed crimes over the telephone. She had always marveled at how much fact he derived from the simplest evidence, like food crumbs that had fallen from clothing allowing him to track a killer to having eaten at a particular restaurant, or determining a man's weight from the impression his shoes left in a garden. Now she was trying to do the same thing but without a familiar frame of reference.

The paleontologist heard a buzzing motor in the distance. It was coming from the direction of Shep's showroom. Dr. Castle looked south. She recognized the distinctive black hull of her old friend's speedboat. Ordinarily, Dr. Castle felt cornered by the passions that drove the old seaman and did her best to avoid them. Right now she was glad for them.

"Is that him?" Tally asked, looking back.

"It is," Dr. Castle said.

"The white knight on a black horse," Tally remarked.

Something else that's upside-down or twisted about, Dr. Castle thought.

She gave Tally a reassuring pat on the shoulder, then went back to the computer. Since it had been shut down without the proper exit sequence, it was running a diagnostics program on each of its systems. She picked up the laptop and sat down. The delay was frustrating.

The heavy feeling in her legs and waist began to dissipate.

Dr. Castle wondered if Tally was right, if the phenomenon was somehow localized. If so, what the hell could it be? It had to be geologic. There was nothing else down there but rock and sediment.

At least, as far as they knew.

The *FreeDome* wireless icon finally appeared. The scientist clicked on it. To her surprise, the computer indicated that it recognized the videocamera.

"Tally, the machines are talking!" Dr. Castle said.

"The camera's still on?"

"Apparently," Dr. Castle replied.

Eagerly, the scientist clicked on the drop-down menu and pressed the UPDATE bar. She waited again as the camera began to download whatever it was seeing as well as whatever pictures had been stored in its memory when the computer shut down. Pictures that were suddenly as precious as any image of a monster.

Pictures that might provide them with clues to the fate of Harold Collins.

CHAPTER TWENTY

WHEN HAROLD COLLINS was finally able to see clearly, he had no idea what he was looking at, or where he was. The physicist knew at once that he was on his back, and floating, but that was virtually all he knew.

Floating? he wondered. *As in "on the surface of the loch"?* It had to be, though he didn't remember going there.

His eyes were open, but that didn't tell him much. Patches of water clung to Collins's visor, creating wiggly patterns on the plastic. It was like looking out a car window on a rainy night. Where there was no water the stars were brilliantly sharp and clear, though they didn't look familiar. There were too many of them to see any patterns or planets. There was no sound except for his own shallow breathing and the water slapping, light and hollow, against his helmet.

His mouth was exceedingly dry, and the helmet was extremely stuffy. It didn't feel as though fresh air were getting in—

No, fresh air was coming in, Collins realized. It was just muggy, warm air, with a slightly acrid smell. It was coming from somewhere to his right. Also coming from that side were occasional drops of warm water. They were splashing his ear. How was *that* happening?

Collins raised his gloved hand to the side of his helmet. He wobbled a little on the water and compensated by leaning slightly toward his left. He felt for the hose. It was still there. What was new was a hole the length of his foot on the top left side of the helmet.

Okay, Collins thought. He would worry about that in a minute. Right now there were larger concerns, such as his own condition. Collins moved his head slowly to the right and then to the left. His neck wasn't sprained or broken. He raised one arm and then another. He did it carefully, so as not to sink or invert himself. His legs were also functioning, though they were bobbing just below the surface because the weights were still attached to his feet. He reached down slipped the weights off and placed them in pouches on his thighs. Physically, all the Harold Collins systems were go. Then he looked at his left forearm to check the electronics.

They looked promising. The computer showed his last recorded depth as seventy-two feet. That was correct. Obviously the readout and memory were still functioning. He punched another button to get the time.

Uh oh, he thought. That couldn't be right.

The digital clock read 8:37 A.M. That would mean it had only been about fifteen minutes since he'd stepped into Loch Ness. The computer had to be malfunctioning.

All right, Collins thought. He needed to contact someone. He tried to speak, but his voice was a raspy whisper, as if he'd been screaming. Maybe he had been. He couldn't remember. The young man worked up some saliva, then wet his lips with his tongue.

"Hello?" he said thinly into the helmet.

There was no answer.

He cleared his throat and tried again. "Hello? Kathryn? Tally? Anybody? Are you out there?"

He waited. No one replied. That wasn't good. If Collins were simply out of range, he probably would have picked up crosstalk, white noise, something. Anything. Obviously, the radio was shot. But that didn't explain why there was no one else around. How could he have drifted without someone finding him? The loch should have been dotted with tourists, fishermen, recreational boaters. Kathryn and Tally should have been looking for him.

Collins was a little more alert than he had been a minute before. He looked up again. What he saw through the still-dripping visor sure looked like dark night. Sharp, clear, two-in-the-morning night.

Wait a second, Collins thought. *Stars . . .*

He had seen them before whatever had happened had "happened." He vaguely remembered telling Dr. Castle something about them.

He didn't remember anything after that. What had happened to the rest of the day? Had he been knocked unconscious and surfaced somewhere else? Maybe he'd been washed into a cove, beneath a rock ledge. Or perhaps he was in a cave and what he was seeing weren't stars but luminous lichen or some kind of Scottish fireflies. But how the hell had he gotten here? And where was "here"?

Collins thought hard and remembered something else. He had been spinning out of control before passing out. And he had seen something else, a big ball of white light. Maybe that light had been real, or maybe it had been caused by banging his helmet against something underwater. He remembered a conversation he'd had with Kathryn about something snagging the lines. Perhaps he'd collided with whatever it was that had gotten entangled in the cables. The Monster? Had he been carried off somewhere, strapped to the creature's back like Ahab on the harpoon-ridden spine of Moby Dick?

No, he decided. His head didn't hurt. And the light he saw had to have been real because it was still here. There was more than starlight picking up the contours of his suit, reflecting off the smooth water. There was a pale white glow over his entire body. It had to be coming from the ball of bright light he had seen before he'd passed out. He lowered his eyes to his feet. He couldn't see anything in the blackness beyond them. The illumination had to be coming from somewhere to his sides or else behind him, just the starlight or whatever that was. Could it be the searchlight of an oncoming boat? A streetlamp? The porch light of an inn on the loch?

It was time to do a more thorough reconnaissance. Collins turned his head slowly to the right and looked across the surface of the water. He saw the dark silhouette of trees and hills about one hundred meters away. No light source there. At least he knew now that he was outside and not lost in a cave or cove. He rolled his head to the left. Nothing there. He used his hands to bat at the water slightly so he could pivot and look behind him. When he had turned about ninety degrees, he squinted as he stared into the source of the light.

Countless gleaming shards scudded across the rippling water. But what caused them was wrong. Way, way wrong. Impossible-wrong.

But there it was.

CHAPTER TWENTY-ONE

D R. CASTLE DID not have time to study the video images further. Not just then. She popped in a blank CD and made sure the incoming pictures were backed up, then went to meet Shep Boucher.

Even as Shep arrived, the men and women of the Loch Ness Volunteer Rescue Service—the LNVRS, pronounced "Lonovers"—were headed toward the site. They came from all directions in over a dozen rowboats, motorboats, and tour boats. Tally was impressed by the speed of their response. She was also impressed that each sailor was watching ahead, making sure that if the missing man surfaced they didn't accidentally run him over. Tally later learned that they were also watching for bubble tracks, in case his air hose had come free and his tank was still jetting air. That might not only prevent him from surfacing by forcing him down, but could shift him around the loch.

Shep Boucher boarded the vessel. Quickly but carefully he donned his own wet suit and scuba gear as Dr. Castle told him what had happened. Tally listened from her port-side post. To Shep's credit there was nothing "I told you so" in his manner or in his responses as he asked questions about Collins's descent: his location, speed, depth, communications, and the aftermath.

"What I really can't understand is what could have made us tilt like we did," Dr. Castle said.

"The Monster," Shep said matter-of-factly.

"Not flotsam of some kind?" Tally asked.

"A clump of underwater branches wouldn't have caused you to list," Shep said. "I'm thinking it could have been a mini-sub, though. Two dealers rent the pedal-operated shells and two of them rent the motorized kind. I phoned them on the way over and left word on answering machines asking if anybody had rented one. You might call the office and see if my sister Eileen heard from anyone."

"My phone went overboard," Dr. Castle replied.

Shep gave her his.

When the seaman was ready, he tested his air, then went to the aluminum ladder at the side of the boat. He unhooked the cable from the severed suit latch and looped it through a hook in his gear belt.

"Did you notice the cable hook?" Dr. Castle asked.

"I did. Cut like butter," Shep said.

"By—?"

"The Devil's own screwblade from the look of it," he said. "Damned if I know. Right now I'm damned if I care. I've a missing diver to find. If you or the others find anything, signal me by starting the cable back up.

"You'll feel that?" Tally asked.

"Like a fish on a line," the Scotsman assured her. "Not everything has to be hi-tech. And keep the other boats away from this side of the vessel. I'll have this area covered."

Dr. Castle and Tally both nodded.

Shep placed his clear face mask on and inserted the

mouthpiece. Then he gave the unspool button a tap. The motor hummed, the winch began to turn, and Shep went to the stairs. He faced the deck. He didn't climb down but slid into the water holding the rails. He hit with barely a splash.

"Good luck!" Dr. Castle yelled as Shep went under.

Tally turned back to the starboard side. She watched as the other vessels continued to arrive. One of the men used hand signals to direct the boats to different sectors.

Tally watched with admiration as the men deployed. *Not everything has to be hi-tech,* she thought.

Her shoulders sagging, Dr. Castle went back to the computer. She sat heavily on the vinyl seat and used the cell phone to call Eileen Boucher-Naughton. Shep's sister said that everyone her brother had called had already phoned back. No one had rented a mini-sub.

"I just thought of something," Tally said. "Ask her if there are any electric cables down there."

Dr. Castle asked Eileen to hold. "Why?"

"I've been thinking about what Harold said right before we lost contact, about feeling electrified and his head getting light," Tally said. "I wonder if his suit tore and a cable could have been corroded—"

"And shocked the water," Dr. Castle said. "Tickled some exposed flesh."

Dr. Castle asked. As far as Eileen knew the only line that ever went under the loch was an old phone cable. It went from east to west about five miles to the north of where the search was taking place. The scientist thanked her. Eileen said that she hoped they found their colleague.

Dr. Castle clicked off Shep's cell phone and returned it to her belt holder. She shook her head as she looked at the computer monitor. Tally came over. The reporter couldn't tell whether Dr. Castle was staring at an image they'd received or was looking through it. The scientist seemed to have had the life sucked from her.

"I wonder if there's anything else we might be overlooking, something in the underwater charts or in the video," Dr. Castle said.

"Do you want me to get the charts?" Tally asked.

Dr. Castle didn't answer. As soon as the video feed had been backed up, the paleontologist accessed a photo-workshop program she used for field analyses. She created a slide show of selected images from Harold's videocamera. There were a dozen slots. The dark, fuzzy pictures changed every two seconds.

"These are a record of what Harold passed through, what he saw," Dr. Castle said. "If I enlarge the video pictures and sharpen them, we may be able to see whatever bollixed things up with the cables, or at least determine the direction Harold went."

Tally was looking at the pictures. "I'm still thinking about what he said, about the tingling. It happened to all of us. There has to be something in that."

"He also said his head was light," Dr. Castle reminded her.

"I know. I wonder, could the tingling have been water pressure on the wet suit? Maybe the headpiece was too tight and he saw stars. Maybe the diving suit sprung a leak."

"Why wouldn't he have reported that?"

"Obviously he wasn't aware of it. A seam could have ripped or split somewhere else. The added weight could have turned him around. Blood rushed to his head, confused him."

"It's possible," Dr. Castle agreed.

"In which case . . ." Tally said, her voice trailing away. She didn't have to finish the sentence. Dr. Castle knew the rest. *In which case Harold's suit would have flooded and he'd be far from his last reported position.*

"Wait," Dr. Castle said suddenly. "I may have been wrong about something I just said."

"What?"

"About his head being light. What he said was 'head light.' He could have been referring to something else."

"You mean a bright light, like a car headlight?"

"Exactly," Dr. Castle said.

"The flashlight on his helmet?"

"Possibly," Dr. Castle said. "Maybe he saw it reflected in something."

"Or it could have been something else," Tally said.

"We already checked for mini-subs," Dr. Castle said.

"Right. Is there anything else that could have caused brilliant illumination at that depth?"

"An underwater flare, but we would have seen one being dropped," Dr. Castle told her.

"What about an old flare that might have fallen from a boat? Could Harold have triggered one somehow?"

"Even if he encountered a flare floating around down there, they have to be pulled to ignite," Dr. Castle said. "He didn't do that." She cancelled the computer slide show and went to the last video images the camera had sent. She had looked at the last few, which showed blackness, but not the ones that came in right before that.

She started a new slide show of every frame but working backward. Everything was black, or near black, until they reached image seventeen.

"There!" Dr. Castle said. She stopped the slide show and clicked on the picture. She enlarged it.

Tally bent closer. "There's something there, but it's very blurry."

The paleontologist cleaned up the image using a pixel filler. The program took information from the surrounding data and dropped it into extremely blurry spots. Then she brightened the image to bring out shadowy details.

"That looks like the edge of Harold's suit," Tally said. She pointed. "See this? It's the tool belt."

"It is," Dr. Castle replied. "He must have dropped the camera. The heavier side was the bottom, where the battery is located. The camera must have turned and pointed up as it fell."

"Wasn't there a line that attached the camera to his belt?"

"Yes."

"Then that means Harold is still down there," Tally said.

The scientist continued to go back, frame-by-frame. The camera had photographed Collins from head to toe as he fell. Dr. Castle stopped on picture twenty-four, a very unsteady image that showed the faceplate of Collins's helmet. She magnified that area. There appeared to be a small but brilliant white flash reflected in the upper right-hand corner of the visor. Dr. Castle did everything she could to clear up the image.

"Amazing," Tally said. "There's definitely something out there. It reminds me of a neutrino flash."

"Which is?"

"Neutrinos are elementary particles created from nuclear reactions in the core of a star," Tally said. "They're emitted along with light. But since neutrinos don't interact with matter very well, they're difficult to detect. In order to see them, scientists build observatories in deep caves and mines that have been filled with purified water. The rock shields out cosmic rays that would otherwise mask the neutrinos. When the neutrinos hit water, they produce a flash."

"Are you seriously saying that this is a neutrino burst? And are they dangerous?"

"I'm saying it half-seriously, because neutrino flashes are nowhere near this bright, and no, they're not dangerous," Tally told her. "What I'm thinking is that this could be something *like* that. A meteorite, perhaps. One that slipped into the water without our seeing it. Still hot, still packing a punch."

"It's possible," Dr. Castle agreed. "A long shot, but possible."

After tweaking the image, the women continued to

study it. It was spherical now, the rays nearly gone. There were dim blotches in the brightness.

Behind them, in the distance, men shouted and engines hummed. The noise seemed so far away. The bottom of the loch felt so much closer.

Suddenly Tally stood upright. "Wait a second," she said. "The stars. Harold insisted that he saw stars."

"Yes, but he couldn't possibly have been right about that," Dr. Castle said.

"I'm not so sure of that," Tally replied.

"What do you mean?"

"I mean, let's toss out common sense for a moment. Do you know what that really looks like to me?"

Dr. Castle turned back to it. "What?"

Tally replied, "The moon."

CHAPTER TWENTY-TWO

---

*T*HE MOON, COLLINS thought as he stared at the night sky. That's what was hanging over him like a streetlight. The blue-white orb was so clear and sharp that Collins felt as if it was only a few feet away. He flicked water at it. The droplets didn't reach. It was a full moon all right, and it was in the sky. But there were two things wrong with it.

First, it didn't look like the moon. Not the moon he knew from years of telescope-watching when he was a kid. It was larger and the features were different. The distinctive Imbrium Basin, a titanic hole which was thought to have been created by an asteroid impact, was missing. So were many of the familiar, distinctive "rays," bright areas created by material ejected across wide distances after meteor impacts. The *mare*, the large dark areas on the surface, had considerably different shapes than he remembered. That was obviously due to the fact that the craters and rays that had defined the edges of the ancient volcanic plains were missing.

How?

Second, despite the fact that it was a full moon, Collins could still see stars. That meant there was nothing going on in the earth's atmosphere to disperse the light: no dust, pollution, volcanic ash.

Both, of course, were impossible.

Collins's first thought was that he had to be unconscious. But water was starting to collect in the bottom of his helmet. His waist hurt as if he'd strained his muscles. He was awake. His second thought was that he was in an isolation chamber and hallucinating. He had spent an hour in one of the coffin-like tanks in college. Maybe he was still in there. Maybe the last six or seven years of his life had all been a vision. It was certainly quiet enough to be an isolation booth. Except for the faintest lapping of water against his suit, the world was absolutely silent. There was water in the isolation tank.

Collins closed his eyes, squeezed hard, then opened them again. Nothing had changed. The water-smeared stars were still above him.

Suddenly, the water lifted Collins several feet and then lowered him again. He was caught totally unprepared and it took him a few moments to steady himself as he settled back down. It felt like a swell or the wake of a boat, but the water was otherwise calm. It was followed by another, even stronger push. Collins wondered if a submarine fissure had released a bubble of gas—

He heard the splash to the right and then looked over. Collins's headlamp shined across the dark water. He saw ripples moving toward him but nothing of whatever had caused them. He rocked on the tiny waves, then felt the bump again, stronger than before.

It was time to go.

The young physicist looked around. He saw coastline to his left. It was much nearer than the one on the right. Turning over carefully so that he was facing down, he held his head stiffly above water as he dog-paddled toward shore. He had decided to keep his leaky helmet and gloves on until he knew where he was and what was going on.

It wasn't easy slogging through the water in his gear. Collins's arms became weary from the added weight and he had to stop and just bob every few feet. Each time he did, he looked around. The "moon" light revealed the silhouette of a landscape considerably different from the one he had left just a few minutes before. There appeared to be high, jagged mountains in the distance. And tall ferns of some sort in the foreground. This wasn't Scotland. The flora and the air seemed tropical. He had to be dreaming. Or on a Star Trek holodeck.

That was it, he decided as he started swimming again. *I've been abducted by extraterrestrials or people from the future, and this is some kind of psychological test. They want to see how earth people react to displacement.*

Collins didn't actually believe that, but it made more sense than what he was seeing.

He felt water push against him from behind. Something was still out there. He resumed swimming. After several minutes Collins felt his knees scrape solid ground. Gratefully, he put his gloves down on what felt like sand. He remained there for a moment before he started crawling ashore. It was sand, only it seemed grittier than beach sand. It was almost like crushed gravel. But it could have been made of sesame seeds for all Collins cared. It was land. His arms were weaker than he'd thought. He crawled forward and dropped down, his face to the right. It occurred to him to shut off his headlamp to conserve the battery. It took surprising effort for him to remove his gloves and feel behind the helmet for the switch. He found it, then lay back down. It felt good just to crash.

He wondered how much time had passed since he'd descended. It seemed like days. What did it matter, anyway? He was here, wherever "here" was, and eventually he would be found. Now he needed to rest. He was spent.

Collins heard something splash behind him. It occurred to him, then, that he had no idea what section of the loch this was, and whether or not there were tides along the shores. If there were, he could fall asleep and be swept away. Or, if there was something in the water, it might be amphibious. Perhaps it would crawl out and get him if it still thought he was here.

With great effort Collins got on his hands and knees and crawled forward. His arms were weak and wobbly, but he managed to reach a patch of what felt like fuzzy grass. It had a mossy smell, damp but not unpleasant. Obviously, the water did not reach this far. He plopped down again, and while wondering if he should be worried about something crawling up and biting him on the finger, he fell asleep.

CHAPTER TWENTY-THREE

KATHRYN CASTLE LOOKED at the bright, featureless glow on the monitor. Either she herself was missing something or Tally Randall had an athletic imagination. The white orb on the screen did not look like the moon. At best it looked like a schoolchild's papier mâché interpretation of the moon, smooth in the wrong places and too lumpy in others.

"This doesn't look like a proper moon," Dr. Castle said. "Forgetting that for the moment, how could Harold be in a position to see the moon if he's underwater, and underwater during the daytime? It's simply not possible."

"But there it is."

"There's something," Dr. Castle said, a bit more testily than she had intended. She took a mental breath before continuing. "Something that only looks like the moon."

"Which would be what?" Tally asked.

"Let's try to find out," the paleontologist replied.

Dr. Castle clicked on a drop-down menu and accessed a

photo-lab program. The encyclopedic file was designed to compare images of dinosaur bones so she could readily identify them in the field. But it also had an extensive library of archaeological and astrological images to allow her to interpret other artifacts she might uncover, from cave art to cuneiform writing. She dropped the image from the videocamera into the ANALYZE slot.

A cartoon clock ticked down onscreen. The computer whirred busily. After nearly a minute, the program thumbnailed seven images. Dr. Castle clicked on them in turn.

A pearl. A goose egg. Big Ben in a fog. A Hubble space telescope image of Jupiter's moon Callisto. A photograph of earth's moon. An automobile headlight. The tail of a firefly.

"A burning meteorite," Tally said continuing down the list. "That's a possibility. A radioactive one to give it some shine."

"I'm sorry, but all of them seem equally improbable," Dr. Castle said.

"Except for the fact that the one I mentioned is there," Tally pointed out.

"Then explain it," Dr. Castle said. "Explain how Harold Collins could have seen and photographed the moon."

"Like I said before, let's go backward. To see the moon on a black field like we have, it has to be night."

"Granted."

"Harold is not here."

"He is not."

"Therefore, he must have been taken somewhere else. Somewhere the moon is shining."

Dr. Castle shook her head. "No. I'm not going from the Loch Ness Monster to alien abductions—"

"I'm not taking you there," Tally protested. "I'm thinking out loud, Doctor. I'm trying to understand what we're seeing and also what we felt. That pulling sensation. The boat tipping to port. The fact that the hooks were severed so completely. The absolute radio silence."

"And where does that get you? Or rather, where does that put Harold?"

"I'm working on it," Tally said.

"Taking into account everything you've suggested, at best—at the *very* best—we have a radioactive substance, possibly a meteorite, to explain disorientation," Dr. Castle said. "That's also one possible explanation for a glow that happens to remind you of the moon. But it still doesn't explain what happened to Harold. Even if your meteorite struck him, pierced his suit and even killed him, we would have heard something. A part of the suit, a part of him would certainly have floated to the surface. Either we or someone else would have spotted it."

"Probably," Tally agreed. "Which is even more evidence that he's gone."

"I repeat: Where?"

"The same place as something else that comes and goes from the loch," Tally said.

"You mean the creature?"

"Yes."

"Are you suggesting that there's a hole down there?" Dr. Castle asked. "A passageway to the other side of the world, from day to night, one that lets animals and people pass to and fro?"

"It sounds stupid, but can you think of a better explanation?"

"I'm sure we can think of several if we keep the animal out of the equation," Dr. Castle said.

"Why should we, though?" Tally asked. "Before you saw it, what was the last sighting?"

"The last reported sighting was about two and a half months ago."

"Then maybe there's some kind of doorway that opens up every two and a half months," Tally said. "It stays open for a day or two then shuts again."

"What kind of 'doorway'?"

"I don't *know!*" Tally yelled. "But Harold is gone, the monster was here, the boat was nearly pulled over, our bodies felt really strange, and metal was vaporized, so forgive me if I look outside the box for answers. I'm also getting a little unstable here," she admitted.

"I noticed that," Dr. Castle said. The scientist's voice was warmer, less challenging than it had been a moment before. "If we're going to help Harold we must remain grounded."

"You stay grounded," Tally said. "I think better under pressure."

"And I think better when the people around me aren't," Dr. Castle said.

"Then next time we should try not to lose one of our team members," Tally said.

"Fair enough," Dr. Castle said. "I suppose I deserved that."

Tally sighed. "No. You didn't. I'm just—"

"Upset. So am I."

The women were silent for a moment.

"Look, we need to stay on topic here," Tally said.

"I agree."

"This place—it's got a lot of secrets. You know that better than anyone. And there are other places like it around the globe, other strange bodies of water. The Bermuda Triangle. The Sargasso Sea. Lake Champlain. Maybe there's something in all of these places we don't understand."

"Such as?"

"I don't know—"

"Salt water, freshwater, geographical location," Dr. Castle said. "Those bodies have nothing in common."

"Nothing apparent," Tally said. "There could be a link we haven't determined, one of your fractal patterns."

"All right, I'll grant you that," Dr. Castle replied. "But figuring that out will take time, and we don't have time."

"Why do you think I'm bouncing around like this?" Tally asked with fresh desperation. "Reason is slow, and I don't want to use it when instinct gets me around faster."

Dr. Castle couldn't dispute the part about reason. But scattershooting wasn't necessarily a better way to get answers. It was like trying to stick a pin in England on a whirling globe.

The scientist looked past Tally. The boats were still making their methodical search of the loch. They were moving in a pattern that described pie slices on the starboard side, with the research vessel at the hub of the pie. The boats were moving but the people onboard were not. They were staring out from the sides, over the prow, off the stern, carefully watching the water. Some boaters had binoculars and were looking farther out. Two were actually in the water using goggles to peer below as the boats moved ahead.

Dr. Castle still believed that whatever had happened to Harold Collins was perfectly reasonable. It had to be. It was just something they hadn't figured out. And she believed that the way to do that wasn't by leaping everywhere an idea took you. Still, she remembered a story her paleontologist associate Tamara Maugham had told her. Tam had read Edgar Rice Burroughs's *The Land That Time Forgot* as a child. The tale of dinosaurs still living on a remote island was improbable in the 1960s, when the scientist first read it. But it taught her to think unconventional thoughts about dinosaurs. Did they have fur? Or possibly feathers? Did they have the capacity to speak? Were they monogamous? It was that kind of thinking that helped to change the view of dinosaurs in the 1970s from ruthless, cold-blooded proto-reptiles to nurturing, possibly warm-blooded family creatures.

Dr. Castle tried the radio again. It was still dead.

Dead. The word resounded in her mind unpleasantly.

If Harold was underwater, he had less than a half hour of air remaining.

Think, she snarled to herself, at herself. *Think think think*—

If reason is going to work you have to move it along faster. What were the elements they *did* have? That was a place to start. They knew where he had disappeared. They knew when. They knew what he was wearing, carrying—

Then it occurred to her. Something they could do that might find him, or at least might find out what had happened to him. It was a little makeshift, but it was all she had.

"There is one thing we can try," Dr. Castle said.

"What?"

"We know how deep Harold went and approximately where he was. What if we were to recover the camera, attach a light, and use the cables to lower it in that same spot? We might be able to see him, or at least recreate what happened."

"I like that," Tally said, brightening. "How do we get it back?"

"The quickest way," she said as she tugged hard on the cable.

CHAPTER TWENTY-FOUR

"**Y**OU BROUGHT ME back to do *what?*" Shep snapped.
The big man was standing on the deck of the boat, his wet suit and face mask dripping. He shielded his eyes from the sun as he looked out at the other vessels criss-crossing the loch.

"We need that camera," Dr. Castle told him. "We want to lower it back along the path he took."

Shep shook his head. Perspiration and lakewater ran down his red cheeks. "You think that's going to find him? With you watching from up here?"

"No," Dr. Castle replied. "We want to see what happens to the camera."

"You're talking in tongues," Shep scowled. "You want to waste your time with more experiments, you do that. I'm going back down."

"Listen, Shep—we've got everything to gain by trying this," Dr. Castle insisted. "We've been studying the videos

Harold took. We thing he was caught in a current of some kind."

"Moving which way?" Shep asked.

"Down," Dr. Castle said.

He made a face. "There's no undertow in the loch."

"I know. But this may have been caused by suction from the fissure," she improvised. "Using the video images he sent as reference, we may be able to find that current—and Harold."

"I criss-crossed the area twice," Shep said. "Where do you think you'll find him?"

"Did you feel anything unusual down there?" Tally asked.

"I felt wet," Shep said. He shook the water from his face, then looked at Dr. Castle. "I also felt anger at you for doing this."

"She said 'out of the ordinary,' " Dr. Castle pointed out.

"No. There was nothing else," he said, still glaring at her.

"Shep, please. I need you to do this," Dr. Castle said. "Harold's a geologist. He may have found some kind of underground cave and gone in. If we can compare what he shot with what we can see through the camera, we may be able to locate him."

"Kathryn, you can stop the performance," Shep said sadly. "Harold Collins is no geologist. I looked him up on the internet. He's a physicist who works for the United Nations. I don't know why you lied to me, and I don't know why you risked his life to keep up the lie. But I don't believe what you're saying. Now if you'll let me go—"

"I'm sorry," Dr. Castle said. "I lied because he was monster-hunting and I didn't want to draw a crowd."

"You got one anyway."

"I *know!*" Dr. Castle cried. "But I'm not lying about the trench, Shep. We believe something's down there."

"There are no places like that in this section of the loch," Shep replied. "You know that. I've been going down there for over thirty years, we've both seen the charts—"

"Christ, we're wasting time!" Tally yelled.

"Exactly," Shep said. As he spoke, he turned toward the rail.

"Shep, please!" Dr. Castle said, grabbing his arm. "We know that Loch Ness is a geologically active region and that the geology changes from time to time. You didn't find him, Shep, you said so yourself. Please let me try this. If there *is* an air pocket or an uncharted conduit that reaches inside the hills, there's only one way we can find that out."

Shep looked hurt. He also looked like he really didn't know how to say no to Kathryn Castle. He craned back to look at the gauge on his tank.

"I've got about thirty-five minutes of air left," Shep said. "That's enough to go down and retrieve your camera. I'll bring it back, then change tanks and continue searching my own way. You can play trail-the-dog or whatever you want on your own."

"Thank you," Dr. Castle said. "Thank you very much. Look for the red ON light on the northwest corner of the ridge. When you spot it, I also need you to do something."

"What?"

"Before you pick the camera up, toss something over it."

"Say again?"

"Pick up a stone, a discarded bottle, anything you find down there and throw it over the camera. Just to make sure that whatever inversion or eddy may have grabbed Harold doesn't grab you."

Shep regarded her. "Is there something else you're not telling me?"

"No," Dr. Castle lied.

"If it makes you happy," Shep told her. "But if you're covering something up and it was the beast that got your friend for breakfast, tossing pebbles isn't going to help."

Shep went back to the ladder, climbed down, then wet his mask. Before he pulled it over his face, Shep looked up at Dr. Castle, who was standing beside the winch. His gaze shifted to Tally.

"I felt tired down there," he said.

"What?" Tally asked eagerly.

"Tired. Arm-weary," Shep said. "More than I ever felt before, as though I'd been swimming for hours. That surprised me."

Before either woman could respond, Shep had fixed the mask on his face and leapt back into the water.

CHAPTER TWENTY-FIVE

I N DECEMBER OF 1996, in Dallas County, Alabama, Kathryn Castle had the worst day of her life.

The paleontologist had found a rare fossil, a very rare skull belonging to the Upper Cretaceous duck-billed dinosaur lophorhothon. Unfortunately, in the months that followed, the courts determined that ownership of the skull itself belonged to a mall developer named Burton Burke, who owned the land on which she had found it. Burke put it in his glass and chrome office as an "oooh-ahhhh" display to impress potential investors in his properties. Though Burke permitted Castle to make a cast of the find, he did not allow her to take the fossil to London and examine it for muscle scarring, capillary networks, or do anything that would advance paleontology if it required cutting or chipping the fossil.

Castle did not think anything could be more frustrating than that time. She was wrong.

Shep found the camera by crawling along the ridge and

looking for the light. While he was gone, Castle had called Eileen to have fresh tanks sent out for him so he could dive again without delay. Dr. Castle also obtained five hundred feet of fine-link engineer's chain from her old friend Ronnie Garrison, manager of the Loch Ness Hotel. Garrison used it on automobile tires during winter snows. She put the chain on a motorboat and brought it out herself. She didn't do that kind of favor for everyone, but she did it for Kathryn Castle. Garrison even helped Tally and Dr. Castle coil one end of the chain around the pedestal of the helm chair. Dr. Castle intended to use the pedestal as an anchor when they lowered the camera, just in case something tried to take it the way Harold Collins had been grabbed.

It was nearly ten A.M., two hours after Collins's descent, when Castle and Tally completed their preparations. They used electrical tape from the repair kit to tape an underwater flashlight to the camera. Before they could lower it, the local constable had arrived to talk to the two women, to ascertain that no foul play had been involved. Dr. Castle gave him the backup diskette so he could see the events for himself, and she promised to visit as soon as they finished their videosearch. The constable had known Dr. Castle for years and was agreeable to that. He did inform her, however, that the other boats were going to reorganize. Now that the diver's air supply had lapsed, they were no longer looking for a lost diver. They were searching for a body and would begin dredging the loch from north to south, against the local current. They expected to reach her area in about an hour. Dr. Castle said they would be done by then.

For reasons she couldn't quite get a grip on, Dr. Castle could not accept the idea that Harold Collins was dead. In fact, the more hours went by without a sign of him the more convinced she became that something very strange had happened. That he was missing but not "lost." She knew what loss felt like. Even before she had seen their bodies on two stainless steel gurneys in the morgue, she had grasped the reality that they were gone. Dr. Castle worked with fossils and extinction every day. She knew the territory, emotionally, intellectually, and psychologically. Harold Collins simply did not "feel" dead.

After giving the surprisingly lightweight chain a good tug and hoping the links were tougher than the cable had been, Tally and Dr. Castle sent the videocamera into the water. This time they lowered it by hand, Tally playing out the chain as they watched the images it sent to the computer. For her part, Tally said that she had not been able to get out of her head what Shep had said before going down for the camera. That his arms had felt heavy.

"Maybe he was just tired, nothing else," Tally said. "It could all be a big weird coincidence."

"Do you really believe that?" Dr. Castle asked.

"No. I'm just talking," she said. "Trying to convince myself."

"Hopefully, the videocamera will give us some missing pieces of the puzzle," Dr. Castle said.

The camera twisted very slowly as it was lowered. Since they weren't using the winch, Dr. Castle was going to have to guess how much chain had gone over. It looked to her as if it had descended about thirty-five feet. There was nothing unusual on the monitor.

The camera continued to descend. The only sounds were from the shouts of men searching for Collins. Even the wind had stopped.

Down twenty-five meters or so there was still just brown water and peat in the monitor. Dr. Castle was beginning to get discouraged. She wished she felt something physically, like the tingling she had felt earlier—some indication that circumstances were the same as before.

"I wonder if having all these people out on the loch is screwing things up," Tally said.

"So you're feeling a difference too," Dr. Castle said.

"Yeah," Tally said. "All the commotion could be changing

the vibes or scaring the Monster or whatever happened before."

"Were we doing anything different?"

"Apart from the fact that we were lowering Harold into the water?" Tally asked.

"Yes, that *is* a big difference, isn't it?" Dr. Castle replied.

"The time of day is different, the temperature is different—god, there are so many variables. Even our mood is different."

"The loch reacting to biorhythms," Dr. Castle said. "Well, why not? Plants are known to react to human emotion, and there are massive amounts of vegetation down there."

"Of course, there could have been something about Harold himself," Tally suggested. "Maybe he did something, or a substance down there reacted to the light on his helmet. We were talking about the creature being photosensitive. Maybe instead of shunning light it's drawn to it."

"That would not be good for Harold, would it?" Dr. Castle asked.

"The stars could have been light bouncing off a highly reflective skin surface," Tally suggested. "Or teeth. Maybe the 'moon' is actually an eye."

"I can't believe that," Dr. Castle said.

"Can't or don't want to?" Tally asked.

Dr. Castle didn't bother replying. They both knew the answer. But she still couldn't believe that the animal was a predator. There simply wasn't enough fish life in the loch to support an animal the size of the one she had seen. On the other hand, there was the issue of man-the-intruder. It was believed that even prehistoric herbivores like triceratops and stegosaurus would take the offensive to protect their nest.

Suddenly, Tally stood upright. Her hands loosened and she allowed the chain to slacken.

"Do you feel anything?" the young woman asked.

Dr. Castle did not. She stood. As the blood flowed more readily to her legs, she felt it. "The tingling," she said excitedly. "It's back."

The scientist went back to the monitor. The camera was beginning to rotate more rapidly.

Tally grunted. "The camera's being pulled!" she said.

"Try and hold it in place," Dr. Castle told her. "We need the images."

"The chain is twisting!" Tally said as the links began to clink against the rail. The chain turned in her hands, nipping bits of flesh from her palms and fingers. She held fast but did not dare wrap the tightening chain around her wrists. In moments her blood made the links slippery. "I can't hold it!" she said.

Dr. Castle went to the port side and grabbed the chain with both hands. She braced her right foot on the side of the boat and started pulling. Hard. It was like hauling someone from quicksand, which she had once had the opportunity to do along the Paraná River on a dig in Argentina. It was uncanny. The camera was fighting to go down.

Just then the chain came free of whatever was holding it. Too free. The women snapped backward several steps. They hauled up what was left of the chain. It clattered up along the hull of the boat until the end dangled free of the water. Dr. Castle drew it in and examined the final link.

"Severed, just like the cable," she said.

"What about the camera?" Tally asked.

Dr. Castle handed the chain to Tally and ran back. While the young woman quickly piled the chain on the deck, Dr. Castle sat down at the computer. There was nothing on the monitor.

"It's dead," Dr. Castle said.

The scientist went into the computer's memory and pulled up pictures from the last few seconds of the struggle. Her legs were still tingling as she waited for the results. When they finally appeared, it took her a moment to realize what she was looking at.

"Tally?" Dr. Castle said. "You've got to see this."

Tally dropped the chain and hurried over. "What is it?" she asked.

Dr. Castle replied, "The most astonishing image I've ever seen."

CHAPTER TWENTY-SIX

I**T SOUNDED LIKE a** trombone being played by a kid in
The Music Man. Raw and unsteady and more full of
breath than musical notes. The single blast woke Harold
Collins from a dreamless sleep. His eyes snapped open and
his heart sent his body on high alert.

The air around him was thick and damp. He was still
wearing his helmet and had to angle his head to look past
the mottled water stains on the visor. The moon had
moved, and there was just the hint of navy blue behind the
trees on the other side of the water. Judging from the location of the moon, he had been asleep for three or four
hours.

The physicist's heartbeat and rapid breathing sounded
louder because of the helmet. The sound didn't come
again. Everything around him seemed still. Collins
twisted the headgear and pulled it off. He had expected
some relief from the stuffiness within the helmet. He
didn't get it. The air outside was warm bordering on hot; it

felt thick in his lungs. There was also a strange smell, like burnt toast. Since the fading stars were diamond clear, it probably wasn't a fire, though Collins did have a flash of a thought: that the Loch Ness Monster might be the biblical Leviathan. Perhaps it had led him down an underwater "rabbit hole" into Hell and that was brimstone he was smelling. It wasn't an explanation the young physicist liked, but it was the only one he had. He still wondered if he had hit his head and was unconscious and dreaming this all. But Collins couldn't remember ever having smelled things in a dream.

Still holding his helmet, Collins studied it in the fast-growing light. He looked at the hole on the left side. It was a wide, neat break that looked as if someone had slashed down with a meat cleaver. He must have bumped something super-sharp without realizing it—a rocky overhang, perhaps. He was lucky. A few inches higher and to the right and the impact would have sliced through the middle of his skull.

Impulsively, he felt the middle of his head to make sure he hadn't been struck. He hadn't been. He was alive and conscious.

And very, very lost.

It was time to get up and have a look around, try to make sense of Wonderland, Hell, Oz, or wherever it was that he'd ended up. Collins put his elbows on the ground and worked himself into a sitting position. He saw more clearly now the silhouettes of tropical-looking trees, velvet-smooth water and, ahead to the right—to the east, he presumed—the crisply delineated start of sunrise. It reminded Collins of dawn on Maui. Which, in turn made him think he was lost somewhere inside his own knocked-out head.

He climbed to his knees and then slowly got to his feet. The sun continued to rise. A paler blue began to appear along the horizon, throwing a hint of light across the terrain.

This most definitely was not Scotland. Ahead, on the opposite side of a wide bay, were palm trees of some kind. They were squatter and darker than any he had ever seen. And they were nothing like any trees he'd seen in Scotland. Along the horizon beyond them were sharp-edged mountains. The mountains of the Highlands were older and softer. These appeared to be extremely tall, like the Rockies, but as the sky turned yellow-blue and details began to emerge, Collins did not detect a single patch of snow on any of the peaks. Several of them had irregular, sharply angled tors that reminded him of Hawaiian volcanoes.

Collins allowed his eyes to roam the brightening skies. Exotic, tropical-looking trees were plentiful, but something surprised him. He didn't see, nor hear, a single bird in any of them. He put his hands to the side of his mouth and yelled. The cry rolled across the water and died without flapping wings or bird-calls drowning it out.

"This definitely isn't right," he muttered. He turned around. Behind him were more trees, and what looked like more mountains behind them. He couldn't tell if it was smoke or clouds gathered around the tops. The trees were in the way. Again, there were no birds. He listened. There were no sounds of *any* kind. Nothing moving but the big, spade-shaped leaves of the tall trees.

Scared now, Collins began to remove his oxygen tanks.

"All right, gang," he said thinking of no one in particular. "What the hell's going on?"

Strange trees. An odd-looking moon. An acrid smell. Snow-free mountains. No birds. He looked down. And what kind of beach was this with fish-tank gravel instead of sand?

Obviously, something unexpected had happened. Nitrogen narcosis and confusion caused by breathing under high pressure were unlikely; he had not gone deep enough. Oxygen deprivation or overload was one possible explanation.

Maybe some joker had put something in his air tanks, some kind of hallucinogen. Though everything sure seemed real. He held his breath. That was something a sleeping or unconscious individual could not do. If a drugged or hallucinating individual tried it, the visual stimulus would be changed by the altered air flow.

Nothing changed. This was real.

Okay, he thought. *First impulses.*

Collins's mind flashed to the underground ocean in Jules Verne's *Journey to the Center of the Earth.* Were it not for the sky, that was where he'd guess he was. Some kind of Rip Van Winkle hibernation. What else could explain how Harold Collins had jumped into the water in Loch Ness and ended up in a tropical world that clearly was not Loch Ness?

Explanations would be easier to come by if you knew where the hell you were, he told himself. *Figure that out and I might learn how I got here and whether it's a two-way street.*

Suddenly, he remembered something that had happened when he had first arrived. Something had moved past him in the water. Since that seemed to be the only animal around, Collins decided he should seek it out. Identifying it, watching it, might give him a clue as to where he was. And if he were going to be here for any length of time, it would also tell him something else. Whether there was anything edible in the water. He hoped it wasn't a dolphin; he would hate to have to kill and eat an intelligent creature. He would also hate to try to catch one in its natural element. Collins was an occasional recreational diver, not Poseidon.

The young man walked toward the edge of the water. He was too curious to be terrified, though he was sure terror would come soon. The water was navy blue with yellow highlights from the growing light of the new day. He looked to the sides as he approached the shore. He was at the mouth of an inlet that opened outward to the sea and a featureless horizon in one direction, ending at a crescent-shaped shore to the north. He turned and faced the forest. He could see now, some twenty meters in, a row of very low-lying floppy-leafed plants of some kind. They led to more of those isolated palms trees. He looked down. There were no shells or driftwood. He had a sick feeling that he had been abducted by some of those mythical English giants he used to read about as a kid and was in a giant-size turtle dish on another planet with fake trees, fake sand, and maybe even a big turtle in the water.

Collins walked to the south some twenty feet, to the point on the beach where he had first come ashore. Though the tide had receded slightly, the white and blue sand-gravel hybrid had retained his knee prints. He walked toward the water, scooped up a handful of the pebbles, and waded into the surf. As he went deeper he was glad to see—or rather feel—that his suit was still waterproof. Wherever Collins was he would probably have to get away the same way he got here. That would mean diving. It would also mean finding a way to repair his helmet. Now that he thought of it, that also meant conserving the oxygen in his tanks. In case he had to spend time underwater searching for an exit. Unless he'd burned through additional oxygen en route, he thought he had about ninety minutes' worth left.

Collins was about to toss the stones into the water underhanded, one after the other, to try and catch the attention of whatever might be out there. Before he could so, something on that open-sea horizon grabbed his eye. There were storm clouds surging in, and quickly. He was surprised to see them on what had looked like an otherwise clear day. There were faint lightning flashes in the charcoal-dark masses. Several fine, almost delicate bolts shot down toward the water.

The storm was coming his way. He did not want to be in

the water when the lightning arrived. He was about to turn back toward shore when he saw something directly ahead of him, something even more surprising. Something that wasn't going to let him get to shore as fast as he wanted.

He saw his videocamera.

CHAPTER TWENTY-SEVEN

THE CAMERA SHOT from the water as if it had been spit out. Another "first impulse": Collins half-expected to see Pinocchio and Geppetto follow it, along with the maw of Monstro the Whale. The camera rose about three feet above the water. There was a small bit of dark chain dangling behind and the camera, which was still inside its waterproof casing. But there was nothing resembling a flotation device attached to it. Only a flashlight, which was new. It appeared to be held on with tape. As quickly as the camera rose, it began to drop. Surprised as he was, Collins realized that the camera was not going to stay spit out for very long at all.

The young scientist half-ran, half-swam toward it. When a person didn't emerge after it, his first and only thought was that Dr. Castle and Tally had obviously recovered it, quickly added the light, and sent it back. Maybe they had figured out what had happened and were sending him a message on the self-contained playback, giving him instructions on how to return.

Collins watched as the camera fell back into the water. It was about twenty feet away. Fortunately, the flashlight was still on. Even when the camera went under, Collins might still be able to locate it.

"Move it, you slow dumb bastard!" he hollered at himself as he plowed through the sea. The diving suit didn't help. Since he had removed his gloves, water poured through the sleeves each time his arms went under.

In the relatively clear water Collins was still able to see the flashlight. Peripherally, he watched the storm rushing in. He judged he had about five minutes before it arrived. That should be enough time to get out, unless the suit became too waterlogged.

And then something bumped him from below. It was big and it literally hefted him from the water. It was also moving toward the camera.

"No!"

He had momentarily forgotten about his seagoing companion from the night before. Collins swam madly for a few feet then sucked up a big breath and dove. He launched himself down with big, ungainly kicks and broad sweeps of his arms. He watched as the flashlight and camera turned and descended slowly. He did not see whatever had nudged him.

His limbs churning desperately, the young man caught up to the sinking camera and grabbed the chain trailing behind it. Then, cocking his legs like a frog, he arched his body upward and kicked hard. The thrust did not carry him as far as he wanted. There was probably more water in the suit than he'd realized, with more pouring in every moment.

Something shot in front of him, causing him to stop short. Then it went under him again and rose. It bumped him up a little, probably by accident. Collins was glad; he was running out of air. But he had presence of mind enough to shut off the flashlight. That'might be what was attracting whatever had hit him.

The scientist was still facing up. He kicked again with both frog legs and rose with agonizing slowness. The surface was there, he could see the brightening blue of the sky even as it gave way to the much darker storm clouds. He just wasn't getting to it very fast, thanks to the damn suit. His chest was beginning to revolt. It wanted to breathe and blamed his brain, caused it to haze over. The scientist lost his bearings, forgot which way—other than "up"—he had to swim. It didn't matter. His body insisted on air, and in the space of a few rapid heartbeats, the only thing that mattered was getting it. His mouth and lungs fought with each other. His lungs said *breathe*, but with some help from his foggy brain, his mouth refused. But Collins knew the dynamic duo wouldn't hold their ground for very much longer.

Then he was lifted upward by a rush of water. He broke the surface and loudly let his chest have all the air it wanted. As his lungs flooded with air, his mind filled with clarity. He saw which way he had to go a moment before he dropped back down due to the weight of the waterlogged suit. His lungs replenished, he made another four-limbed commotion in that direction.

The thing sideswiped him again, from the back left. This time Collins saw it as it sliced through the water. The animal resembled a long-necked tadpole the size of a crocodile. A very large one. It passed ahead of him, then turned majestically and swung back at him. It appeared to have the mouth of a crocodile too. And now it was open.

Collins had the videocamera in his right hand. The chain was about eighteen inches long. He grabbed the free end in his right hand and tugged at it as he continued to kick with his feet. He was hoping to get close enough to the shore to be able to stand. The creature continued to swim directly at him. If the sharp teeth were any indication, it was certainly a carnivore.

So much for the Loch Ness Monster not eating me, he thought.

From what Harold had seen, there were no other fish this close to shore. Just him. After several brushes, the creature had obviously decided that Harold wasn't a log or a fellow whatever *it* was. Perhaps its tiny eyes weren't so effective underwater. Perhaps that's what those get-to-know-you bumps had been about.

Translation: The physicist was a suitable meal.

Collins continued to pull and jiggle the chain. It was looped around the camera. As he fussed with it, the chain came free. He hooked the camera to his utility belt, then held the other side of the chain with his left hand.

Whatever the animal was, it had flippers instead of crocodilian feet. They paddled in big, rotating swipes as the animal neared. Collins reached water that was shallow enough for him to stand. He got his feet under him. To his left, in the not-far-enough distance, he saw a puff of light in the water. A lightning strike. He *had* to get the hell out of the water.

The creature charged him, its jaw opened almost at a right angle. Collins ducked as low as he could but kept his arms raised with the length of chain stretched between them. As the lower jaw passed under the chain Collins stepped forward, dragging the chain toward the mandible joint. He socked the chain in hard, then released it, simultaneously dropping to his belly. The chain had snagged there. He could feel the animal thrashing. Collins did not know whether it would hold, nor did he care. As his lungs began to complain again, Collins scrambled forward along the rough sea bottom. His limbs felt like they were stuck in wet cement. He watched for the shore as he stumbled ahead, holding his breath—

And then he felt himself batted ahead, hard. The concussion knocked the air from his lungs and he rolled forward. He protected the camera by putting his hands around it, banging them up in the process. When he came to rest he was on his back, facing the surface.

This is where I came in, he thought.

Only this time his brain was swimming and his body was not. Time to reverse that. He pushed off with his feet, his lungs empty and crying, and crawled the few feet it took to thrust his face into the air and inhale. Then he fell back down on his belly. Painfully, he hooked the video-camera to his equipment belt and got back on his hands and knees. He opened his eyes. His head was above water. His hands were below it. They were bleeding, trailing wispy tendrils of blood.

"Shit, shit, shit," he panted.

The young man half-crawled, half-scampered forward, splashing in the surf as the creature charged yet again. Collins heard the rush of water, a crack of thunder in the distance, the snap of jaw on chain, and then the thrashing as the beast retreated from the too-shallow water. Obviously, it was not amphibious.

Score one lucky break for his team.

Collins's arms shook as he crept the last few feet to shore. Then they gave out. He fell on his chest, leaking water from his sleeves. He was breathing heavily but happy to be breathing at all as he cherished the hot, foul, wonderful air. Somewhere below his feet, in the water, he still heard splashing and movement. It lasted for a few moments more, then stopped. Either the creature had been able to dislodge the chain or it had given up and gone away, or both.

Lightning popped to his right. Thunder followed. With effort, Collins turned over and dragged himself from the water. He couldn't be more wet than he already was, so he wouldn't bother seeking shelter from the rain. However, even though Collins hadn't heard any noises from the foliage, he did not know for certain whether there were any

predators about. He decided to stay relatively close to
shore in case he needed to get into the water. Plopping
himself next to his air tanks, Collins scooped out a hole in
the beach, placed them inside, and covered them so they
would be less likely to attract lightning. Then he removed
the camera from his belt, took off the watertight container,
and opened the small fold-out monitor. He wanted to see if
there was a message from the loch.

He rewound the tape just a few seconds to conserve battery power. Then he hit play. He saw the suddenly welcome
murk of Loch Ness. Then the image began to shake and a
strange thing happened. It began to spin. The graphics
looked as if a painting had been placed on a potter's wheel,
the paint still wet and splattering everywhere. Only instead
of paint it was pixels flying. After a moment the picture
stopped turning quite as violently—but it was no longer
Loch Ness. It was here. It showed the spiny tail of the
crocodile-thing and the surface of the water above it. It
showed a lens-eye view of the camera popping into the air,
falling, and then Collins's struggle to reach the shore. He
didn't bother to watch that.

Apparently, Dr. Castle and Tally didn't think they had
time to send a message. Or else it didn't occur to them to
record one. Why should it? For all they knew he was at the
bottom of the loch and they were simply trying to find him.

More flashes struck the water, and then a heavy rain
began to fall. Winds rushed in, blowing the warm drops at
an angle this way, then that. The bellowing of the wind and
the lashing of the trees by the rain seemed very loud, perhaps because they were the only sounds in town.

Collins put the camera back in its waterproof container.
Then he removed his diving suit to let it drain. The rain
actually felt good. Even though it was warm, it was less
warm than the air. It cooled the hot wet suit he still had on.
Allowing himself to relax, he took a moment to study the
clouds. They seemed different than the clouds he was

familiar with. They were busier somehow, as if the air were roiling harder, faster. That probably meant the rising thermal currents were moving faster and meeting colder air higher than normal, in thinner air, something that was giving the storm system added vigor.

A maelstrom above and some kind of maelstrom below, Collins thought as the big drops drummed him. He wondered if there were a correlation. Probably not, though the electrical discharge of the storm might have some impact on whatever was going on under the surface. After all, many scientists believed that lightning strikes on ancient seas transformed amino acids into the first life forms. Perhaps they also did something to the chemistry of this section of the loch, though the notion that Collins was somewhere under Loch Ness, or beside it, or anywhere in the vicinity of it, seemed increasingly remote.

But if not the loch, where am I? And how did I get here?

The scientist turned the small camera over in his hand. It had definitely come from Dr. Castle, who was somewhere else. Come with a great deal of force judging by the way it had been expelled. And things probably could go the other way. Whatever that creature was he had tangled with, he was willing to bet it or a close cousin was the Loch Ness Monster. Snatched from here and deposited there, as he and the videocamera had been, but going the other way.

Snatched by what?

He gazed out at the storm clouds. Snatched by a very powerful but limited electrical field of some kind. He had watched the video. It had showed a sort of quantum event that had distorted the world around the camera without, apparently, affecting the mechanism of the videocamera— or himself. He suspected that the field was strong enough to prevent Dr. Castle and Tally from receiving radio messages that originating on this end.

Thinking about the physics kept Collins from dwelling on his predicament—not just being stranded who-knew-where, but the fact that he had nothing to eat or drink.

Well, duh, he thought. *That isn't true.*

It was raining. Collins had his helmet. He could use it as a receptacle. He would probably need the water more than he would need the radio, which the rain would probably short out.

Collins clawed out a shallow well in the beach and put the helmet in it upside down. He sat back, watching as rainwater quickly filled the interior up to the gash. The familiar *plop plop* of the heavy drops was reassuring. Whatever had happened to him, he was still in a place that supported life. That gave him hope. Instead of contemplating his personal situation, Collins tried to "stay scientific," as one of his professors used to say. He couldn't let emotion or desire creep into the project. In this case, the emotions were panic and terror. The immediate project was staying safe. The longer-term project—and he didn't know how long-term that could be—was getting home. Though the young man had to admit that as dire as his situation clearly was, he felt a small sense of accomplishment. He was alive and relatively safe. The struggle with the crocodile thing had prioritized his dangers.

At least for the moment.

CHAPTER TWENTY-EIGHT

"**D**O YOU REMEMBER what you were asking me about yesterday, when you first arrived?" Dr. Castle asked.

"About . . . ?"

"Unknown life forms," Dr. Castle stated.

"What about them?"

Tally sounded impatient. She *was* impatient. The mystery of the loch was less important to her right now than finding Harold. Unfortunately, there was nothing they could do but what they were doing: analyzing the data the camera had sent back. Meanwhile, the search crews were doing their part. Dr. Castle had moved the boat to an area slightly north of where Collins had descended. That allowed the dredging crew to come through. They were moving in a straight line across the loch. So far, they hadn't found anything. Tally took that to be a good sign. As long as there was no body, there was hope. Even though Harold's air would have run out by now, Tally was holding on to the idea that he could have found an underwater air pocket or surfaced somewhere else.

"You asked about the possibility of discovering a previously unknown life form in the loch," Dr. Castle said.

"Of course I remember," Tally answered. "Why?"

"Because we've found it," Dr. Castle said. "Only it may be closer to the coelacanth model than I imagined."

"I'm not following you," Tally admitted.

The paleontologist pointed to the monitor. "This appears to be the dorsal posterior of a prehistoric tail," she said.

There was excitement in Dr. Castle's voice. Not agitation as before, but genuine passion. Tally took a closer look. She saw blurry bumps and a series of swept-back spines. They were leaning forward on what looked like the back end of a reptilian tail.

"Judging from the size of the spines, what we're seeing is a half-meter-long section. Look at these," Dr. Castle said, moving her finger along the image. "Note the distinctive vertical ridges, the bulge out in the center for defensive swings against potential predators."

"I see that," Tally said. "Question: Does this help us figure out where Harold has gone?"

"Very possibly," Dr. Castle said. "If it's a modern-day life form it means there are areas within the loch of which we're unaware, possibly a cave system where Harold could have gone."

"You said 'if' it's a modern-day life form," Tally said. "Is there another option?"

"There is, if we're considering all options," Dr. Castle said. "This tail has elements that are reminiscent of the thecodont *Scleromochlus taylori,* a lizard ancestor of many modern amphibians and reptiles."

"An *ancestor* of modern amphibians?"

"That's right."

"Okay," Tally said. "And your explanation for it being here is what?"

"I don't have one," Dr. Castle said.

"Then let me suggest one, from the gut," Tally said. "A hoax. Someone is feeding you images over the internet."

"I don't have a wireless internet connection," she said.

"I mean, before today," Tally suggested impatiently. "Something that was snuck into your computer memory and was triggered by the camera."

"Why?"

"All academicians have enemies," Tally said. "Maybe you've got one or two who really want to embarrass you."

"I do," Dr. Castle agreed. "But what about the rest of what has happened today? Harold is missing. Something tugged on the camera and cut the chain. When we lost Harold the boat nearly inverted. We are both feeling a strange aura or magnetism, if you will. That is not a hoax."

That was true. "Then what does it mean?" Tally asked.

"You said something a moment ago. You asked for an explanation about how the creature could be 'here.' I'm not so certain it is."

"Come again?"

"We've got what appears to be a dawn-lit sky," Dr. Castle said, pointing to the monitor. "Obviously, that's not Scotland. It's afternoon here. We saw what looked like the moon in an earlier image. It was daytime here."

"The time frame is all off," Tally said.

"Correct," Dr. Castle said.

"Forgive me for being dense, but what does all of this add up to?"

"You had a good idea before when you suggested working backward from a conclusion," Dr. Castle told her. "However improbable it seems, the evidence suggests that we have not only tapped into a different time zone but also a different era."

Tally looked into the scientist's gray eyes. "Time travel. That's what you're suggesting."

"I didn't suggest it," she said. "This did." She tapped the monitor causing the colors to swirl.

"I don't believe it," Tally replied. "I can't believe Harold was 'beamed' to some other world. There has to be another explanation."

"What? Or, less to the point, why?"

"Because things like that don't happen," she said.

"How do you know?"

Tally had no answer to that. With a sigh she left Dr. Castle and returned to the railing. She picked up the chain and finished winding it around the chair. When Tally was done, she stood for a moment and watched the boats search for Harold. She hated to admit it, but Shep had been right. They never should have let Harold do this. They'd acted as if this were a motorboat outing on the Long Island Sound. It wasn't. They had sent an inexperienced, frightened young man wearing unfamiliar equipment into the dark loch. What the hell had she been thinking?

Tired, frustrated, and angry, Tally found herself feeling about Kathryn Castle as she felt about her mother: that the older woman had pushed her into doing something she hadn't wanted to do. Only this time it wasn't about going to this college or that country club function or dating some Joe Asshole III.

"Tally?"

The young woman didn't look over. "Yes?"

"He's out there, and we're going to find him."

"I know. That *slomo taylor*, or whatever it was, is giving him mouth-to-mouth until we can get to him."

"Tally—"

"Or maybe Harold crawled inside its belly like Jonah."

"You're not thinking," Dr. Castle said.

"Oh, but I am. Too much. And what I think is that we

should talk to Shep and see how we can help with the search."

"I have a better idea," Dr. Castle said. "If I'm right, we're dealing with a phenomenon that may be triggered by electricity."

"What makes you think that? There was no electricity around the day you were out here."

"The animal I saw could have been here for days," Dr. Castle said. "We also don't know what's happening on the 'other side,' if there is one. Electromagnetism in the rocks, electrical storms, an ion wave like Harold was describing. What we *do* know is that we saw two reactions today, and the videocamera was operating both times."

"But the camera was not generating a lot of electricity," Tally said, "and none of it would have been leaking into the loch."

"Which brings me to the next point," Dr. Castle said. "Whatever this phenomenon is, it could be triggered by low energy or low frequency waves in any form."

"Like the low gauge explosion that triggers a nuclear blast," Tally said.

"Good analogy. Yes. Exactly like that," Dr. Castle said. "If that's true, then there's no reason we can't attempt to recreate the phenomenon."

"And do what? Send someone through to look for Harold?"

"Not immediately—"

"Even if you *are* right about all this, how do we know it's a two-way street? How do we know this very hypothetical electric doorway will even open to the same spot in time and space? The videocamera could have ended up in the Ice Age or in this same water last Tuesday or next month or who knows when? So could Harold, if he tries to come back."

Tally felt a psychic kick in the head when she said that. The idea that someone could play Chutes and Ladders with time and space was too much to process.

"All of what you just said is absolutely correct. I couldn't have put it better," Dr. Castle replied. "Which is all the more reason to investigate what happened down there."

"And how do we do that?" Tally wanted to know. "Trying to send something else through the opening probably won't tell us anything. It'll be like pouring water down a drain."

"I agree," Dr. Castle replied. "We need to be a little more clever." She had climbed from her seat and gone below.

"What do you have in mind?"

"The one thing we can send down that actually helps us by getting pulled into this other place," the paleontologist replied. "Sound."

Dr. Castle returned with a folder. She selected a chart and showed it to Tally. "Remember the point on the bottom of the loch where the fissure seemed to just stop?"

Tally said she did.

"What if that was a result of a long-standing misinterpretation of data?" Dr. Castle said. "Suppose a section of the floor of Loch Ness did not return an echo during an earlier expedition—"

"It might show up as a sort of black hole that the echo receiver interpreted as a mass," Tally said.

"Exactly. And it so happens that the spot is very close to where we are," Dr. Castle went on. "Certainly close enough for a phenomenon, a rift in time or whatever this could be, to have snagged Harold and the camera. Or released the creature I saw."

"A dinosaur," Tally said.

"It would appear so, wouldn't it?" Dr. Castle replied.

The scientist's reply wasn't so much a statement as a challenge. It dared Tally to come up with a better explanation for the animal, for all of this. And once again Tally found herself wavering. When she was in school, one of Tally's journalism professors used to tease her by saying that she would make a brilliant reporter because she was so easily moved by arguments pro and con.

You'll have no choice but to report both sides accurately because you'll never come down on one, Dr. Natasha Lane had told her.

Tally didn't know whether that was a good thing or a bad thing, but it was certainly a true thing. Harold Collins had sold her a crazy story in an uncrazy way and got her to go to Loch Ness. Five minutes ago Tally had been convinced—yet again—that Kathryn Castle was a nutburger. Now the paleontologist had a good idea that made the most outlandish idea seem reasonable.

"How do we do this?" Tally asked.

Instead of replying, the scientist turned to the radio.

CHAPTER TWENTY-NINE

THE RAIN PASSED quickly, faster than any big pour Harold Collins had ever experienced. That included the savage storms that blew into Maui from Maalaea Bay and crossed the island within an hour. And Collins had never seen a storm where the lightning was so . . . "frizzy" was the word that came to mind. Whatever comprised or influenced the atmosphere here—dust, elements, chemical compounds, temperature fluctuations, or some combination of those—was like nothing Collins had ever encountered in the South Pacific, North America, or Europe. He wished he had a prism so he could study the spectrum of the sky, of the clouds, of the lightning. He was willing to bet there was a higher than normal carbon dioxide content in the air. A lack of free oxygen might make it difficult for the lightning to mount the kind of displays with which he was familiar. If so, it could be a result of the oxygen being locked in the H_2O.

By the time the heaving clouds had passed inland, the

sun had cleared the horizon. Part of Collins wished it
would start to rain again. If he thought it was hot when he
arrived, he was wrong. It was hot and extremely muggy
now. It had to be at least one hundred and ten degrees and
certain to get hotter as the sun crept higher. It was definitely not a time to be wearing his wet suit. Stripping it off,
he sat on the beach in the longjohns he had worn to prevent
chafing. Sipping a little water from his helmet, Collins
looked out at the bay and contemplated what he had seen
on the videocamera.

The tail end of one body of water and the front end of
another. They were totally different. Between them was literally a swirl of visual data. In addition to the images, there
was the camera itself. Though it had been moved physically from one place to another—as he had been—apparently none of the internal electronics had been affected any
more than his own insides had been damaged crossing
over. At least, as far as he knew.

Crossing over, Collins thought.

How easily he accepted that notion as opposed to the
idea that he was unconscious or stuck inside some kind of
dream. Or even dead. That was certainly a possibility.
Except for the monster, wouldn't his idea of heaven be an
exotic beach somewhere? Or maybe it was hell. Perfection
with a fatal flaw that would terrorize him throughout eter-
nity.

On the other hand, such a ready acceptance of a timeslip
or dimensional shift of some kind shouldn't surprise him.
The concept that time and space could be warped was
nothing new in quantum physics. The belief that there
could be one or more "mirror universes" or "temporal
warps" on the opposite side of a massive gravitational field
had been theorized by Albert Einstein and Karl Schwarz-
schild as far back as 1916. However, most physicists
had always believed that such fields were out in the remote
universe somewhere, created by black holes or other

massively dense objects. If they were any closer, the gravitational fields would tear the earth apart.

Or so the theories went. That was the beauty of science. One day's canon was the next day's cannon fodder.

So it was possible, if not without theoretical impediments, that he had gone through a powerful field of some kind to somewhere, some-when else. Scientists believed that the monstrous gravitation of any singularity—a point where matter has infinite density and infinitesimal volume, causing all existence around it to be fully distorted by its vast gravitational forces—would destroy anything that tried to go through them, even light. And if it did get through, there was no way of knowing whether an object or particle could ever return. Theory did not establish whether the hole would be stable in reference to any other time or even any other dimension. For all Collins knew, he could be on Earth X, a world where the surface was eighty or ninety or ninety-nine-point-nine percent water with five-hour days and two-month years.

Yet Collins had a problem with this idea. If he had passed through a singularity of some kind, something deep in the loch, how could it have gone undetected? Or was it detected and the signals simply misunderstood? If that were the case, how could it be strong enough to shift time and space, yet not destroy him and the relatively fragile videocamera?

Unless we weren't pulled into the object itself, he thought. *What if we hit the event horizon, the point of no return, and went* around *the object itself, like flat rocks skipping across water?*

Collins picked up his helmet, taking care not to spill the water. Once again, he examined the hole in the side. Then, he set the helmet back in the sand, reached for his diving suit, and looked, for the first time, at the severed ends of the cables. They, too, had been cut with a scalpel-sharp slice.

By what? he asked himself. What force could keep him from being drawn into a singularity?

Collins let his mind run free. The images from the videocamera suggested that a rapid spinning had taken place, not just of the objects but of light itself. What could have caused that?

Just a small amount of electricity might do it, he thought. A small amount of leakage from the camera or his suit computer might stimulate a reaction from a powerful singularity, like a gnat buzzing a giant. However small or thin that electrical leak was, it could have a different charge from the singularity. It could have generated sufficient kinetic energy and angular momentum to form a barrier, one that renewed its physical structure from nanosecond to nanosecond. If so, it would act like oil on a slick road. Hitting it would send him in another direction. At the same time the impact would act as a straight, spectral-line cutting tool. It would have the same effect as falling off a motorcycle onto the road and scraping his helmet along the street at extremely high speeds on a super-heated, very smooth street.

If that proves to be the case, what are my chances of getting back? he wondered.

Even if the singularity led home, how could Collins be sure that next time the passage wouldn't take a slice out of his chest or belly or left-hand pinky? Then there was the problem of finding the singularity, if it did exist. Even if there were some way to go down and attempt to map the singularity with his computer or camera, he only had a very limited air supply and battery power. He would probably not have enough time to define the parameters of the opening.

"Maybe I can persuade Toothsome to go into the singularity for me," he thought aloud.

Now that he thought of it, the animal had probably

already done that. This creature, or one like it, must have been the Loch Ness Monster Dr. Castle had seen. Its forebears must have been the Loch Ness Monster other generations had observed. Perhaps Toothsome was hanging around here because it liked what it smelled in the future and was looking for human prey. Or maybe the water had tasted better. Or maybe it was cooler.

"Maybe I should rig a saddle and try to ride the thing back to the future," he mused.

Collins wondered if the lightning strikes had opened the door for them. Probably. That might be a way for him to get back—assuming he could find the singularity and wasn't electrocuted wearing metal oxygen tanks and waiting for the door to open.

How frustrating it was. Not just being stuck here but having an explanation for one of the world's greatest mysteries and being unable to tell anyone.

Collins wondered if Tally or Dr. Castle had figured any of this out. Perhaps they had, especially if the camera had continued to broadcast as it vanished. There was no reason to think it hadn't. The lens would still have been talking to the camera software as it transitioned. And the software would still have been in touch with the onboard computer. He doubted if they got more than a flash of the other side, but a flash was all they would need to realize that he was no longer where he had been a moment before.

The young physicist sat and looked out at the water. Hot sweat stung his eyes, and he wiped it away with the back of his hand. The sun baked his skin. As he watched the sparkling water, he wished he could take a refreshing swim. Just that right now, nothing more. But he didn't know if Toothsome might be down there, waiting. At some point he would have to deal with that. At some point soon he would have to deal with capturing *something* to eat, whether it was Toothsome or some other marine life, and hope that their systems didn't possess bacteria that would kill him.

"Before starvation does, that is," he said. And before it became too savagely hot to move. Toothsome's skin would make a good tent. If nothing else, it was waterproof.

Collins pushed himself up from the hot gravel. He left the camera there. He wondered if it had enough battery power left to send back to Dr. Castle with a message. Maybe he could do what they apparently had, send the camera into the water and hope it would get snagged.

"Failing that, you can always use a piece of gravel to scratch a message on your oxygen tanks and leave them to be discovered by them in the future," he said to himself. " 'Send sandwiches and a Mountain Dew. Oh yeah, and look for my fossilized skeleton where there used to be a jungle. It'll be the one, with the fossil of what turned out to be a poison berry in its mouth.' Hey," he thought with an sudden blend of terror and delight. "Everything I've said since I got here may be the first words ever spoken on planet earth."

The delight quickly faded as the sense of isolation settled in. If everything he had surmised was true, he was not only the first human on earth, he was the only human.

"Unless you've gone into the future," he thought aloud. This could be a time when humans and land creatures had died out and all that was left on earth were plants and marine life.

"No," he told himself. "That was a very young moon in the sky." It hadn't yet been battered by the asteroids to create the man-in-the-moon image we know. And since the moon's not volcanically active, those craters couldn't have been covered over. This was the past all right, a couple hundred million years deep.

He sighed.

"And you're already talking to yourself. That is definitely not a good thing to have happening."

The young physicist decided he had to stay busy. Exploring the immediate area was a good place to start. Leaving his helmet and camera behind, he turned and walked toward the foliage.

CHAPTER THIRTY

IT TOOK NEARLY three hours for Dr. Castle to get the equipment she needed and put it in place—three hours during which the LNVRS had had no success finding any trace of Collins. Tally was encouraged, confused, heartsick, and anxious, but glad there was no reason to give up.

And wondering, in spite of herself, if their wildest ideas might somehow be true.

The sonar transducer was kept and maintained by a local man, Sean Davies. The retired game warden had agreed to store it for the Academy of Applied Science following their 1975 expedition. After a series of public gaffes involving reputed Nessie photos, they had forgotten that the sonar device and the raft were there, and now Davies rented them out to interested explorers. He even had a hand-painted sign on his garage offering reasonable rates for the machine that had helped take the famous "flipper" photograph of the monster, a picture that showed what was supposedly one of the creature's extremities but had later been proven to be just shapes on the bed of the loch. That photograph had been part of a series that had inspired Sir Peter Scott of the World Wildlife Fund to give the creature an "official" name: *Nessiteras rhombopteryx,* which was itself a bit of skullduggery, an anagram for *Monster Hoax by Sir Peter S.*

Dr. Castle paid Davies one hundred pounds in advance for two days' rental, though she told Tally that she intended to stay on the loch until she had what she wanted. If they needed supplies, she or Tally would take the dinghy to shore to get them.

The raft was a sturdy, ten-meter blue inflatable with two seats. The sonar transducer sat on two pontoons attached to the back of the raft, with what Davies called "the business end" of the sonar tube itself in the water. The transducer had a range of a half-kilometer and could target objects as small as one quarter of a meter long. Data received by the unit was sent to a paper printer in the raft. The paper itself was gridded. The submerged mouth of the sonar could be targeted to zoom in on any area of the grid the user selected. The printer was tucked inside a thick, red plastic case. The wiring was waterproof.

As Dr. Castle explained to Tally when they returned to the site where Harold had vanished, sonar—an acronym for SOund NAvigation and Ranging—sends out audio pulses, which bounce off objects in their path, returning a new set of pulses. Sonar serves two basic functions. First, it can take a fairly detailed snapshot of a region. The length of time each signal takes to return to the source is assigned a number. That number represents a color or gray tone. The greater the distance, the darker the corresponding gray tone. As a result, the bottom of a chasm looks the darkest in a sonar-generated photograph. Second, sonar can be used as a tripwire. When something passes in front of the audio "ping," the object changes the sonar pulses that bounce back to the transducer. That shift can be used to activate a camera and strobe to take a picture, which will hopefully capture an image of whatever is passing by. Unlike sonar photographs, which take time and patience to generate but can cover a much wider area in much greater detail, the tripwire system uses sonar technology to provide a traditional snapshot.

Dr. Castle had a third use for the sonar. One that she and Tally were sure had never been attempted.

Tally agreed to ride in the raft, which Dr. Castle would tow behind the boat. The object was to survey in minute detail the area where Collins had disappeared. They were hoping to find the source of "the aberration" as Dr. Castle had begun calling it. Tally preferred to think of it as "the drain," as in "things get sucked down it and don't come back."

Shep Boucher had radioed when he saw that they had borrowed the sonar equipment.

"That's a clever way of finding a body," he told Dr. Castle. He sounded sincere.

"Thanks," she replied.

"Watch for the tanks," he said. "The creature would not have swallowed those." He still sounded sincere.

When they reached the spot where Harold had gone down, Tally took one of the walkie-talkies. She climbed down the stern ladder into the raft. Dr. Castle followed. Together, they made sure the sonar was pointed in the right direction. Then Dr. Castle returned to the boat. Tally sat in one seat and placed the printer in the other. She opened the case, then unfolded the sonar chart of the region. If they decided to shift the focus of the sonar, or zoom in closer on an area, all Tally needed to do was adjust the dial on top of the two-foot-long cylinder. It was like working the focus on an old-fashioned telescope, before everything was digitized. Tally placed the chart in her lap and turned the sonar on. After running a self-diagnostic, the printer began chugging out paper slowly, a scan line at a time, just like the prehistoric dot matrix printers she had used in high school.

"Is it operating?" Dr. Castle asked over the walkie-talkie.

"Perfectly," Tally replied.

Ordinarily Tally wouldn't have the patience for this any more than she did with dial-up internet, local-stop subway trains, or people who couldn't make decisions on what to order in the deli. But being away from the go-get-'em energy of New York made everything seem less urgent. Which was strange, considering that a man's life was at risk.

The black-and-white image continued to build, the printer head moving one way, then the other. It reminded Tally of when she was a kid and liked to clear her Etch A Sketch of all its silvery coating. After five minutes, when there was nearly an inch of map, Tally saw that they were focusing on an area about a dozen meters from where they wanted to be. She adjusted the transducer accordingly. The stacked paper coughed out an inch of white, then started the process again.

Tally waited. She concentrated on the printout, but her world was mostly sound. There was the clack of the printer, the low hum of the sonar device, and the soft lap of the water on the raft. She heard the occasional shouts of men on boats and in the water itself, as they suggested new places to search, called for right of way, or organized a small flotilla to start dragging a new section of the loch. Over the walkie-talkie she heard Dr. Castle call for Harold on the radio, then listen. Then call. Then listen. Then suggest yet again that he tap if he couldn't speak, then listen. There was nothing but the most opaque silence from the radio.

After a while it sounded as if the small choppy waves were laughing at Tally. They collected around the raft and made glugging little snickers each time they smacked the sides.

"We're going to beat you," she muttered.

"Sorry, I didn't get that," Dr. Castle said over the walkie-talkie.

"Nothing," Tally replied. "Talking to myself." She wondered why that seemed stranger than thinking to herself.

The young woman looked down at the printer. There was just over an inch of imaging. They were nearing the area where the previous echo chart had showed the impossibly smooth, solid wall to be. That was where Dr. Castle seemed to feel the "aberration" might be located. Tally radioed that she was comparing the emerging page to the sonar chart.

"What are you seeing?" Dr. Castle asked.

"I'm a couple of scan lines from where the original chart says your wall should be."

"And?"

"So far it looks the same. I'll let you know what shows up."

The image continued to click out line by line. As Tally watched it, she began to feel a little anxious. She didn't know if she wanted the image to be the same as or different than it had been on the previous chart. A change would almost certainly help them to locate Harold. It would also mean that they had found a potentially explosive situation that might change the way they looked at the world. Forever. Tally hadn't bargained for that. She was still adjusting to living outside her parents' world. Finding no change would allow them to continue searching for Harold along more traditional lines, as the others were doing.

Tally didn't know which way things would go, but she needed to know what she wanted to see. So she decided to do a trick her Grandfather Bates had once taught her. She pulled a coin from her pocket and flipped it. Heads meant that the new chart would be exactly like the old chart. Tails meant they were on the trail of the aberration. While the coin was in the air, Tally let her gut tell her which way she hoped it landed.

Tails, she thought as she caught the coin in her palm and closed it. Slowly, she lifted her fingers. She got tails.

Relieved, Tally looked at the printer. She watched as the sonar scanned the region where the previous expedition had found the blank wall.

She got tails.

CHAPTER THIRTY-ONE

THE ACRID SMELL Harold had noticed upon coming ashore became much more pronounced the further inland he ventured. It occurred to him that it might actually be coming from the thick soil beneath his feet. Walking across it seemed to release the smell. It could be rotted vegetation, though it smelled more like sulfur. Whatever it was, he didn't like it.

The vegetation began about a quarter-mile away. Collins had decided to put his wetsuit on before entering the region. The last thing he needed was to brush up against some form of poison whatever and end up with a painful rash or bite from some kind of microscopic tic.

The low-lying plants had big floppy leaves about a foot long and nearly a foot wide. They glistened with a saplike substance which, he assumed, acted like sunblock. It let the photosynthetic nutrients in while keeping the ultraviolet rays out. As he moved through them, he realized that he was probably the first thing other than the wind to move them.

He half-expected them to curl up, snap out at him, and say something nasty like flowers from *Alice in Wonderland*. Or maybe they'd grab him and shove him down into some unseen maw. Maybe that was why there was nothing moving around out here. It all got eaten.

Easy, boy, Collins thought. If these plants were carnivorous, there would be some kind of animal life around here. Otherwise, the plants would have become extinct. He wondered, though, if they might be edible. If not the leaves, perhaps the roots were. He was going to have to look into that before very long.

The foliage went on for perhaps another quarter-mile. It was considerably muggier here than it was on the beach. That was no doubt due to the reflective quality of the leaves. Sunlight probably bounced from one to the other before dissipating.

Thinking about the sunlight, Collins noticed that the leaves were glistening less than when he'd first entered the field. He looked up. There were thin gray clouds moving in from ahead. He had seen formations like those before, though he couldn't remember where. Being tired and dehydrating quickly didn't help him to focus. Hopefully, he'd have a better view of the western horizon when he reached the trees ahead.

It took Collins about a half-hour to clear the low-lying plants. By the time he had reached the forest of pre-palms or faux palms or whatever they were, the composition of the soil had changed dramatically. It went from being like the gravel-grained surface on the beach to a blacker, finer surface. He bent and scooped some up, let it run through his fingers. The particles were small, gritty, and very dry. They reminded him of the soil in some regions of Hawaii. He wondered if he was on an island. He rose and continued walking.

The trees were clustered closely together and were sharply curved. They reminded him of bunches of bananas.

They were about seven feet tall and had bark like pineapple skins, and from what he could tell from the few fronds he found on the ground, the leaves were nothing like those on the lower plants. They were dagger-shaped and covered with very thin, short white hairs, almost like fur. They were also extremely thick. The trees probably recovered evaporated water through the hairs. Or possibly the hairs sensed seasonal changes and spurred internal changes in the trees. Beneath the hairs the leaves themselves seemed leathery. Whatever they were, he had never seen anything like them before. If this was the distant past, Collins doubted whether structures so fair as the hairs would have survived in the fossil record.

It was cooler among the trees, which made wearing the wetsuit slightly more tolerable. The deeper he went into the woods, the more he encountered occasional sharp-edged rocks, much to the chagrin of his bare feet. He assumed the reason there had been none on the beach was because the surf and rains had eroded them. They were shielded here by the canopy of leaves.

After another half-hour or so of pleasurable shade, he neared the edge of the woods. He found himself on a ledge that overlooked a broad, dark plain. There were a few patches of plants down there, but he discerned no other living things. Collins realized then that he was standing on some kind of natural dam that held the sea back from spilling into this depression. However, that was not the most startling thing about the vista. Not at all.

Beyond the plain, approximately ten or fifteen miles distant, was a row of three mountains. The central peak was maybe ten thousand feet high, the others a little more than half that. All of them looked as if someone had taken a machete across the top, leaving the distinctive caldera of recently-active volcanoes.

One of them was smoking. Gray smoke. In his direction. *Of course!* Collins thought. That was where he'd seen gray "clouds" like the ones he saw before. On Hawaii. Only they weren't clouds, they were plumes of smoke from volcanoes. Collins realized, suddenly, that the natural dam that he stood on had probably been formed within the last ten or twenty years when lava met the sea and solidified. Plants and trees quickly took root on the rich volcanic soil. The plain below was a former lava field. It had obviously been "hot" more recently than the area above it, since there were only a few plants there.

Frightened now, Collins turned back toward the beach. The fact that the volcano was smoking could mean nothing. Volcanoes often woke, smoked, then went back to sleep.

"Volcanoes in *your* time," Collins reminded himself. If this were an earlier age, volcanoes in this time, sitting atop a younger, hotter earth, might behave differently.

Collins didn't know where he was going. If the volcano was getting ready to erupt, being on the beach probably wouldn't help him. Though it didn't appear as if the lava from previous eruptions had reached that far, the ash certainly had. And that was what killed you. The lung-burning suffocation.

He had to get out of here.

Moving quickly through the trees and then the plants, Collins wondered how many scientists would willingly give up their lives to be where he was. They'd get all mushy at the prospect of seeing a prehistoric creature living, moving, thriving. They'd leap at the chance to explore the ancient world, a world where there were no phones, no bills, no pressures other than maybe to fish and collect rain water and hope that a volcano didn't vaporize or entomb you. Most would probably run the risk. Someone once did a poll of planetary scientists asking how many would take a trip to Mars if they knew they wouldn't be able to return. Nearly seventy-five percent said they would go.

Collins would not have been one of those.

What the physicist enjoyed most about science was crunching data and working with other scientists and going places with his mind, without ever leaving the room. He had come to Loch Ness because he was desperate, because he wanted to commune with other scientists, because he needed to do something to get UNIT Omega some attention. He hadn't bargained on ending up in one of H. G. Wells's nightmares.

Perspiration was rolling down every part of his head, from hairline to nape. He cleared the foliage and began tugging off the top of the wet suit. The sun was high and really hot now. He was going to have to go in the water and cool off regardless of what Toothsome might do. Collins also hoped it rained again soon. He didn't see any rivers or streams, and that helmet full of water, filled only to the hole in the side was not going to last very long.

By the time Collins had reached the shore, he had removed his wet suit. He waded into the surf. He sat down, navel-deep in the water, and kept an eye out for Toothsome. The water was warm but very refreshing. The young man cupped some of it in his hand—a fair hand, he saw, somewhat ashamed, a hand that had not known a hard, outdoor life—and let the water splash over his head. That felt good so he got on his hands and knees and dunked the top of his head in the water. He shook it around, let his hair go wild in the water. That felt even better. And he didn't even have to worry what he looked like, whether his hair was messy or not. Combed hair might not be necessary for another half-billion years because there was no one here to see it.

When Collins sat up again, the salty drops that landed in his mouth reminded him of just how thirsty he was. He spit them out and went back to the beach, sat next to the helmet, and filled his mouth with water. He held it there before swallowing. It tasted delicious, clean, and better because it was *earned*. He felt smart having used his helmet to catch water. Now that he thought of it, maybe he could use the helmet to catch fish. If there were any, that is.

"Smart! Smart! Smart!" he yelled as loud as he could, as if he were his own cheering section at the Harold Collins Bowl. His voice was quickly lost on the empty beach.

"The only words on earth, momentous yet insignificant," he said. He looked along the shore. The quiet and isolation was maddening to contemplate. There were no footprints save his. No shells. No seaweed. No sails on the horizon. No buildings in the distance. No oil rigs. No piers. No people. No ideas except those that were in his head.

No God?

Or was *he* God? Was he the origin of all religion, a racial memory that would live on in the genetic code of plants and Toothsome? It was possible. He was here in a paradise with a devil locked on the outside and hell brooding to the west. And it was possible that whatever he did here would affect the course of all future events. His sweat, his waste material contained DNA. The creatures that would one day become human beings could have arisen from that, created in "his own image" from the dust of the beach or forest. Or maybe it wasn't that complex. Some creature he might kill could have ended up as the mother of all mammals. For all he knew he might have already screwed up tomorrow by moving through the foliage and disturbing plants that would have protected a spot of land where the first insect would have broken through the surface and sired every cockroach that ever plagued New York. Perhaps he had done terrible damage to the future by redirecting or harming Toothsome, by introducing a chain into the ecosystem.

Or perhaps none of that was relevant. History might be immutable and everything he did could already be part of the historical record.

Perhaps there was a god and that god was using him.

All of those thoughts were pushed to the side as Collins heard something he didn't expect to hear. A constant pinging, like someone hitting a triangle under the water. It possessed a mechanical quality, like the sonogram he once employed to find impurities in the sulfuric acid he used to clean metal in some of his undergraduate laboratory work. If it weren't a naturally occurring sound, it could be coming from Loch Ness.

Could it be sonar? Collins wondered.

That would fit his theory of low-frequency impulses gliding off some kind of singularity to skip through time and space.

Were Dr. Castle and Tally looking for him? If so, they might not realize there was an opening in time or space or both. They might just be scanning the area and moving on. He had to get through the hole, or at least let them know he was here. What did he have? What could he use?

"*Think,* asshole!" he cried as he jumped to his feet and waded back into the water.

Then it hit him.

Collins turned and half-ran, half-stumbled to the center of the beach. That was where he had left his wet suit and the one thing he could still use to communicate with the future. Snatching the wet suit in one hand, he grabbed the videocamera in the other. Turning it on himself, he ran back to the water.

CHAPTER THIRTY-TWO

"KATHRYN, I'M GETTING something really strange from the printer."

Tally held the walkie-talkie in her left hand and the edge of the printer paper in her right. She had already informed Dr. Castle that the shape of the "wall" was coming in different from the original sonar reading. The paleontologist had told her to keep watching to see how different the shape of the region was. The southeastern end, where Tally was located, was smaller than in the previous reading, with a rounder rather than flat contour. That could have been due to shifting sands, erosion, or falling rocks. But what she was seeing now was more than simply a geographical redistribution.

"Explain 'something really strange,'" Dr. Castle said.

"It looks like incoming!" Tally said excitedly. "I'm reading a lighter gray spot in the middle of the black wall. Only it isn't just lighter—the gradations are getting brighter with each click, and there's an apparent size change from east to west as the sonar scans it."

"Brighter and wider definitely means something's moving closer to the surface," Dr. Castle agreed. "Shape?"

"Lumpy," was the word that came to mind as Tally looked at the partially scanned shape. "Like coal. It's getting bigger and whiter. Whatever it is, it's rising very fast."

"Which side of the boat?" Dr. Castle asked.

"Right sight—starboard," Tally said, trying to get her sea brain to work with her sea legs.

Dr. Castle broke from the radio and went to the starboard side. Tally had a clear view of the side of the boat and also looked in that direction.

"Keep talking to me," Dr. Castle said. "What does the sonar say?"

Tally looked at the paper. "The object's still coming," she replied. "Should we get someone over here to help in case it's Harold?"

"No time!" Dr. Castle called back. "Wait—I see something!"

The raft wasn't stable enough for Tally to be able to stand, so she leaned on the side and looked out. Huge bubbles were beginning to rise, like the kind she'd seen in films of volcanic eruptions. They didn't so much pop as collapse, as if they were being sucked down again immediately after forming.

"Should I keep the sonar operating?" Tally shouted, not bothering any longer with the walkie-talkie.

"Yes," Dr. Castle replied. "If the passage is reopened, that has to be what did it!"

"But if things are being spit out, they might also be sucked back! That might not be a good thing!"

Tally and Dr. Castle exchanged long-distance looks. Tally had her hand on the dial. She could almost hear the scientist thinking, *What would be worse? Risking cutting Harold in half by shutting the door or having him come through and then be dragged back?* If the bubbles were being imploded, there could be a severe backwash—

"Cut it!" Dr. Castle replied.

Tally twisted the dial just as she heard a loud splash from the front of the main boat. Something broke the water like a cannonball. Without hesitation, Dr. Castle snatched the fish net from the hooks along the cabin wall. As the scientist ran back to the railing Tally saw something rise five or six feet above the surface of the loch. It was a glistening, oddly-shaped black object that hung in the air for a moment before dropping straight down again. Tally hoped it wasn't Harold Collins, charred and compacted from his travels.

By the time the flat black object struck the water, Dr. Castle was there with the fish net. She managed to get the long aluminum pole into the water and swung the nylon net beneath the object. But the black mass was larger than the net, and Dr. Castle was having trouble hauling it in. She called for help, but her call wasn't necessary: Tally had already untied the mooring rope from the raft, pulled the oars from under her seat, and begun rowing in toward the front of the boat. She rowed in sure, steady strokes that moved the raft smoothly through the water without upsetting the printer.

"Is it heavy?" Tally called over her shoulder when she was about ten feet away.

"No, just ungainly," she replied.

That was a word her mother would use. Tally would try not to hold that against the scientist.

As Tally neared the net, she swung the raft around so the front was facing the object. She closed in on the object, put the oars on the floor of the raft, and knelt on the side. She reached for the oily-looking lump. There was no steam coming from the water, so the thing probably wasn't very hot. Of course, it could be highly radioactive, in which case she was a dead person anyway. Whatever it was, the thing looked familiar—

"Damn me," Tally said as she got her hands around it.

"What is it?" Dr. Castle asked. She used the net to help maneuver it. "Is it from Harold?"

"It's his wet suit!" Tally said. She backed over to the seat and unbundled the makeshift package. The arms and legs of the wet suit had been knotted securely around something.

"Is that all?" Dr. Castle asked. "Just the suit?"

"No," Tally said. She looked up at the scientist as she finished pulling the suit open. "There's something inside."

"What?" Dr. Castle asked.

Tally looked up at her. "It's the videocamera."

CHAPTER THIRTY-THREE

IN THE VERNACULAR of a sport in which Harold Collins had very little interest and knew only because his father had been ferociously devoted to it, the move had been a jam.

Or was it a stuff?

He couldn't remember now. And it didn't matter, since basketball hadn't been invented yet.

As he had run toward the water just a few minutes before, Collins had used the videocamera to tape a message to whoever found it—presumably Dr. Castle and Tally.

"I'm hoping that you're making those sounds I'm hearing—maybe you can hear them in the background too—and that I can still hear them underwater when I get there," he had said, panting as he sloshed into the water. "I appear to be in a prehistoric environment, I mean a *really* prehistoric one with nothing but plants on land and monster fish in the water. Nothing in the sky except a moon that hasn't gotten badly battered yet and smoke from a line of volcanoes. I was brought here by some kind of anomaly that appears to be affected by electricity—the storms here are very fast and hit the water with a kind of 'tassel lightning' for lack of a better term. If I didn't think it would tear the earth to pieces, I would suspect there's a miniature black hole in the center of the earth causing a warp in time and space along the event horizon. Maybe it's just the butt-end of one, or some kind of microscopic wormhole. Whatever it is, I'm not sure how big the opening is or how long it lasts, but obviously I got through and the camera made it and so are the sounds. Keep them coming as long as you can—if this camera gets through, start them up again and maybe I can follow them back."

With that, he bundled the camera in his wet suit to protect it from whatever buffeting it might take, and then he dove. He thought he might even have a chance of getting through himself, and he had decided to seize the chance if it were presented. But Toothsome had appeared from the mouth of the bay and charged him. Or maybe the creature had been angered by the sound and was attacking that. Collins really didn't know. All the scientist had time to do was go to where the sound was loudest, swim toward it, and thrust the package down. He hoped it was sucked through. He couldn't stay around to see if it disappeared. Toothsome was too close. If the camera did not get through, Collins figured it would float to the surface. Or, if Toothsome tried to make a meal of it, some of the remnants of wetsuit and electronics would get spit out and float up.

He had scrambled back to shore, as he had the day before, and clawed frantically along the gravel to get out. Which probably saved his life. He lacerated his bare knees and palms and left a blood trail for some local predators to follow. He had not met the opal-red eel-like creatures before. Perhaps they were day feeders. In any case, when they showed up, Toothsome was briefly distracted. He gobbled them down in a few decisive snaps instead of chasing the larger prey. That bought Collins the time he needed to get out of the water.

Upon reaching the shore, Collins suddenly heard the pinging stop. Hopefully, that meant the women had received his package and they had shut the sounds down to study it.

Hopefully.

Collins didn't let his mind wander to what else it could mean. Maybe some Viking blowing a trumpet had opened the aperture and was just now trying to figure out what the hell had popped from the water. Or some rocker in three thousand A.D. might have been playing a futuristic synthesizer at a loch-side party when the weird-looking parcel popped through.

No, he would hope for the best. The anomaly was a hardwired link, and they had received the package.

The physicist wished, in retrospect, that he had asked Dr. Castle to send a shark cage through the opening. He was willing to bet the monsterphobic Shep probably had one stored somewhere. Though he wondered if even that would be enough to protect him from Toothsome. Each time that huge jaw came down on an eel-thing, Collins felt a forceful push from the rush of displaced water. If he ever got back, he wanted to go to a museum, find a fossil of this thing, and kick the everlasting hell out of it.

As soon as Collins was a few feet up on the beach, he turned and looked out at the surface of the sea. Toothsome had finished his meal and swam back out to deeper water. He had been thorough: Collins did not see any pieces of eel-thing in the water. The creature's tail broke the surface with a wicked snap, then his dorsal ridges appeared, arching gracefully before he submerged. Collins continued to watch. There were no pieces of black rubber, no glass or plastic or microchips. He didn't know if the message had gotten through, but at least the camera didn't appear to have been eaten.

Breathing heavily from the exertion, Collins sat down and dropped on his back. The cool seawater had felt good, but already the sun was beginning to bake him again. He reached over and pulled his diving suit on top of him. As bad as the heat was, he'd feel a lot worse if he got a wicked sunburn. He didn't even know what kind of ozone layer the planet had. For all he knew the ultraviolet light could be coming in at lethal doses. There was nothing he could do about it at the moment, so he decided to think about the more urgent matter of escape. Now that he had apparently proven there was an anomaly of some kind, it would be good to figure out exactly what it was.

"If the anomaly is activated by electricity, various stimuli must affect it differently," Collins said to himself. "Maybe the aperture is wider depending on the higher or lower frequency, or the greater the intensity or duration." That would explain how he managed to get through. Or how Toothsome or any of his monster-size cousins managed to make the passage. Lightning might create a different size aperture than sound.

Collins heard a rumble and sat up. He looked toward the southern sky. There were dark clouds on the horizon. They appeared to be gathering for a fresh assault. Storm systems obviously worked on a very different timetable here than they did in the twenty-first century.

That could be a good thing in terms of letting him get home. Each storm would give him a fresh run at the interdimensional window. But it could also be a bad thing. If Collins tried to go through the anomaly during a storm, he would have to deal with electrified water in addition to Toothsome. It would be better to wait and see if Dr. Castle and Tally tried the sonic approach again.

Collins heard another rumble, different from the first.

"That's not good," he told himself. This one was louder, closer, and coming from behind him. It had to be the volcano.

Maybe it did this all the time. He had no way of knowing. But he didn't like it.

Heat, hunger, no shelter, and no information. And Collins had thought working at the United Nations was bad. Still, he was encouraged by two things. First, he had made it here intact, meaning that a trip to somewhere else could probably be undertaken. Second, he had resourceful and dedicated allies somewhere, in some future, trying to help him. Compared to the level of support he had received at the United Nations, he was as good as saved.

In theory, anyway.

CHAPTER THIRTY-FOUR

D R. CASTLE WAS openly, overly enthusiastic as Tally climbed aboard with her precious cargo. She handed Dr. Castle the wet suit. The scientist turned it over quickly and examined all sides. It was pretty well chewed up.

"Obviously this took a beating, either going or coming through a very narrow passageway," Dr. Castle said.

"But it proves that wherever Harold is, he probably wasn't badly injured getting there," Tally said as she reached the deck. "Otherwise, he couldn't have sent this to us."

"Correct."

"Under the right circumstances, he can probably make it back," Tally said.

"Clearly. The question is, what constitutes the right circumstances?" She set the tattered wet suit on the helm and reached for the camera. "Let's see if he had anything to say."

"Harold? Have something to say?" Tally joked as she handed Dr. Castle the camera.

Both women chuckled. It was a short-lived tension reliever.

The paleontologist opened the collapsible viewing monitor. Strong fingers, which had probably been so steady when cleaning fossils, were trembling now. The older woman held the camera so that both of them could see it clearly. They went slack-jawed as they watched the video. They heard what Harold was saying, about where he thought he was and how he got there. But Dr. Castle was utterly amazed by what she was seeing.

"Those plants behind him—they look like forms of *Zosterophyllophytes* and *Tremerophytes* we've found fossilized in this region," she said.

"From what era?"

"The Devonian, about half a billion years ago," Dr. Castle said. "The trees could be *Archaeopteris*—the first trees. We're looking at the first trees on earth, Tally! This is unbelievable!"

"What were the land masses like then?" Tally asked.

"There were just two continents, supercontinents, really—Gondwana and Euramerica."

"Where was Scotland?"

"In Euramerica, which was made up of modern-day North America and Europe," Dr. Castle said. "They were joined near the equator, most of their surface underwater. South of them was most of South America, Australia, India, Antarctica, and Africa."

"So in order for Harold to be on land, he had to have been shifted in time and place," Tally said.

"Apparently so, unless he's on an island somewhere," Dr. Castle said, shaking her head and staring. "And fortunately so, I might add," she said. "Otherwise he would have drowned or possibly been eaten by the placoderms, which were rather ferocious and large-jawed—"

She fell silent.

"Kathryn?" Tally said.

"They were very large-jawed fish, some of them armor-plated," the scientist continued. "Just like the animal I saw in the loch. It's all falling together, Tally. We have discovered a direct portal to the mid-Devonian era. I don't know what it is or how it is, but this is simply astonishing."

"So we know it's there," Tally said. "Which brings us back to the question how do we get him *here?*"

"We have to assume he's waiting for us to turn the sonar back on," Dr. Castle said.

"Right," Tally said.

Dr. Castle nodded toward the wet suit. "Unfortunately, none of us knows whether that will be enough to get him through."

"I have to believe it provides more punch than whatever his suit was generating that brought him through the first time," Tally said.

"But the suit may not have been acting 'alone,' so to speak," Dr. Castle said. "There may have been storms on the other side that provided the bulk of the power. Or it could have been the ancestor of electric eels. I've written about the modern-day *Electrophorus electricus*. They grow to be about eight feet long. Their forebears were considerably larger."

"So what we should do, then, is just turn the sonar on and let Harold decide when to come back."

"There are only about two hours of battery power left," Dr. Castle said. "We don't want to burn that up and strand him in the past for the hours it will take to go back to shore and recharge."

"In the past," Tally shook her head. "It's too damn creepy. If we don't get him back, his skeleton could be fossilized somewhere beneath us."

"We'll get him back," Dr. Castle assured her. "Let me think about this for a minute."

The paleontologist rewound the video. She jacked the camera into her computer and began uploading the images. She watched it for a second time as she did, paying more attention now to the blurry surroundings than to Harold and what he was saying.

"Uh-oh," Dr. Castle said.

"What's wrong?"

The scientist hit the PAUSE button on the video camera. She took a closer look at the image on her monitor. She stopped the download and brought up her graphics enhancement software.

"What are you looking at?" Tally asked.

"Just a moment," Dr. Castle said.

Tally watched as the scientist sharpened the picture. Collins was holding the camera at arm's length and pointing it at himself. Dr. Castle leaned toward the top left corner of the image, over Harold's right shoulder. There appeared to be an open sea or ocean there. And above it very black, low-lying clouds—

"Only they're not storm clouds," the scientist muttered as the image shifted into much sharper focus.

"Excuse me?" Tally said.

"Look at these," she said, pointing.

Tally looked at the dark mass in the sky. "I see it."

"He must be on an island," Dr. Castle said. "He was transported in time but *not* in space. Four hundred thousand years ago this entire region from the tip of Loch Ness to the North Sea was on the cusp of a three-hundred-mile stretch of volcanoes. We believe these mountains were in a state of more-or-less constant activity for thousands of centuries. Some of them were located underwater beneath a sizeable body of water known as the Casterberg Sea. That has to be what we're seeing here," she said, pointing to the water. "And the island Collins is on must have been formed by them."

"So we know where Harold is," Tally said. "But you just said those clouds are not storm clouds. If not—"

"They're volcanoes," Dr. Castle replied. "Erupting volcanoes."

CHAPTER THIRTY-FIVE

THE RUMBLING GREW more insistent as the minutes passed. It came from behind Collins and from the south. Each time a mountain bellowed, the sands of the beach vibrated. They reminded Collins of the men in the electric football game he used to play with his father. The sands wriggled and mixed and fell and then stopped—until the next outburst, which usually came before the echo of the last one had died.

Worse than the frequency was the power of the blasts. There would be a loud bang followed by several softer ones. Then an even louder bang, then several softer ones. The smoke was constant, but each series of explosions seemed to chug a little more into the sky. Nothing billowing; not yet. They were still just snaking gray wisps. But he knew from the volcanoes of Hawaii that the mood of a mountain could change quickly.

Worse than the power of the blasts was that Harold Collins could do absolutely nothing about them, or about his own predicament. The next move was up to people who would not be born for several hundred million years, give or take. He couldn't even put on his diving suit and wait for another burst of sound or a flash of electricity or something else to come through from the future. He would sweat himself to dehydration, and he hadn't collected enough water to compensate. Even if he put the suit on, what would he do? Go down and knock on rocks?

Hello, is there a fragment of white dwarf under you? No? Have you seen one around?

He didn't think his wrist computer would generate sufficient power to stimulate the anomaly. Even if it did, he doubted the aperture would be sufficient to allow him through. And while he did all of this, of course, he would be burning through his oxygen supply. He might need that air to get home.

"Speaking of which . . ." he thought, looking back. He had to figure out a way to fix the damn helmet. Otherwise he wasn't going anywhere. He put part of his mind to that problem. The rest stayed where it had been since the twenty or thirty minutes that had passed since he'd pushed the camera into the sea. During that time Collins hadn't been able sit still, lie still, or stand still. If nothing else, pacing cooled the sweat that was coating his body from scalp to ankle. He was trying to concentrate on the mystery of the anomaly, in particular why it was so much closer to the surface here, only about twenty feet down, than it was in the twenty-first century.

Or maybe that was illusional. Perhaps the event horizon occupied the same location in time-space respective to some baseline other than the sea bottom. That would make sense. An object that was positioned in a theoretical infinite number of times and spaces would not necessarily use a section of the earth's crust as its defining boundary.

"Unless—" the young man said, stopping and staring into space with sudden realization.

And then it fell into place.

"It has to be," he said.

What if it were the other way around? What if the singularity predated the earth? What if it were closer to the surface in this time because the surface had not had as much time to—

"Build up," he said.

If the anomaly predated the earth, the components that created our world probably accreted *around* it. Perhaps the chunks of asteroid and heavy gasses were attracted to the singularity by its intense gravitation. A black hole would be too powerful for a planet to be constructed around. It would simply have sucked the matter into it. But that wasn't the only cosmic phenomenon this could be.

"There was a universe of stars that existed before our second-generation sun was born," Collins thought aloud, the same way he had when he was in college and had a theoretical problem to solve. Talking also helped him to think over the rumbling of the volcano. Thinking gave him something to do other than worry; escape was out of his hands. It was up to lightning or sonic blasts from Loch Ness. "Many of the first-generation stars went nova and spewed out the heavier elements that comprised the next generation of stars. But some of those early stars did not explode. Some shrunk and became super-condensed white dwarf stars that, in theory, could easily tear a hole in timespace."

But that alone didn't solve the mystery of the Loch Ness anomaly. A white dwarf would be nearly the size of earth. And the gravitational pull would be so intense that the atoms of anything that came near it would be torn into their component quarks, down quarks, hadrons, and other elementary particles.

"Which means . . ." he thought triumphantly.

The white dwarf could not be an entire white dwarf but a part of one. The question then was how was it destroyed?

There was only one force known to science that could do that.

Suppose you have a binary star system, one star dying before its companion, he thought. Most stars in the known universe were binaries. It wasn't unlikely. *If that dead companion became a black hole, it would swallow its partner. What if that partner was already a white dwarf? Suppose parts of the white dwarf were tough enough to survive a really rocking-and-rolling passage through the heart of darkness? And suppose those shards or particles or motes of white dwarf were scattered around time and space by the black hole?*

That could explain the missing black matter of the universe, the unseen mass of matter that scientists theorized had to exist—having observed measurable gravitational forces exerted on the universe that far surpassed the visible mass of the universe—but could not find.

"White dwarf dust thrown all over the universe could serve as a nexus for the accretion of other stars or planets," Collins thought. "The particles would be strong enough to attract matter and would probably tear it apart, *unless* their energy were trapped by the inertial force of approaching matter. That trapped force could create a shell around the white dwarf particle, similar to the repulsive force generated by 'like' ends of two magnets. That shell, that force field, would be perfectly stable unless it were imbalanced by some outside force. Conceivably, the white dwarf could be 'tickled' into action by the application of energy. The stimulus might cause the harmonious time-space balance to become momentarily unhinged. For one moment the gravitation might become more intense in one spot, causing anything around it to come under the time- and space-bending influence of the white dwarf particle.

"Like I was," Collins ruminated.

Yet given the infinite combinations of location and era, why would the doorway between his time and this time—and on the same world—open repeatedly, regardless of the level of stimulation? A perfectly formed white dwarf should not play favorites with any specific time or place. It should form reality-warping bonds with all of them.

"Unless there's an imperfection," he said excitedly.

That one he liked. If a white dwarf were pulled through a black hole, the pieces might not emerge smooth and even, as a "normal" white dwarf would be. Maybe the white dwarf inside the earth was rotating, slowly or rapidly—it didn't matter. Maybe each time the imperfection clicked around, it was like a scratch on a CD. The laser in the player couldn't go past that spot. Maybe the chute between here and the present was a one-only event.

"Or there could be two, or three, or ten imperfections attached to the same white dwarf particle but at different spots on earth," he speculated. Each one might open somewhere or sometime else.

It was all very thrilling. A cosmic gem that scientists had wanted to study for years, a white dwarf, could conceivably be right below his feet. Right below Dr. Castle's feet.

And right below Toothsome's underbelly, unfortunately.

Collins frowned. He just now realized that the rumbling had become more or less constant, the tail end of one roar giving way to the opening blast of the next. He looked back.

"What the hell?"

The smoke was no longer wispy and gray but charcoal gray bordering on black. And it was rolling toward him over the treeline, rolling up, and rolling out. It looked almost like a fat mushroom cloud.

Suddenly, Collins heard a sound behind him like steam rushing from a locomotive. He turned and saw churning white smoke rushing toward the seven-foot-high tree line. It was far below the black cloud. He ran back in that direction, crashing through the brush and those palm tree wanna-bes. As he pushed through the last line of trees, he saw one of the mountains not just spitting smoke straight up, like a locomotive announcing its departure, but also blasting it through a large vent low in its side.

As the white cloud rolled toward him, Collins heard two loud bangs to his left. Turning, he ran toward the beach. He cleared the trees and looked out to sea. Several miles out he saw two other gray clouds rising from the water, each one sending ruffs of steam rushing in all directions.

"A ring of fire," Collins said fearfully.

There must be a chain of volcanoes in this region. Not that the existence of the others mattered. If the volcano beyond the forest blew, Harold Collins would be dead within minutes.

Collins ran back to the beach. He had zero ideas about what to do next. He couldn't outrun a volcano, and the diving suit wouldn't offer much protection. Even if it saved him from the rain of suffocating ash, he didn't have very much air left in the tanks.

The physicist had gone from "as good as saved" to "as good as entombed" in just a few minutes. Hopefully—and it was less than a hope, really; it was more like a dream—in the fast-changing world of Harold Collins, someone would find a way to reverse that.

CHAPTER THIRTY-SIX

"**T**HIS DOESN'T LOOK good," Dr. Castle said.

The two women were looking down at the computer monitor. Dr. Castle was still sitting, and Tally was standing beside her. The paleontologist had finished downloading the video and was studying the frames for other signs of volcanic activity.

Tally felt as if they had been out here for days, even though it had been less than seven hours. Then again, time was suddenly a very different concept to her. For all Tally knew, it passed at different speeds from spot to spot and clocks were in on the conspiracy.

"What's wrong?" Tally asked.

"The video lasts a total of forty-one seconds," Dr. Castle said. "During that time, the plume advances along the top of the picture. It does not sink."

"Meaning?"

"It's being driven upward by superheated gasses."

"Hot air rises," Tally said.

"Exactly," Dr. Castle replied. "This mountain is in the process of erupting somewhere beyond the horizon. Not just venting but getting ready for a major outpouring. And if, as I suspect, the volcano is linked to others, they may all be ready to disgorge."

"Is that really worse than just one?" Tally asked.

"Very much so," Dr. Castle replied. "Because we're dealing with the sea, Harold not only has to worry about hot ash and lava but scalding steam and tsunami-generated waves that could obliterate that beach he's on."

"Someone has to go in after him," Tally said.

"No. Even if we wanted to take that risk there isn't time to get another suit," Dr. Castle replied. Her voice was clipped, tense. "I'm not even sure we can open the anomaly wide enough to accommodate two people."

"It accommodated a monster!"

"Yes, when it was powered, in all probability, by intense forces on the other side. We are not guaranteed that kind of cooperation."

"Well, we obviously have to do something," Tally said. "What about Morse code? Maybe Shep or one of the others can send a signal. Harold's dad was in the Navy, he might know what we're trying to tell him."

"That he's in danger? I think he knows that by now. Besides, if this volcano is becoming active, Harold may not be able to hear a thing. We'll have to send a very loud signal through and hope for the best."

"We'll have to do that anyway, to make sure the tunnel opens wide enough," Tally said.

"That's true," Dr. Castle said. She took a slow breath. "He's probably waiting for us to do something. We'd better turn it on."

"Wait," Tally said. She looked over the railing at the raft.

"What is it?" Dr. Castle asked.

"The sonar was used underwater by the AAS, wasn't it?"

"Yes," she said. "They anchored it to the floor of the loch to trigger their cameras."

"Then that's what we have to do," Tally said.

"What do you mean?"

The young woman climbed down. "We need volume so he can hear, and so we can open the gate as wide as possible. What we have to do is turn the sonar on, lower it into the loch, and target the area where we think the anomaly is located. Where the graph says the wet suit and camera came from."

"I like it," Dr. Castle said. "But we have to hurry."

"I'll need a monkey wrench to pry this loose," Tally said as she stepped into the raft.

Dr. Castle reached for the tool chest under the helm. "You realize that the battery will only give us about ten minutes at top intensity."

"I'm betting that when Harold hears the sound he'll seize the moment and try to get through. What about the animals he's facing out there?"

"Well, that could be a problem, and not just because they're carnivorous," Dr. Castle said. She found a wrench and a pair of pliers. She hurried to the ladder and went down. "If they maneuver or communicate using echolocation, the noise could upset them."

"As in 'disorient' or 'piss off'?"

"Either," Dr. Castle admitted. "If the sonar happens to sound like a wounded animal, it could also attract more predators to the area, especially if they're moving out to sea away from the volcanic region. On the other hand, the sonar could scare them off, and the activity of the volcano could send them running in the other direction. I just don't know."

"I'm an optimist," Tally said. "I like the second scenario better."

Amidst grunts, swearing, and torn finger flesh, the women finished removing the bolts and carefully lifted the sonar from its platform. Dr. Castle went back on board to retrieve the chain. There was a hook on the back of the sonar for a guideline. However, the sonar weighed about fifty pounds and was somewhat unwieldy; the women decided that the chain would have to be secured to the ladder, which was the closest stable site. This was not going to be a very precise operation. In theory, though, it didn't have to be perfect. All they needed to do was get the sonar as near to the opening as possible and generate as much noise as possible.

And then do two things more.

First: hope that Harold got through.

Second: hope that a swarm of pissed-off creatures didn't follow him.

CHAPTER THIRTY-SEVEN

"THERE ARE TWO reasons to go with your instincts," Harold Collins's father once told him. He said it when they were playing the board game Stratego, a game where toy soldiers face the risk of stumbling onto bombs concealed on a board. "First, your instincts are usually right. Second, don't waste time and effort fighting them. There's no guarantee the results will be any better." More often than not that advice had served Collins well on tests and games, and in dealing with people.

The good news right now was that Harold didn't have time to think, just to go with his instincts. The bad news was, his instincts weren't telling him what to do other than *Get into the water and find your way out of here*.

Unfortunately, he couldn't do that. He needed help to get the aperture to open. Even if he went back in the water to look for the opening on his own, tried to use his computer, Toothsome might still be out there. Searching while on the run from a man-eater was not likely to breed success.

Still, Collins thought, *a few minutes from now it might be the only game in town.*

The ground was shaking violently now, shifting the sands so hard with each punch that he nearly lost his footing. He decided to go back and put on his diving suit and also to rig a patch for the hole in his helmet. He had come up with an idea he hoped would work. One more "might" in a long series of them.

Collins ran back to the area of ground vegetation. The leaves, especially the leathery ones from the trees, might be sturdy enough to use as packing material. The sands felt warm but not hot on his bare feet. That was a good sign. The beach was not getting ready to go magma on him. He did not have a lot of time, but at least he had some.

As Collins approached the garden, there was a clap that was so loud it hurt his ears. It was like someone had put his head in a metal trash can and banged it. But the sound didn't come from beyond the forest. It had come from the south. Collins looked over in time to see the blue horizon turn black, then red, as a volcano far out at sea went megaton ballistic. It sent a fat column of flame and smooth ugly smoke into the stratosphere. At the same time steam rolled from the sides of the eruption, just as it had from the mountain to the west. Unlike Toothsome, who had oily skin and breathed in the water, Collins's flesh and lungs would be boiled when that cloud reached the bay area.

Collins turned and ran back to the beach. The steam was crossing the water like a giant breaker, white and frothing. He was in an absolute panic. He was going to have to pull on his suit and get into the water and hold his breath as he dove at the spot where he had come through. With luck, and odds in the googolplex-to-one vicinity, he wouldn't be cooked, eaten, or drowned.

"I'm sorry what I thought about maybe being God," he panted as he ran. "I'm not. I didn't mean that. I'm just a jerk."

Suddenly, he heard it again. The sound from the hole.

The blessed blast from the future. Only it was not a series of pulses as before. It was a single burst. Dr. Castle and Tally must have gotten his video and figured out how to open the doorway wider, with a concentrated sound. He smiled with pride as his mouth shook with terror. It was the strangest sensation he had ever experienced.

"Thank you, God!" he shouted as he reached his suit.

As Collins pulled the diving suit on he thought, *helmet, helmet, helmet*. He could reach the anomaly on this side without air, but he risked drowning on the other without it. The tanks weren't designed for mouth-breathing. The oxygen needed to come through the helmet. He had to do something. Quickly. There wasn't time to go back to the garden.

"Think!"

He wished he hadn't sent the wet suit through. A slice of rubber would have worked fine—

"The weights!" he shouted.

They were rubber and fit over the bottom of the boot. Dropping to his knees, he picked one up, drank the rest of the water in the helmet, then stuck the weight inside, over the hole. It was difficult to place it precisely as the ground began to rock like a subway car. There was a deafening blast behind him. He didn't have to turn to know that one of the mountains beyond the forest had just blown. His shadow vanished along with the sun. It was time to go.

Collins pushed the thick rubber slab against the opening. It fit the hole but there was no way to hold it there—

"Use your head," he thought.

Literally. If he pushed his head to the side he could press it there.

No, he thought. If he turned to look at something, that might be enough to cause the buffer to fall away.

"Unless the pressure is greater on the inside than on the outside—that will hold it," he said. He would turn the oxygen up as soon as he went in the water. That might make him a little lightheaded, but the added pressure per square inch might keep the weight in place against the water pressure.

No guarantees, but it was a shot.

Collins pulled on the suit, boots, the second weight and gloves. Whatever had blown from the volcano behind him was raising the temperature rapidly. His body was literally lifted from the ground by another series of blasts. He got on his knees, threw the oxygen tanks onto his back, adjusted the harness, and turned the air on full. Then he crawled toward the water. He didn't dare stand. If the patch fell from the hole now, there was no way to put it back. He had to keep his head pressed to that side.

As Collins began to have a tiny ribbon of hope, he saw an animal's tail break water. Toothsome was back. Obviously, the creature wasn't happy with the situation at sea. No doubt the water was heating up significantly. Collins look past the animal. He saw a patchwork of fins, dorsal spines, and tails breaking the surface as other sea animals sought haven in this natural harbor. But Collins couldn't let that stop him. He didn't know how long Dr. Castle and Tally would be able to keep the aperture open. He had to get out there.

Leaning his head against the weight in the helmet made Collins feel like broken-necked Ygor in the Frankenstein movies. The increased air pressure was making his head pound. But he'd survive. Collins continued to crawl until he was underwater. The helmet leaked, but only slightly. It was barely enough to dampen his hair. He continued ahead until he was able to stand. Though his left foot rose from the seabed, the weight in his right boot and in the helmet helped keep him underwater. He continued ahead, following the hollow, tuba-like sound coming from the anomaly. He peered ahead, looking for the telltale swirl of matter around the event horizon. He didn't see it. Not yet. What he did see, even with the clouded skies and the helmet light doused, were Toothsome and his friends. They were milling in the deeper waters. But the water wasn't so deep that they wouldn't see him. If he couldn't get through them, finding the singularity would be moot.

And then it hit his off-kilter head. He could use a decoy like the one he'd inadvertently discovered earlier.

Collins pointed his left hand down and removed his glove. The increased air pressure kept water from coming in. He tucked the glove under his arm, knelt—keeping his left arm facing down—and fished through the gravel. He found a small wedge-shaped stone and dragged it across the back of his hand. Blood rose thickly in a snaking line. He used his gloved hand to nurse the sides of the wound, squeezing out more blood. Then he put his glove back on and hurried to the south, away from the blood. When he was about twenty or thirty feet away from where he'd entered the water, he turned and continued out to sea.

As Collins had expected, Toothsome remembered his smell and came after him—at least, the "him" that Collins wanted the monster to chase: the blood. He could see the animal's tail whip up, then down, then swat from side to side as the creature rushed toward shore. Collins also saw other creatures head for the spot. Whether they smelled the blood or were simply hoping to get a piece of whatever Toothsome killed, he didn't know. He did know that it was going to create a hell of a logjam along the shore. With luck, Toothsome would have trouble getting back before Collins was gone.

The physicist continued out into the bay. He checked the wrist joint on his left hand to make sure there was no leakage. It wouldn't be in his best interests to have the monsters follow the trail of blood back to him. Fortunately, the wrist seal was secure.

Well done, he told himself. *You'll bleed to death inside your suit instead of being eaten.*

Hopefully, the loss of blood wouldn't cause him to black out either. That would make his head slump and let his helmet leak.

The volcanic clouds threw the underwater world into near-blackness. Collins had no choice but to turn on his halogen lamp. He wasn't sure how the creatures would react to light, but it didn't matter. He had also kept the flashlight from the videocamera. He removed that from his tool belt and turned that on as well. Since he couldn't turn his head without turning his body, the second light would help him see. The extra volts might also give him another square inch or two of space in the anomaly. That could make the difference between losing or keeping the tip of a toe or nose.

His rapid pace kicked up clouds of black silt that rose above his waist. He had to hold the flashlight high to see above it. Small, strange fish moved around him. They looked like barracuda an inch or so long. They seemed agitated, perhaps by the eruption, perhaps by the sound which was getting louder the deeper he went. The fish flitted this way then that, but always rushed away as he approached. Collins wondered if they perceived him as a menace, hated the light, or were running from Toothsome. The scientist felt a constant tingling in the small of his back, like the giant was going to ease up behind him at any moment and crush his pelvis.

Or bite me in half at the thighs, leaving my right leg anchored because of the weight and my left leg floating free. Paleontologists will wonder about that when they find me in the future. "What was one leg doing in Scotland and another in Mexico?"

Collins didn't know what was behind him, but he knew what was ahead. Some forty feet away and twenty-five feet down he saw the vortex. As far as Collins could ascertain, it was pretty much where he had emerged the night before. It was approximately two feet high and four feet in diameter at the mouth. The vortex looked like a waterspout in cylindrical form. It was comprised of water that was somewhat darker than the surrounding sea; Collins suspected that the spout contained matter from both the present and the future loch. *The anomaly must cause the two time periods to overlap in some way,* he thought. No doubt the movement and discoloration was what had attracted Loch Ness Monsters for as long as they'd been passing between the two eras. They thought it was prey. And if storms and volcanoes were as prevalent as they seemed, perhaps animals were driven to this bay with some regularity in search of shelter or sustenance.

Collins was beginning to feel the effects of the added air flow and the loss of blood. It wasn't just headaches but weakness. He decided to concentrate his energies on getting himself above the vortex. Once he was there, he could position himself above it and hope that the weight in his one boot and helmet, plus the suction of the anomaly, were enough to carry him down.

Collins left the seabed and started to swim. So did his vision. But he kept his eyes on the vortex and his head against the patch. It occurred to him that if he were spit out with the same ferocity as before, the jury-rigged patch on his helmet might not hold.

One thing at a time, Collins reminded himself. He had to get through to his own time before he could worry about drowning in the loch.

The light on the helmet revealed the vortex nearly below him. The swirling mouth seemed to expand slightly as he neared. It must have been responding to the light. Photons. That made sense. They would go sliding off the singularity just as electricity did. He cranked his arms and legs as hard as he could to get over the mouth. The seas were churning around him, and he was knocked roughly to one side. He had to concentrate to keep his head against the patch. He looked in the direction of the eddy and saw

columns of bubbles diving downward. The volcano must
be spitting superheated rocks into the bay.

It was definitely time to go.

Collins kicked his feet hard, swept his arms ahead, and
got himself above the vortex. The sound from the future
was very loud here, but he wasn't close enough to be
pulled in. He didn't waste time righting himself but swam
toward the opening headfirst. He was about twenty feet
away, nineteen, eighteen—finally, he felt himself turned
and pulled down the same way he had been before. He kept
his arms at his sides and his legs straight and pressed
together so he wouldn't lose them, or any parts of them. He
saw into the funnel of the vortex. It was dark there. No
stars this time, no moon. He was looking down, but what
he was really seeing was up into Loch Ness.

Collins felt a punch in the left ear and then his head
filled with terrible noise. He realized after a moment that
water was gushing against his temple. He must have
moved his head and the weight must have come loose. The
air pressure hadn't been enough to hold it. If that's what
had happened, there was nothing Collins could do about it.
Besides, the Loch Ness Monster regularly survived the trip
without exploding in a vacuum or suffocating. Perhaps he
would too.

Collins felt himself dropping, twisting. Or maybe it was
the world and time that were twisting around him, he
couldn't be sure. He saw muddy colors all around him,
whirling drab greens and browns, heard the sound of the
rushing water. He screamed but could not hear that. Then
he heard nothing, saw nothing, thought nothing . . .

The next thing Collins knew was that he was rushing
forward. He felt weightless, almost noncorporeal, as though
he were strapped to the nose of a jet in a power dive. The
only sensory input was the cool pressure against his left
ear, against his chin and neck, legs and chest. It was the

seawater pouring in. His arms were too heavy to move, but he didn't think he could have lifted them anyway. He was being propelled forward into the darkness . . . hopefully into the time and place where his journey had begun.

CHAPTER THIRTY-EIGHT

"CUT THE SONAR!" Dr. Castle yelled. "Kill it!"

The scientist was standing at the helm, looking at an area near the boat where she had seen large bubbles appear. It was an area directly above where they had deduced the anomaly to be. There was a now-familiar tugging in her legs as the abnormality or anomaly or whatever it was worked on her nerves or circulatory system or both. A moment later the paleontologist saw a spongy shape rising to the surface. The shape was largely obscured by the bubbles or moving water. Dr. Castle watched anxiously as the underwater tumult increased, sending up more and larger bubbles. Finally, the shape broke the surface just starboard of the prow. It turned out to be what the paleontologist had thought: Harold Collins's diving suit, apparently with Harold Collins still inside, if the flash of flesh she saw through the visor was not a trick of the amber late-afternoon light. The suit popped up, not as dramatically as the camera had, but rising headfirst a few inches above the surface before dropping straight down. Dr. Castle wanted the sonar shut down before the anomaly had a chance to suck Collins back down.

Or before anything else came through.

This morning she would have done just about anything to see the Loch Ness Monster. Not now. She was also glad that Harold had come through before the sonar itself was drawn to the other side. She wondered what that much energy, applied directly, would have done to the gateway.

Dr. Castle's legs returned to normal almost at once. She rushed to the radio and punched in the frequency of the boat Shep was on.

"Shep, are you there?"

"Yes," he said. "I was about to ring. What's the commotion?"

"Harold's here!" Dr. Castle replied. "We need help!"

"On the way," Shep replied.

Once again Shep Boucher was a professional. No needless questions, no extraneous chat, no judgmental remarks. Dr. Castle turned from the radio, ran to the ladder, and climbed down.

Tally had remained in the raft. She was in a good position to get to Harold. He was floating on his back, coughing, weakly trying to remove his helmet, and sinking slowly. Tally oared toward him, leaning over the front of the raft as she reached him and getting her arm around his neck and right shoulder. She pulled him up against the raft and held him there.

"I need help down here!" Tally yelled.

Dr. Castle hurried down the ladder. Things like this used to be easier for her. Her lower back and legs ached from standing for so much of the day, the pain worsened by that last tug from the gravitational force. She felt a flash of envy watching Tally move so easily to help her stricken comrade while her own tendons screamed and her joints popped. But those feelings were replaced by a sense of pride. Tally was not thinking about the risks to herself. Her only concern was for a man who had annoyed her more often than not in the brief time they'd been together.

"His helmet's full of water!" Tally shouted.

Screw it, Dr. Castle thought as she made her way down the ladder. She could see the young woman struggling to keep Collins's head from sinking beneath the water. Inspired by Tally's example of prodigious effort, Dr. Castle dropped into the water. She swam to the raft, grabbed the side, and dragged herself to the side of the stricken young man.

"I'm going to lean my weight down on this side," the paleontologist told Tally. "When the raft dips, pull him in."

"Will do," Tally replied.

With effort, Dr. Castle straightened her arms, hoisted her weight up, and let it all come down on the side of the raft. It bulged downward enough so that Tally could pull Collins's head and torso in. Hooking her right arm around the side, Dr. Castle stretched her left arm under his butt and pushed up. His thighs cleared the lip of the raft and Tally was able to pull him in. As she did, water poured from a hole in the left side of the helmet.

While Dr. Castle got into the raft, Tally twisted the broken helmet off. She dropped it into the raft. The five-pound weight from the boot was tucked into Collins's collar. Dr. Castle couldn't wait to hear how it had gotten there. Tally removed it as Dr. Castle straddled him and pressed on his chest. Collins coughed and spit up water on Tally. The scientist wondered if all this water was from the loch or whether some of it was from the prehistoric sea. If the latter, if there were extinct algae or microbes in it, the paleontologist couldn't begin to contemplate what effect it might have on the biosystem of Loch Ness. The newness of this situation was at once exciting and horrifying.

"Harold, talk to me," Tally said as she tapped his cheek hard. She was kneeling behind his head.

"Put your hands on his cheeks, try to warm him," Dr. Castle suggested.

Tally did so, rubbing vigorously. Collins's eyes were shut and he was breathing weakly. Meanwhile, Dr. Castle removed his boots. The water drained out as she did so. She decided to leave his suit on, since at the moment, that was the only thing keeping him warm.

Off to the east, Shep and two men were speeding over in a motorboat.

"Come on, Mr. Wizard," Tally said. "I couldn't shut you up before. Now I can't get you to talk. Let me know you're okay."

"No," he whispered without opening his eyes.

Tally smiled through the wet hair framing her face. " 'No' you're not okay or 'no' you're not going to let me know?"

"Yes," he mumbled.

With effort, Tally and Dr. Castle paddled the raft toward the vessel as Shep and his crew pulled up alongside. The seaman had changed into a flannel shirt and jeans. His moves were strong and efficient as he shifted from the boat to the raft.

Tally climbed onto the ladder first, then reached down to help Dr. Castle up. The scientist waved her off, staying behind as Shep knelt beside Collins. Another man, the young game warden, Carroll Charlotte, remained in the boat.

"Radio Thatcher," Shep said to Charlotte. "Tell him we're bringing in a man who appears to be suffering from exposure, though I don't understand how that can be." He looked up at Tally. "Toss down some blankets, will you? They're on the cot below."

"Coming," she replied.

"Car?" Shep yelled to the boat.

"Yes?"

"Toss me your canteen!"

The game warden did so. Shep unscrewed the cap.

While Dr. Castle gently opened his lips, Shep poured water in. Collins gagged, swallowed, pressed his lips together repeatedly, then was still again.

"He's probably exhausted," Shep said.

"And hungry and wet," Dr. Castle added.

"So are you, Kathryn," Shep said. "You should get into something warm."

"I'm okay," she said.

He reached into his pocket and pulled out a handkerchief. "At least dry your face," he said. He grinned. "And don't worry. That's the one I use to polish my binoculars."

"Thanks," Dr. Castle said.

She accepted the white cloth and wiped the water from her face and neck. Then she continued what Tally had started, rubbing Collins's cheek. While she did that, Shep turned his attention to the diver's gloves.

"There's blood dripping from the wrist lock," Shep said as he unscrewed the left-hand glove.

Dr. Castle leaned over and gently picked up the young man's arm. The blood was from an ugly gash along the back of his hand. She used the handkerchief to bandage it while Shep removed the right-hand glove. All the while Collins remained very still. Every now and then he would let out a gentle moan.

"Where did you find your lad?" Shep asked her as he removed Collins's boots.

"He was in the water. But he must have been ashore somewhere," Dr. Castle said.

"Odd we didn't see him." Shep cocked his head toward the submerged sonar unit. "Did that help you find him, then?"

"Yes," Dr. Castle replied.

"How, if he was ashore?"

"He must have gone back in the water to try and reach us," Dr. Castle said. "That was when we picked him up."

"I suppose there are nooks along the waterline where a man can get lost if he doesn't know the loch," Shep said. "Maybe Mr. Collins got disoriented when he hit his head." Shep pointed to the helmet. "He must have taken quite a knock to bust that topper."

"Very true," Dr. Castle said.

"He's lucky he didn't drown."

That was true too. He was also lucky he hadn't been scalded, eaten, or dismembered by the time portal on the return trip. Dr. Castle didn't say that, of course, though she did exchange a knowing look with Tally, who was obviously thinking the same thing.

"Though it's strange," Shep continued. "His nose and forehead almost look sunburned."

"He must have scraped them when he hit his head," Dr. Castle replied.

"I don't think so," Shep said. "In fact, I don't 'think so' about any of what you're saying. But we'll worry about that later."

Tally returned with the blankets and tossed them down. Dr. Castle helped Shep remove the diving suit and bundle the young man up. While they gingerly shifted the physicist to the motorboat, Tally climbed down. She joined Shep in the motorboat while Dr. Castle returned to the other vessel. She watched as the smaller boat tore toward shore, the other sailors waving, a few saluting, and all beginning to dismantle the search.

Their job was ended.

For Dr. Castle and the others, the real work was just beginning.

CHAPTER THIRTY-NINE

"**Y**OU APPEAR DISTRACTED," Tally said to Collins.

The three were sitting by the large, arched fireplace in the cozy, wood-paneled lounge of the inn. Collins had arrived several minutes before, after taking a long nap.

He had not been checked into the local ten-bed hospital, since the doctor could find nothing wrong with him, save for mild dehydration and a wicked sunburn on his shoulders, thighs, face, and feet. Water and some homeopathic aloe-lotion concoction took care of both. All Collins wanted to do after that was make a phone call and then rest. And he had done both, though his sleep was troubled by a washing machine somewhere in the cellar. Every time it came on, the building hummed slightly and he woke, ready to run. He had a feeling that he was suffering from post-traumatic stress and would never again feel a rumble—whether a subway train, a thunderclap, or a household appliance—without flashing back to that alien beach on a young, restless world.

Now the young man was sitting in a deep, very stable arm chair holding a can of Coke in his bandaged hand. He was dressed in jeans and a big, fluffy Loch Ness sweatshirt that Tally had picked up from the gift shop. The women were wearing sweaters and sitting on a small sofa drinking tea.

"Sorry," Collins replied. "I'm just sitting here thinking how amazing it is that just a few hours can totally change your life."

"For the better or worse?" Tally asked.

"Probably a lot of both," Collins said, managing a weak smile. "I don't know yet how it's all going to shake out. What I *do* know is that household appliances are definitely on my list of 'things that have gotten worse.'"

Tally made a puzzled expression.

"Frankly, there's no need to apologize or explain," Dr. Castle remarked. "You've been through a great deal."

"We all have," he said. "I still can't believe you got me out of there."

"Brains and luck," Tally smiled.

"Speaking of what you went through," Dr. Castle said, "I must hear more about the things you saw, heard, smelled, and felt back there. Everything you can recall. You're exhausted, so I won't press you on this now. But I urge you to jot some notes or talk into a tape machine, make some kind of record before you forget any of the details."

"I assure you, Kathryn. I won't forget a thing," Collins said.

"In the meantime," Tally said, "you didn't die, weren't seriously injured, didn't lose a friend. Which is why I don't understand how you can look so depressed. You came here to explore the unknown, and you did. The anomaly is still down there. We can go back, do further studies, apparently without changing the future. Or, if we do, it's already part of our past. The implications of what you've discovered are beyond imagining."

"I know," Collins told her. He took a swallow of soda from the can. The one-two hit of sugar and caffeine felt wonderful. "Before I went to sleep I called Samuel and told him to get his butt over as soon as possible. He'll be here in the morning. We're going to need help with this. A lot of it."

"Did you tell him what happened?" Dr. Castle asked.

"I told him I discovered something down there that I needed to discuss with him on-site. I didn't tell him what happened. He wouldn't have believed me. I'm going to need help convincing him."

"Understandable," Tally said. "If I hadn't seen the video, you'd need help convincing me." She sat there shaking her head. "Dinosaurs. You saw dinosaurs. My god, what a story this is."

Dr. Castle leaned toward Tally. "Actually, Tally, what Harold encountered was not a dinosaur," she pointed out.

"Oh?"

"A dinosaur is a member of the orders Saurischia or Ornithischia—respectively possessing a reptilian pelvic girdle or birdlike pelvic girdle. They were primarily land animals and they existed during the Mesozoic era, which includes the Triassic, Jurassic, and Cretaceous. What Harold saw, and what I saw in the Loch the other day, seem to be early Paleozoic forerunners to dinosaurs."

"Well, take that, me," Tally said.

"Good lord," Dr. Castle said. "I didn't mean it as an upbraiding. I was just—talking, that's all."

"I know," Tally assured her. "I was just teasing."

"Ah," Dr. Castle said. She sat back.

"Anyway, that's what I get for working on contemporary natural science articles instead of natural history," Tally said.

Collins took another draft of Coke. He stared at the sofa as if he were looking through the women.

"Talk to us, Harold," Tally said. "Don't keep things inside. What are you thinking about?"

"Nothing important," he assured her.

"Does that mean you won't share with the class?" she pressed.

He grinned. "At this moment I was thinking about the helmet—which, by the way, I fully intend to pay for, along with the other gear."

"I already took care of that," Dr. Castle said.

"Then I'll reimburse you," Collins said.

"Not necessary," Dr. Castle replied.

"Harold, what about the helmet?" Tally pressed.

He snuggled into the seat. "I was looking at it 'back then,'" he said. "It took a pretty good whack. So did the wetsuit. I'm kind of sitting here thinking how lucky I am it wasn't me."

"Amen to that," Dr. Castle said, raising her teacup as an offering.

"But I'm also thinking about other stuff," he said quietly. "Mostly faith stuff and quantum physics stuff."

"Such as?" Tally asked.

"Oh—like whether someone was looking out for me. Hard-nosed agnostic Harold Collins found a little religion back there. I was wondering if there was a god, wondering if I had gone to heaven or hell. But then I also think about the quantum physics possibilities," he said. "What if, in passing through the anomaly, I didn't end up in earth's past but in the present in another dimension? Is there any way I'll ever know that?"

"By exploring," Tally said. "Harold, that's what you're in business to do. Not just at the United Nations but in your chosen profession."

"I know that," Collins said. "But I'm scared. You know how scientists are. You work for years to knock electrons from an atomic orbit and then—oops!—you're J. Robert Oppenheimer worrying about how you've helped to create a nuclear bomb."

"And saved millions of lives by ending World War II,"

Tally said. "Besides, you didn't do anything controversial. You found what appears to be a hole in time. That's not a bad thing."

"We'll see," Collins said. "What about you?" he asked Tally. "What do you see as your role in this not-bad thing."

"My role?" Tally asked. "I don't get it."

"You want to write about it."

"No. I want to sit on the greatest story of our time and never tell anyone," she replied.

"What do you think will happen once you've published a report?" Collins asked.

"With luck, I'll win the Pulitzer Prize and become the talk of my mother's country club," she replied.

"Seriously," Collins said.

"I am serious!" Tally assured him. "What do you think I came here for? To get a story. I've got one."

"I have to say, Tally, Harold's hit on something I've been fretting over as well," Dr. Castle said.

"What is this, suck Tally through a professional anomaly night?"

"Not at all," the paleontologist said.

"We're just talking," Collins said.

"Yeah, about muzzling me. No way. N-O way."

"Please, hear me out," Dr. Castle said. "To begin with, on a very personal scale, have you thought about what will happen to the loch?"

"No, but I'm guessing that tourism will go way, way, waaay up," Tally said. "That's what this place is all about, isn't it?"

"To a degree," Dr. Castle said. "But I'm concerned that what will happen is the same thing that happened to your state of Texas when the internal combustion engine was invented."

"Right. Economic growth," Tally said. "Big time. That can't be avoided. You've got a puzzle that will keep scientists busy for decades, possibly for centuries. One that will expand human knowledge in ways we can't begin to imagine. Paleontologists will be able to study early life or other-dimensional life or whatever it is. Geologists will study early earth. Astronomers will study the early heavens. The net effect is a big gain for human knowledge. And possibly, just possibly, we may find a source of energy to replace the split atom that troubles you so much," Tally said to Harold.

"Maybe," Collins said. "What I'm concerned about has nothing to do with local disruptions. It has to do with large-scale disruptions in time. Who knows if we didn't do that today?"

"Harold, if you had done something major to the time flow, we would have heard about it right now. We might not even be here."

"Maybe we aren't," he said.

"Huh?"

"How do you know there wasn't a fourth member of our party when we climbed into the boat this morning?"

"Oh, please," Tally said.

"I'm serious. Suppose this person was never born because of something I did in the past, so all knowledge, every trace of him or her has been erased. For that matter, how do we know you weren't an old man and I wasn't a young woman? And that's if you're only thinking in a linear fashion," Collins went on. "How do you know I didn't spin off a different time line by going back, and that we're living in it? Quantum theory suggests that the act of traveling through time in reverse can create a new pathway, like when you cut grass in the opposite direction from the way you've been going and it really stands out."

"That's your scientific model?" Tally said. "Mowing the lawn?"

"No, but I figured it would be easier for you to understand than modular functions and their relation to KSV loop diagrams and interacting strings," Collins told her.

"Touché," Tally said. "And you know what? You're right.

I don't know whether any of that happened while you were gone. It could be we'll head for the airport tomorrow and find out that it's a boatport or dirigibleport because the Wright Brothers never lived."

"Or there may be a suborbital hyperjet port because someone did live who invented air travel a century earlier," Collins pointed out.

"It could be that," Tally agreed. "Or a place for big kite travel. Or maybe it *was* all that before and now it'll be airplanes. But I'm betting it won't be. My gut tells me that time is frozen and that everything you or future loch-hole travelers did in the past was already done in the past."

"Maybe," Collins said.

"Y'know, that's about the twelfth 'maybe' you've said in the last couple of minutes," Tally noted. "Which is one reason I'm not scared. Your 'maybe' is as good as my 'why not?' "

"Very possibly. As I said a few minutes ago I was just sitting here thinking about all this, is all," Collins said.

"Fine," Tally said.

Everyone took a moment to calm down.

"In the meantime," the young woman went on, "my point, if I may re-make it—and which you've actually supported with this discursive chat—is that what happened here today has given science a hell of a lot to do. It will propel humankind forward as it propels some people backward." She shook her head quickly. "There's so damn much here. I may need to write an introductory series about the implications of time travel. Ease people into the idea. Ending the series by printing a frame grab from the videotape showing Paleozoic flora is going to be a coup."

"If you end up doing any of that," Dr. Castle said.

"Hello, Doctor!" Tally said. "We've moved on from that nonissue. I haven't heard anything to convince me I shouldn't."

"Simply this," Dr. Castle said. "If you write about this

before the proper safeguards are in place, who knows what could happen?"

"What kind of safeguards to prevent against what kind of eventuality?" Tally asked.

"For one thing, disrupting the integrity of the past, keeping someone from doing what was done to the *Titanic*," Dr. Castle said. "Researchers found it and then capitalists started hauling up pieces to put on display. What's to prevent some impresario from exploiting the anomaly to capture a prehistoric animal and bring it to the present, put it on display?"

"Uh—laws?" Tally said.

"Laws don't stop smugglers," Collins pointed out.

"No, they don't," Dr. Castle said. "We don't know what diseases may come through with them. What impact their removal from the past may have on future history, despite what your 'gut' tells you. We just don't know enough to make this discovery public."

"And I say we have a responsibility to share what we've found with the public, not hide it from them."

"That's the response of a journalist, not a scientist," Dr. Castle said.

"Well, duh."

"Tally, I hear you. But I still think this is one of the things I need to talk to Sam Bordereau about," Collins said.

"Talk to Daddy," Tally said with disgust. "Cripes, I could've stayed home and got this kind of fascism from my mother."

"This isn't a dictatorship," Dr. Castle said. "It's a forum. We are all expressing concerns, ideas, and ambitions. I think the minimum that I'm suggesting is that you wait. Wait at least until we know more before writing that the Loch Ness Monster is a primeval beast that periodically wriggles through a lightning-activated hole in time, pokes around, then goes back again. If that is, in fact, what happens."

"You know, Dr. Castle has a point," Collins said. "From

a journalistic point of view, what exactly *do* you say?"

"I'll report on what I've seen and what I've experienced."

"You're going to be making some pretty extreme claims," Collins said. "Where's the evidence your editor will want to see? Sure there's strange foliage on the videotape, but that can be faked. Hollywood does it all the time. You've got sonar readings, but there are probably explanations other than a powerful gravity well of some kind."

"You're right, Tally," Dr. Castle said. "We have discovered one of the most amazing finds in history. What kind of scientists, what kind of *people* would we be if we didn't take a breath and have a hard look at the discovery and its implications? I'll answer that," the scientist went on. "We'd be rich. We'd be famous. In my case, my reputation would be restored. But there are larger issues. And we must make certain we've examined those before taking the next step—which will, of course, include writing about the expedition."

"As for Samuel," Collins said, "what organization would be better equipped to manage this find than the United Nations?"

"A scientific one," Tally suggested. "My museum, for instance. I know you guys paid for this, but my fear is that the UN would turn Loch Ness into another Area 51."

"Which is what?" Dr. Castle asked.

"A facility in Nevada where the United States government is reportedly playing host to a flying saucer and its crew," Collins said. He was silent for a moment. "You know, something just occurred to me."

"What?" Tally asked.

"That the Area 51 flying saucer, if it exists, might have contained human beings from the future. Passengers who came to our era by the time portal I used."

Tally regarded him. "I can't tell if you're being serious or talking about hyperjetports again."

"I'm being very serious," Collins said. "For all we know, every flying saucer sighting throughout history could have originated on earth, not another world. But earth of another time period."

"The anomaly *would* still exist in the future, wouldn't it?" Dr. Castle said.

"Yes. The question is whether it only works from point to point, like the present to 500 million B.C.," Collins said, "or whether this time is just a local stop in a time subway that stretches to 3199 A.D. and then to 5401 A.D. and who knows where else? It could even be that future scientists have found a way of using the anomaly to pick different times or places to visit."

"There could be something to all that," Dr. Castle agreed.

"Yes there could," Tally said. "But you still haven't given me a good reason not to write about what we *do* know. And don't go on about that faked footage business, Harold, because it's a nonissue. We have photo experts who can verify what you shot. As a matter of fact, we can even send cameras through to take more pictures. You can't ask me not to write about this. And if you do, I won't listen. This is what I came to do. It's what you asked me to do."

The fire crackled loudly, or maybe it only seemed that way. Tally sat back angrily. Collins took a swallow of soda. He felt like a traitor. Hell, he *was* a traitor, to her. But this wasn't the time to worry about hurt feelings.

"May I suggest something?" Dr. Castle said.

"Please," Collins said. "I don't seem to be doing very well."

"You said what needed to be said," she submitted. "Now I suggest that we go to bed and talk about this when we're rested. Tally, you weren't planning to file any kind of story tonight, were you?"

"We're a monthly," the young woman grumped.

"Fine. Then we'll talk again over breakfast."

"Why? You just said that Harold said what needed to be said. What more is there to say?"

"Another 'said'?" Collins suggested.

Tally half-smiled. Then she laughed. So did Collins. It felt good.

"Okay, fine. I *could* use some sleep," Tally told him. "But that doesn't mean I'm going to feel different in the morning."

"You might," Harold said.

"What makes you think so?"

"Because I haven't told you everything that's been going through my mind," he replied.

"Oh?" she asked.

That got Dr. Castle's attention too.

"All of this talk has got me thinking," Collins said. "Thinking that what I saw today, what we experienced today, is just a part of something that's so huge that you may not want people to know about it."

CHAPTER FORTY

BASED ON THE position Samuel Bordereau held at the United Nations, combined with Harold's few references to him, the Frenchman was exactly what Tally had expected he would be. A slick, charming, well-groomed, perceptive if not deeply curious man who wore sunglasses on an overcast day—including inside the hotel—and had exactly the right clothes to wear to Loch Ness, down to the tartan scarf.

Tally had spent the early morning in her room, making notes and answering e-mails. Contrary to Kathryn's prediction, things did not look better after a full night's rest. If anything, she was more outraged than before that she was being asked to sit on the story. As for Collins's parting words the night before, Tally believed he was sincere about the scope of this thing. But that didn't change the fact that what little they knew was worth reporting. She had studied in science journalism class

how every step of the U.S. space program had been
front-page news for the ten years prior to the moon landing. This was no different.

The young woman decided not to say anything more
until she heard what Bordereau had to say. She had looked
up his bio online. The UN official sounded sufficiently
public relations–savvy to strongly overrule Harold and
Kathryn in the matter.

Tally had brunch on the loch-side promenade with the
late-sleeping Kathryn, the two of them talking mostly
about the history of the Loch Ness area going back to the
Ice Age. Obviously, Dr. Castle didn't want to talk about
journalistic responsibility either.

Harold Collins spent the morning in his room. The
women did not know whether he was sleeping or working,
but they decided not to bother him. Like the anomaly, he
had a way of sparking weirdness that Tally was not in the
mood to deal with. Not now, anyway.

Bordereau arrived at the inn at noon in an official UN
helicopter. He had called Collins from his cell phone
when he was just a few miles away. Collins notified Tally
and Dr. Castle, who were outside to meet him. Collins
was not.

As happy as Bordereau was to meet the women, he was
concerned about Harold Collins—genuinely concerned,
Tally was pleased to note. He asked where his friend was
and asked to be taken to him immediately. As the women
led him to the lobby, Harold Collins came walking out to
meet them.

"Welcome to Scotland," Collins said with a smile.

The men shook hands. Bordereau was openly surprised
that Collins seemed so fit.

"I thought you were hurt," Bordereau said in a French
accent that was rose-sweet despite the hint of anger.

"I am," Collins replied. He held up his bandaged hand.

"Seriously, I mean," Bordereau frowned.

"I am," Collins said. "My mind is never going to be the same."

"This is a joke of some sort," Bordereau said.

"Not at all," Collins told him.

"Then I'm very confused," Bordereau said. "Why am I here? What's going on?"

Tally took him by the arm. "Two questions with one answer," she said as she led him to the lounge. "Only I think you'd better sit down to hear it."

The group sat where they had the night before, Bordereau taking the armchair and Collins dragging over a wing chair to sit beside him. Tally simply sat back and listened while Harold and Kathryn brought Bordereau up to speed. The United Nations official had obviously heard many individuals tell personal tales of danger in exotic locales. But his concerned, practiced "I'm listening and I feel your pain" face became more and more suspicious as the story went on. By the time Harold had reached the part about drawing the prehistoric animals to shore with drops of his blood—a part which Tally had not heard before—the Frenchman was shaking his head.

"This is a joke," he said.

"It isn't," Collins replied.

"There cannot be a hole in time."

"It isn't a hole," Collins told him. "Strictly speaking, if my calculations are correct, its a hive."

That took Tally and Dr. Castle by surprise.

"A hive?" Tally said.

"I worked on this most of the night, did a lot of math," Collins said. "And what I believe I encountered is just one facet of a multifaceted gravitational phenomenon. Tally, Kathryn, you felt the increased gravitation on the boat."

Both women nodded.

"It was greatly diminished but still present over a distance of seventy-two feet," Collins said. "I tried to

calculate the parameters of an object that could generate a
gravitational force powerful enough to open a wormhole
through time and annihilate the atomic structure of a portion
of the diving helmet, yet exert only a modest force on the
boat."

"You mean, a naked singularity should have destroyed
us," Tally said.

"You, Loch Ness, Scotland, and probably the rest of the
earth along with a good portion of the solar system,"
Collins said. "The opposing gravitational force of the earth
would not be sufficient to contain that power. It would take
the gravity of time-space itself to do that."

Tally started shaking her head. "No," she said. It had hit
her, where he was going with this. Only she couldn't process it. "You're talking about other dimensions."

"Exactly," he said.

"I'm sorry, but you've lost me," Dr. Castle said.

"Not me," Bordereau said. "I'm still at the terminal."

Collins sat forward. He was excited and obviously trying hard to dummy the science down. "We believe that
time and space are warped around gravitational monsters
like black holes and a white dwarf stars. That's a part of
relativity. They suck in matter, they suck in light, and
they also suck in time and space. We suspect that the
fields of incoming time-space are so intense that they
actually feed on one another—like isometrics, the left
hand holding the right hand and pulling it toward the
chest, as it were."

"You mean, if 'Monday' is getting pulled into a singularity, it could bump into 'Tuesday,' " Tally said.

"Precisely," Collins said. "Away from the singularity
'Monday' and 'Tuesday' are distinct. Closer to it, the tunnels merge in a fourth-dimensional formation. 'Monday'
merges with 'Tuesday' at a certain point. 'Tuesday' may
merge with 'Next Tuesday' at another point. If you want
to try and picture it, imagine a giant rubber-band ball with

the white dwarf particle in the center, the bands around it, and earth around that. Except that the bands are not physical. They're temporal. Still, they remain distinct and provide enough of a barrier to keep the white dwarf from eating up the earth. However, if you apply a bit of energy, the gravity of the white dwarf gets a slight boost that allows it to chew a small, temporary hole between adjoining rubber bands."

"Holy shit," Tally said.

"Yes, but that's only for starters," Collins said. "I said I worked out the math. Given the diminution of gravity levels from the event horizon to the boat—that is, the weakening of the pull through seventy-two feet of water—I've calculated that the force diluting the power of the white dwarf is the equivalent of roughly ten thousand rubber bands."

"Ten thousand," Tally said. "Of which the road to your prehistoric beach is just one."

"That's right," Collins said.

"Meaning there are nine thousand, nine hundred, and ninety-nine other stories in the naked singularity," Tally said.

"Give or take a few hundred," Collins said.

Tally was speechless.

"Harold, would all of them be centralized here?" Dr. Castle asked.

"I don't think so," Collins told her. "Otherwise, the odds are I would not have been able to travel from point to point twice. These are just the point at which two of those bands happen to merge, possibly due to imperfections in the white dwarf, either in its structure or spin, assuming that it's rotating."

"So where would the others be?" Tally asked.

"They could be anywhere," Collins said. "Roswell, New Mexico, for example, may be connected to the future. The Bermuda Triangle may be joined to a pre-accretion void where planes and boats just tumble into space. Mt. Everest could be a tunnel to a Neanderthal time, from whence the Abominable Snowman comes and goes."

"So there are ten thousand time tunnels on earth?"

"Yes, but they may not all be in this time or this dimension," Collins said. "Where it gets really interesting is when you think about destinations other than time. Dragons or gryphons, for example, could be common life forms from some other dimension."

"Question," Tally said.

"Sure."

"How does your head not hurt from all this?"

Collins smiled. "It does. But it's like the muscle burn other people get from exercising. I love the pain."

"Somehow that doesn't surprise me," she said.

"And I suppose," Bordereau said, "that you have some kind of documentation to back all of this up. Just a tiny, tiny bit of proof." He made a small size gesture with his index finger and thumb.

"We have video images from the prehistoric beach," Collins said.

"You do?" Bordereau said.

"Yes. I didn't want to show them to you at the start because you might have thought we faked them. I wanted you to believe me first, then view them with an open mind."

"Believe you," Bordereau said as he slumped in his chair and shook his head. "How can I?"

"How can you afford not to?" Collins asked.

"Yeah," Tally said. "Especially since there's a reporter here who does believe and who wants to tell the story to the world."

No one spoke for a very long time. Finally, Bordereau asked if there was a bar at the inn. Dr. Castle said she could use a visit herself and would take him there. The two of them rose.

Collins and Tally stood with them. He motioned discreetly for her to stay behind.

"If it's all right with you, I'd like to go back to my room to do more calculations," Collins said. "I want to see if I can use the present to 500 million B.C. as a baseline, a yardstick to measure the reach of some of those other theoretical rubber bands."

"Sure," Bordereau said. He faced the physicist. "You really believe everything you just told us?"

"I do, Samuel."

"Where is the video?"

"In my room," Dr. Castle replied.

Bordereau sighed. Twice. "I want to see it before we go to the bar. I still have serious doubts about everything you've told me. It's easier to believe you took a hard knock on the head and imagined the rest."

"But then there's the other evidence," Dr. Castle pointed out. "Harold's long disappearance. The helmet, which I have in my room. The video. The gravitational effect on the boat, on us. Tally and I weren't knocked on the head. We didn't imagine that."

"No," Bordereau agreed. "We need to talk about this more after I've digested what you just told me. In the meantime, can I trust you all not to say anything of this to anyone?"

Collins and Dr. Castle nodded. They looked at Tally.

"I'll be quiet for the time being," she told Bordereau. "At least until you've had time to do your digesting."

"Thank you," he said in that gracious accent of his. He regarded Collins. "You know, maybe there's a reason the United States government denies the existence of an unidentified flying object in Roswell."

Samuel Bordereau and Dr. Castle left, the latter turning and giving Collins a reassuring smile as they walked away.

Tally was not quite as generous. "So. You were a busy little boy last night."

"I was."

"Between us mice—not that I'm suspicious or anything, I just wanted to make sure—you *do* believe what you told him, right? That wasn't just a ruse to get more funding or something like that."

"Actually, I have suspicions that go beyond that, but no evidence to back it up. So, for now, that's all I want to say."

"Suspicions as in, 'Uh-oh, the earth is doomed' or 'Wow, this is neat!'?" Tally asked.

"The latter," Collins said. "The hive concept, the rubber-band ball or whatever you want to call it—all these tunnels running through time and space and other dimensions. Structures like these may be the real building blocks of the universe. One ball may connect to the other, that to the next, the next to the first, and so on in all kinds of multidimensional forms."

"Okay," she said. "But frankly, Harold, in all of that, and in everything you said to Samuel—who is completely adorable, by the way, though I wouldn't trust him out of my sight—I didn't hear one good reason for me to *not* write about what happened here."

"I didn't mean to present you with one," Harold said. "However, I do have a suggestion."

"Which is what? That I keep a diary and not let it be opened till we're all dead? Like the Nixon tapes?"

"Better," he said, "and possibly more lucrative. Possibly even bringing you more fame and acclaim."

"You have my attention," she said.

"Write it up as fiction," he said.

"You're not serious," she said.

"Sure I am."

"As in the great American novel?"

"No, as in a great science fiction novel," Collins replied.

"Or a series of them, depending on what else we discover while studying the anomaly. It would be an interesting way to disseminate the story, selling it to the most naturally receptive minds in the general public."

"But then people wouldn't believe it," Tally said.

"Do they believe in Area 51?"

"Some people do."

"But more people watch shows like *The X-Files* and *Stargate* and hear their message," Collins said. "They want to believe in cover-ups and conspiracies, that there are more things in heaven and earth than are dreamed of in classrooms and textbooks. Also, their creators get richer than most reporters."

"Are you sure you're not just trying to live out your own writer-guy fantasies?" she asked.

"Maybe a little," he said. "I might throw a thought in here or there. But think of the contribution you'd make. You could be a modern-day Robert Lewis Stevenson. *Dr. Jekyll and Mr. Hyde* was fiction, but he was right about people being devils and angels in one body. He psychoanalyzed the human psyche before Freud invented the idea. You can prepare the world for ideas that are beyond their current experience. That would also help you understand it, give you a creative outlet, and maybe a Hugo instead of a Pulitzer, but that ain't so bad. And your imagination might give us some leads as well."

"Us?"

"You and me."

Tally considered this. "Y'know, under ordinary circumstances I'd think I was getting hustled."

"But?"

"I think you believe what you're telling me," she replied. "That this is good for me, for the team, and for the Sally and Joe Public."

"I do," he said.

"And then one day I can write the true story behind the fictionalized story and blow everyone away."

"If you want to spoil things," he said.

"Spoil them?"

"Sure," he said. "No one remembers the real-life Trojan War except for a few archaeologists. But everyone knows Homer and *The Iliad*."

"Good point," she said, nodding. "I like this. I like it a lot."

"Thanks. That one came to me last night, before I started figuring out all the rest of this."

"Aww . . . you care," Tally said.

"Actually, I was also worried," he told her. "This is a big deal. We can't afford any missteps."

"I think I liked it better when you were looking out for my fame and future," she said.

"Sorry," he replied. They started toward the hallway. "When I find the wormhole that takes me back to five minutes ago I'll change that."

"I still don't think you can do that," she told him.

"What?"

"Change a thing that is already in the past," she said. "It's there. Whatever Toothsome did yesterday, five hundred million years ago, is all he ever did on that day five hundred million years ago. You didn't change the course of history."

"Maybe," Collins said. He grinned. "The good news is you can make it however you want when you tell the story. That's what novelists do."

Collins turned to go to his room. Tally went to join the others in the bar adjoining the lobby. Unlike Bordereau and Dr. Castle, she didn't need a drink. She wanted the company.

You don't want a drink and you want to be with people, she thought. *What kind of a novelist are you?*

A frightened one, she had to admit. They had discovered a means of traveling through time and possibly through space. Whether Collins was right about anything else, he was right about one thing:

This was a big one.

EPILOGUE

THE HORIZON-SPANNING CLOUD of steam rolled toward the beach, encountering the first rain of sizzling volcanic ash as it did. The geysers of white-hot ash kept spewing as the steam kept rolling. Where they met, the steam cooled the ash and caused it to fall into the sea. Walls of cooler steam rose and swirled and spun toward the cloud and landed like dancers on a stage.

The shoreline changed as the water evaporated. The animals that had followed Toothsome were stranded along with the larger creature as the shoreline receded farther and farther into the harbor. In frustration, furious at having lost the bright slow-moving prey, Toothsome turned and snapped at them, killing those nearest him and feeding on them. He moved his giant flippers but was unable to turn. He tried to breathe but gasped as the water around him vanished into the air. Only his thick skin, which protected him from large and small predators, saved him from being burned.

And then something happened. As the initial heat rose, cooler air began to settle. The ash mixed with the steam and pulled it to the ground. A soft, watery mud began to form around Toothsome. He could not get back to the sea, but he could move in the mud, somewhat. There was sufficient depth and water so that he could draw breath.

Darkness came, and then light. The volcanoes caused waves that washed to where Toothsome lay. They carried more food to him. And more pockets of water. Eventually, there was sufficient water so that he could return to the sea. But whenever food in the harbor was scarce, he would swim toward the shore and waddle as far as he could go. Eventually, waves brought food to him and dropped it in the little puddle-like traps he made with his flippers.

In time, he mated. When he did, his mate followed him to the shore. And fed as he fed. And lived as he lived. And laid her eggs in one of the shallows Toothsome had excavated. And as those animals grew, they did not go into the water as much because food came to them and it took less energy to wait for it than to hunt and pursue it.

And then one day a spawn of Toothsome did not go into the water at all, but struck out in the other direction, toward the greenery, to see if those things that moved in the wind but did not run could be eaten. . . .

When an elite prosecutor faces the most lethal predator she's ever encountered, it all comes down to a choice between justice and . . .

RETRIBUTION

Turn the page for a taste of one of
the most exciting debuts in years!
Jilliane Hoffman's first novel,
Retribution,
is guaranteed to have you holding
your breath until you turn the very
last page.

**On January 5, 2004,
retribution will be claimed!**

PROLOGUE

June 1988
New York City

CHLOE LARSON WAS, as usual, in a mad and blinding rush. She had all of ten minutes to change into something suitable to wear to *The Phantom of the Opera*—currently sold out a year in advance and the hottest show on Broadway—put on a face, and catch the 6:52 P.M. train out of Bayside into the city, which was, in itself, a three-minute car ride from her apartment to the station. That left her with only seven minutes. She whipped through the overstuffed closet that she had meant to clean out last winter, and quickly settled on a black crepe skirt and matching jacket with a pink camisole. Clutching one shoe in her hand, she muttered Michael's name under her breath, while she frantically tossed aside shoe after shoe from the pile on the closet floor, at last finally finding the black patent-leather pump's mate.

She hurried down the hall to the bathroom, pulling on her heels as she walked. *It was not supposed to happen like this,* she thought as she flipped her long blond hair upside down, combing it with one hand, while brushing her teeth with the other. She was supposed to be relaxed and care-free, giddy with anticipation, her mind free of distractions when the question to end all questions was finally asked of her. Not rushing to and fro, on almost no sleep, from intense classes and study groups with other really anxious people, the New York State Bar Exam oppressively intruding upon her every thought. She spit out the toothpaste, spritzed on Channel No. 5, and practically ran to the front door. Four minutes. She had four minutes, or else she would have to catch the 7:22 and then she would probably miss the cur-tain. An image of a dapper and annoyed Michael, waiting outside the Majestic Theater, rose in hand, box in pocket, checking his watch, flashed into her mind.

It was not supposed to happen like this. She was sup-posed to be more prepared.

She hurried through the courtyard to her car, rushing to put on the earrings she had grabbed off the nightstand in her room. From the second story above, she felt the eyes of her strange and reclusive neighbor upon her, peering down from behind his living room window, as he did every day. Just watching as she made her way through the courtyard into the busy world and on with her life. She shook off the cold, uncomfortable feeling as quickly as it had come and climbed into her car. This was no time to think about Mar-vin. This was no time to think of the bar exam or bar review classes or study groups. It was time to think only of her answer to the question that Michael was surely going to ask her tonight.

Three minutes. She had only three minutes, she thought, as she cheated the corner stop sign, barely making the light up on Northern Boulevard.

The deafening sound of the train whistle was upon her

now as she ran up the platform stairs two at a time. The doors closed on her just as she waved a thank-you to the conductor for waiting and made her way into the car. She sat back against the ripped red vinyl seat and caught her breath from that last run through the parking lot and up the stairs. The train pulled out of the station, headed for Manhattan. She had barely made it.

Just relax and calm down now, Chloe, she told herself, looking at Queens as it passed her by in the fading light of day. Because tonight, after all, was going to be a very special night. Of that she was certain.

PART ONE

CHAPTER ONE

June 1988
New York City

THE WIND HAD picked up and the thick evergreen bushes that hid his motionless body from sight began to rustle and sway. Just to the west, lightning lit the sky, and jagged streaks of white and purple flashed behind the brilliant Manhattan skyline. There was little doubt that it was going to pour—and soon. Buried deep in the dark underbrush, his jaw clenched tight and his neck stiffened at the rumble of thunder. Wouldn't that just put the icing on the cake, though? A thunderstorm while he sat out here waiting for that bitch to finally get home.

Crouched low under the thick mange of bushes that surrounded the apartment building there was no breeze, and the heat had become so stifling under the heavy clown mask that he could almost feel the flesh melting off his face. The smell of rotting leaves and moist dirt overwhelmed the evergreen, and he tried hard not to breathe in through his nose. Something small scurried by his ear, and he forced his mind to stop imagining the different kinds of vermin that might, right now, be crawling on his person, up his sleeves, in his work boots. He fingered the sharp, jagged blade anxiously with gloved fingertips.

There were no signs of life in the deserted courtyard. All was quiet, but for the sound of the wind blowing through the branches of the lumbering oak trees, and the constant hum and rattle of a dozen or more air conditioners, precariously suspended up above him from their windowsills. Thick, full hedges practically grew over the entire side of the building, and he knew that, even from the apartments above, he could still not be seen. The carpet of weeds and decaying leaves crunched softly under his weight as he pulled himself up and moved slowly through the bushes toward her window.

She had left her blinds open. The glow from the street lamp filtered through the hedges, slicing dim ribbons of light across the bedroom. Inside, all was dark and still. Her bed was unmade and her closet door was open. Shoes—high heels, sandals, sneakers—lined the closet floor. Next to her television, a stuffed-bear collection was displayed on the crowded dresser. Dozens of black marble eyes glinted back at him in the amber slivers of light from the window. The red glow on her alarm clock read 12:33 A.M.

His eyes knew exactly where to look. They quickly scanned down the dresser, and he licked his dry lips. Colored bras and matching lacy panties lay tossed about in the open drawer.

His hand went to his jeans and he felt his hard-on rise back to life. His eyes moved fast to the rocking chair where she had hung her white lace nightie. He closed his eyes and stroked himself faster, recalling in his mind exactly how she had looked last night. Her firm, full tits bouncing up and down while she fucked her boyfriend in that see-through white nightie. Her head thrown back in ecstasy, and her curved, full mouth open wide with pleasure. She was a bad girl, leaving her blinds open. Very bad. His hand moved faster still. Now he envisioned how she would look with those long legs wrapped in nylon thigh-highs and strapped into a pair of the high heels from her closet. And his own hands, locked around their black spikes, hoisting her legs up, up, up in the air and then spreading them wide apart while she screamed. First in fear, and then in pleasure. Her blond mane fanned out under her head on the bed, her arms strapped tight to the headboard. The lacy crotch of her pretty pink panties and her thick blond bush, exposed right by his mouth. *Yum-yum!* He moaned loudly in his head and his breath hissed as it escaped through the tiny slit in the center of his contorted red smile. He stopped himself before he climaxed and opened his eyes again. Her bedroom door stood ajar, and he could see that the rest of the apartment was dark and empty. He sank back down to his spot under the evergreens. Sweat rolled down his face, and the latex suctioned fast to the skin. Thunder rumbled again, and he felt his cock slowly shrivel back down inside his pants.

She was supposed to have been home hours ago. Every single Wednesday night she gets home no later then 10:45 P.M. But tonight, *tonight,* of all nights, she's late. He bit down hard on his lower lip, reopening the cut he had chewed on an hour earlier, tasting the salty blood that flooded his mouth. He fought back the almost overwhelming urge to scream.

Goddamn mother-fucking bitch! He could not help but be disappointed. He had been so excited, *so thrilled,* just counting off the minutes. At 10:45 she would walk right past him, only steps away, in her tight gym clothes. The lights would go on above him, and he would rise slowly to the window. She would purposely leave the blinds open, and he would watch. Watch as she pulled her sweaty T-shirt over her head and slid her tight shorts over her naked thighs. Watch as she would get herself ready for bed. *Ready for him!*

Like a giddy schoolboy on his first date, he had giggled to himself merrily in the bushes. *How far will we go tonight, my dear? First base? Second? All the way?* But those initial, exciting minutes had ticked by and here he still was, two hours later—squatting like a vagrant with unspeakable vermin crawling all over him, probably breeding in his ears. The anticipation that had fueled him, that had fed the fantasy, was now gone. His disappointment had slowly turned into anger, an anger that had grown more intense with each passing minute. He clenched his teeth hard and his breath hissed. No, siree, he was not excited anymore. He was not thrilled. He was beyond annoyed.

He sat chewing his lip in the dark for what seemed like another hour, but really was only a matter of minutes. Lightning lit the sky and the thunder rumbled even louder and he knew then that it was time to go. Grudgingly, he removed his mask, gathered his bag of tricks, and extricated himself from the bushes. He knew that there would be a next time.

Headlights beamed down the dark street just then, and he quickly ducked off the cement pathway back behind the hedges. A sleek silver BMW pulled up fast in front of the complex, double-parking no less than thirty feet from his hiding spot.

Minutes passed like hours, but finally the passenger door opened, and two long and luscious legs, their delicate feet wrapped in high-heeled black patent-leather pumps, swung out. He knew instantly that it was she, and an inexplicable feeling of calm came over him.

It must be fate.

Then the Clown sank back under the evergreens. To wait.

CHAPTER TWO

TIMES SQUARE AND Forty-second Street were still all aglow in neon, bustling with different sorts of life even past midnight on a simple Wednesday. Chloe Larson nervously chewed on a thumbnail and watched out the passenger-side window as the BMW snaked its way through the streets of Manhattan toward Thirty-fourth Street and the Midtown Tunnel.

She knew that she should not have gone out tonight. The tiny, annoying voice inside her head had told her as much all day long, but she hadn't listened, and with less than four weeks to go before the bar exam, she had blown off a night of intense studying for a night of romance and passion. A worthy cause, perhaps, except that the evening hadn't been very romantic in the end, and now she was both miserable and panic stricken, suffering from an overwhelming sense of dread about the exam. Michael continued to rant on about his day from corporate hell, and didn't seem to notice either her misery or her panic, much less her inattention. Or if he did, he didn't seem to care.

Michael Decker was Chloe's boyfriend. Possibly her soon-to-be ex–boyfriend. A high-profile trial attorney, he was on the partner track with the very prestigious Wall Street law firm of White, Hughey & Lombard. They had met there two summers ago when Chloe was hired as Michael's legal intern in the Commercial Litigation Department. She had quickly learned that Michael never took no for an answer when he wanted a yes to his question. The first day on the job he was yelling at her to read her case law more closely, and the next one he was kissing her hot and heavy in the copy room. He was handsome and brilliant and had this romantic mystique about him that Chloe could not explain, and just could not ignore. So she had found a new job, romance had blossomed, and tonight had marked the two-year anniversary of their first real date.

For the past two weeks Chloe had asked, practically begged, Michael if they could celebrate their anniversary date after the bar exam. But instead, he had called her this same afternoon to surprise her with theater tickets for tonight's performance of *The Phantom of the Opera*. Michael knew everyone's weakness, and if he didn't know it, he found it. So when Chloe had first said no, he knew to immediately zero in on the guilt factor—that Irish-Catholic homing device buried deep within her conscience. *We hardly see each other anymore, Chloe. You're always studying. We deserve to spend some time together. We need it, babe, I need it.* Etc., etc., and etc. He finally told her that he'd had to practically steal the tickets from some needy client, and she relented, reluctantly agreeing to meet him in the city. She'd rushed into Manhattan all the while trying to quiet that disconcerting voice in the back of her head that had suddenly begun to shout.

After all that, she had to admit she wasn't even surprised when, ten minutes after curtain call, the elderly
usher with the kind face handed her the note that told her
Michael was stuck in an emergency meeting and would be
late. She should have left right there, right then, but,
well . . . she didn't. She watched now out the window as
the BMW slid under the East River and the tunnel lights
passed by in a dizzying blur of yellow.

Michael had shown up for the final curtain call with a
rose in his hand and had begun the familiar litany of
excuses before she could slug him. A zillion apologies
later he had somehow managed to then guilt her into dinner, and the next thing she knew, they were heading across
the street together to Carmine's and she was left wondering
just when and where she had lost her spinal cord. How she
hated being Irish-Catholic. The guilt trips were more like
pilgrimages.

If the night had only ended there, it would have been on
a good note. But over a plate of veal marsala and a bottle of
Cristal, Michael had delivered the sucker punch of the evening. She had just begun to relax a little and enjoy the
champagne and romantic atmosphere when Michael had
pulled out a small box that she instantly knew was not
small enough.

"Happy Anniversary." He had smiled softly, a perfect
smile, his sexy brown eyes warm in the flickering candle-
light. The strolling violinists neared, like shark to chum. "I
love you, baby."

Obviously not enough to marry me, she had thought as
she stared at the silver-wrapped box with the extra-large
white bow, afraid to open it. Afraid to see what wasn't
inside.

"Go ahead, open it." He had filled their glasses with
more champagne, and his grin had grown more smug.
Obviously, he thought that alcohol and jewelry of any sort
would surely get him out of the doghouse for being late.

Little did he know that at that very moment he was so far from home, he was going to need a map and a survival kit to get back. Or maybe she was wrong. Maybe he had just put it in a big box to fool her.

But no. Inside, dangling from a delicate gold chain, was a pendant of two intertwined hearts, connected by a brilliant diamond. It was beautiful. But it wasn't round and it didn't fit on her finger. Mad at herself for thinking that way, she had blinked back hot tears. Before she knew it, he was out of his seat and behind her, moving her long blond hair onto her shoulders and fastening the necklace. He kissed the nape of her neck, obviously mistaking her tears for those of happiness. Or ignoring them. He whispered in her ear, "It looks great on you." Then he had sat back in his seat and ordered tiramisu, which arrived five minutes later with a candle and three singing Italians. The violinists soon got wind of the party downtown and had sauntered over and everyone had sung and strummed "Happy Anniversary" in Italian. She wished she had just stayed home.

The car now moved along the Long Island Expressway toward Queens with Michael still oblivious to her absence from the conversation. It had started to sprinkle outside, and lightning lit the sky. In the side-view mirror Chloe watched the Manhattan skyline shrink smaller and smaller behind Lefrak City and Rego Park, until it almost disappeared from sight. After two years, Michael knew what she wanted, and it *wasn't* a necklace. *Damn him.* She had enough stress in her life with the bar exam that she needed this emotional albatross about as much as she needed a hole in the head.

They approached her exit on the Clearview Expressway and she finally decided that a discussion about their future together—or lack thereof—would just have to wait until after she sat for the bar. The last thing she wanted right now was the heart-wrenching ache of a failed relationship. One stress factor at a time. Still, she hoped her stony silence in the car would send its message.

"It's not just the depo," Michael continued on, seemingly oblivious. "If I have to run to the judge every time I want to ask something as inane as a date of birth and Social Security number, this case is going to get buried in the mountains of sanctions I'm going to ask for."

He pulled off onto Northern Boulevard and stopped at a light. There were no other cars out on the street at this hour. Finally he paused, recognized the sound of silence, and looked over cautiously at Chloe. "Are you okay? You haven't said much at all since we left Carmine's. You're not still mad about my being late, are you? I said I was sorry." He gripped the leather steering wheel with both hands, bracing himself for the fight that hung heavy in the air. His tone was arrogant and defensive. "You know what that firm is like. I just can't get away, and that's the bottom line. The deal depended on me being there."

The silence in the small car was almost deafening. Before she could even respond, he had changed both his tone and the subject. Reaching across the front seat, he traced the heart pendant that rested in the hollow of her throat with his finger. "I had it made special. Do you like it?" His voice was now a sensuous inviting whisper.

No, no, no. She wasn't going to go there. Not tonight. *I refuse to answer, Counselor, on the grounds it may incriminate me.*

"I'm just distracted." She touched her neck and said flatly, "It's beautiful." The hell she was going to let him think that she was just being an emotional bitch who was upset because she didn't get the ring she'd told all her friends and extended family she was expecting. He could take what she said and chew on it for a few days. The light changed and they drove on in silence.

"I know what this is about. I know what you're thinking."

He sighed an exaggerated sigh and leaned back in the driver's seat, hitting the palm of his hand hard against the steering wheel. "This is all about the bar exam, isn't it? Jesus, Chloe, you have studied for that test almost nonstop for two months, and I have been really understanding. I really have. I only asked for one night out . . . Just one. I have had this incredibly tough day and all during dinner there has been this, this tension between us. Loosen up, will you? I really, really need you to." He sounded annoyed that he even had to bother having this conversation, and she wanted to slug him again. "Take it from someone who has been there: Stop worrying about the bar exam. You're tops in your class, you've got a terrific job lined up—you'll do fine."

"I'm sorry that my company at dinner did not brighten your tough day, Michael. I really am," she said, the sarcasm chilling her words. "But, let me just say that you must suffer from short-term memory loss. Do you remember that we spent last night together, too? I wouldn't exactly say that I have neglected you. Might I also remind you that I did not even want to celebrate tonight and I told you as much, but you chose to ignore me. Now, as far as having fun goes, I might have been in a better mood if you hadn't been two hours late." Great. In addition to the guilt pangs her stomach was digesting for dessert, her head was beginning to throb. She rubbed her temples.

He pulled the car up in front of her apartment building, looking for a spot.

"You can just let me out here," she said sharply.

He looked stunned and stopped the car, double-parking in front of her complex.

"What? You don't want me to come in tonight?" He sounded hurt, surprised. Good. That made two of them.

"I'm just really tired, Michael, and this conversation is, well, it's degenerating. And quick. Plus I missed my aerobics class tonight, so I think I'll take the early one in the morning before class."

Silence filled the car. He looked off out his window and she gathered her jacket and purse. "Look, I'm really sorry about tonight, Chloe. I really am. I wanted it to be special and it obviously wasn't, and for that, I apologize. And I'm sorry if you're stressed over the bar exam. I shouldn't have snapped like that." His tone was sincere and much softer. The "sensitive guy" tactic took her slightly by surprise.

Leaning over the car seat, he traced a finger up her neck and over her face. He ran his finger over her cheekbones as she looked down in her lap, fidgeting for the keys in her purse, trying hard to ignore his touch. Burying his hand in her honey-blond hair, he pulled her close and brushed his mouth near her ear. Softly he murmured, "You don't need the gym. Let me work you out."

Michael made her weak. Ever since that day in the copy room. And she could rarely say no to him. Chloe could smell the sweetness of his warm breath, and felt his strong hands tracing farther down the small of her back. In her head she knew she should not put up with his crap, but in her heart, well, that was another story. For crazy reasons she loved him. But tonight—well, tonight was just not going to happen. Even the spineless had their limits. She opened the car door fast and stepped out, catching her breath. When she leaned back in, her tone was one of indifference.

"This is not going to happen, Michael. I'm tempted, but it's already almost one. Marie is picking me up at eight forty-five, and I can't be late again." She slammed the door shut.

He turned off the engine and got out of the driver's side. "Fine, fine. I get it. Some great fucking night this turned out to be," he said sullenly and slammed his door in return. She glared at him, turned on her heel, and marched off across the courtyard toward her lobby.

"Shit, shit, shit," he mumbled and ran after her. He caught up with her on the sidewalk and grabbed her hand. "Stop, just stop. Look, I'm frustrated. I'm also an insensitive clod. I admit it." He looked into her eyes for a sign that it was safe to proceed. Apparently, they still read caution, but when she did not move away he took that as a good sign. "There, I've said it. I'm a jerk and tonight was a mess and it's all my fault. Come on, please, forgive me," he whispered. "Don't end tonight like this." He wrapped his hand behind her neck and pulled her mouth to his. Her full lips tasted sweet.

After a moment she stepped back and touched her hand lightly to her mouth. "Fine. Forgiven. But you're still not spending the night." The words were cool.

She needed to be alone tonight. To think. Past her bedroom, where was this whole thing headed anyway? The streetlights cast deep shadows on the walkway. The wind blew harder and the trees and bushes rustled and stirred around them. A dog barked off in the distance, and the sky rumbled.

Michael looked up. "I think it's going to pour tonight," he said absently, grabbing her limp hand in his. They walked to the front door of the building in silence. On the stoop he smiled and said lightly, "Damn. And here I thought I was so smooth. Sensitivity is supposed to work with you women. The man who's not afraid to cry, show his feelings." He laughed, obviously fishing for a smile in return, then he massaged her hand with his and kissed her gently on the cheek, moving his lips lightly over her face toward her lips. Her eyes were closed, her full mouth slightly parted. "You look so good tonight I just might cry if I can't have you." *If at first you don't succeed . . . try, try again.* His hands moved slowly down the small of her back, over her skirt. She didn't move. "You know, it's not too late to change your mind," he murmured, his fingers moving over her. "I can just go move the car."

His touch was electrifying. Finally, she pulled away and opened the door. Damn it, she was going to make a statement tonight and not even her libido was going to stop her.

"Good night, Michael. I'll talk to you tomorrow."

He looked as if he had been punched in the gut. Or somewhere else.

"Happy anniversary," he said quietly as she slipped into the foyer door. The glass door closed with a creak.

He walked slowly back to the car, keys in hand. Damn it. He had really screwed things up tonight. He really had. At the car, he watched as Chloe stood at the living room window and waved to him that all was okay inside. She still looked pissed. And then the curtain closed and she was gone. He climbed in the BMW and drove off toward the expressway and back toward Manhattan, thinking about how to get back on her good side. Maybe he'd send her flowers tomorrow. That's it. Long red roses with an apology and an "I love you." That should get him out of the doghouse and back into her bed. With the crackle of thunder sounding closer still and the storm fast moving in, he turned onto the Clearview Expressway, leaving Bayside way behind him.